He cleared his th... his hands to cup...

Words still didn't com... swirled around in his head, mingling with the good ones and mixing with the present. After a heavily weighted minute, it was Raven who spoke. Just one word, but somehow, she made it sound like an ache.

"Lucien."

It was all he could take. Overcome, he dipped his face down and pressed his mouth to hers. For a moment, she was still. Just receiving the kiss. Her lack of reaction very nearly made Lucien pull away. Then—as if she sensed his intention to separate— her hands came up and landed on the back of his neck, holding him there. And more important, she came alive. Her lips moved with his, tasting and exploring, setting off the metaphorical fireworks that had waited under the surface for what felt like a millennium.

Earlier, Lucien had thought the brief contact between their lips had been a kiss. He'd been wrong. So very mistaken.

* * *

If you're on Twitter, tell us what you think of Harlequin Romantic Suspense! #harlequinromsuspense

Dear Reader,

Lucien and Raven are two characters who have been in my head for a long time, and I'm delighted to finally bring them to life in *Serial Escape*. This story actually has many elements that I like to find in the books that I read myself. There's an escaped serial killer...a second-chance romance...and a mature hero with a gruff exterior.

Lucien is pretty sighworthy, if I do say so myself. And I love my wonderful heroine, Raven, as well. She's been through hell. She's lost those closest to her. She's rebuilt her life. And she has a nice solid wall around her heart. She's tough and kind and knows what she wants, too. All of which makes her a perfect match for Lucien.

Happy reading,

Melinda Di Lorenzo

SERIAL ESCAPE

Melinda Di Lorenzo

If you purchased this book without a cover you should be aware
that this book is stolen property. It was reported as "unsold and
destroyed" to the publisher, and neither the author nor the
publisher has received any payment for this "stripped book."

HARLEQUIN®
ROMANTIC
SUSPENSE™

Recycling programs
for this product may
not exist in your area.

ISBN-13: 978-1-335-62667-7

Serial Escape

Copyright © 2020 by Melinda A. Di Lorenzo

All rights reserved. No part of this book may be used or reproduced in
any manner whatsoever without written permission except in the case of
brief quotations embodied in critical articles and reviews.

This is a work of fiction. Names, characters, places and incidents
are either the product of the author's imagination or are used fictitiously.
Any resemblance to actual persons, living or dead, businesses,
companies, events or locales is entirely coincidental.

This edition published by arrangement with Harlequin Books S.A.

For questions and comments about the quality of this book,
please contact us at CustomerService@Harlequin.com.

Harlequin Enterprises ULC
22 Adelaide St. West, 40th Floor
Toronto, Ontario M5H 4E3, Canada
www.Harlequin.com

Printed in U.S.A.

Amazon bestselling author **Melinda Di Lorenzo** writes in her spare time—at soccer practices, when she should be doing laundry and in place of sleep. She lives on the beautiful west coast of British Columbia, Canada, with her handsome husband and her noisy kids. When she's not writing, she can be found curled up with (someone else's) good book.

Books by Melinda Di Lorenzo

Harlequin Romantic Suspense

Undercover Justice

Captivating Witness
Undercover Protector
Undercover Passion
Undercover Justice

Worth the Risk
Last Chance Hero
Silent Rescue
First Responder on Call
Serial Escape

Harlequin Intrigue

Trusting a Stranger

Harlequin Intrigue Noir

Deceptions and Desires
Pinups and Possibilities

To all those who've given love a second shot.

Chapter 1

The thump of Detective Lucien Match's rubberized soles against the equally rubberized treadmill belt somehow rode a line between cathartic and jarring.

Tap-bounce, tap-bounce. Bounce-tap.

Tap-bounce, tap-bounce. Bounce-tap.

The rhythm didn't change.

It didn't get faster or slower.

He never missed a beat, not even when his cell phone buzzed on the little tray in front of him. He cast a glance down at the slim device and saw that it was his boss, who knew damn well that Lucien was on vacation, because he was the one who'd ordered the break in the first place.

Tap-bounce, tap-bounce. Bounce-tap.

Tap-bounce, tap-bounce. Bounce-tap.

He always kept up his steady, five-kilometer-per-hour pace for the full sixty minutes. It wasn't easy, and he didn't consider himself a natural runner. His body wasn't leanly built, and in all honesty, he probably would've been better suited to weight lifting. But he'd learned as a rookie that being able to run for an extended period of time came in handy when chasing criminals through the streets of Vancouver, BC. Far handier than being able to bench one-eighty. In spite of the way it looked on TV, there weren't a ton of unreasonably fit petty thieves and drug dealers lurking around, just waiting to lead cops on wild, citywide runs. In fact, most gave up after a block or two because they had no choice. Zero cardio endurance. Plus—even if he'd felt inclined to—adding any kind of weight system to the already cramped condo was a laughable idea. Lucien would've had to give up something important to make the space. Like maybe the bed.

He chuckled to himself at the thought, then grabbed his water bottle from the holder and took a hearty sip, still without a pause.

Tap-bounce, tap-bounce. Bounce-tap.
Tap-bounce, tap-bounce. Bounce-tap.

His eyes flicked idly around the area as he continued to run. He had the treadmill set up in the middle of the living room. The spot between the couch and the wall was just the right width to accommodate, and when Lucien wasn't actively running, he folded up the behemoth of a machine and tucked it into a corner. It was a bit crowded, but the lack of space wasn't a burden. It was a good thing, actually. No lawn maintenance. Little housework. Executive living, they'd called it when he moved in.

The condo had come mostly furnished, too. It'd been outfitted with the same couch that sat there now, and the coffee table and lamp were also standard. The kitchen was a stocked with cutlery and dishes, and a very plain, two-person table-and-chairs set took up the corner opposite the small fridge. In the bedroom were a wide dresser and a sturdy bed frame. Lucien had provided his own mattress, as well as the wall-mounted television set which was currently playing some old action flick in silence, and also the treadmill beneath his feet.

Tap-bounce, tap-bounce. Bounce-tap.

Tap-bounce, tap-bounce. Bounce-tap.

His phone buzzed again, this time with an incoming text, and Lucien aimed his gaze toward it a second time.

PICK UP YOUR DAMN PHONE, read the message under his boss's name.

He looked from his cell to the timer on the display. There were still eighteen minutes left in his sixty.

"You can wait that long," he muttered, his voice just barely tinged with exertion.

Grudgingly, he acknowledged that a part of his unwillingness to answer was just childish spite. This past Friday, Lucien had been called into HR, where he'd been lambasted for not taking any of his accrued time off for the last three years in a row. The official policy was a use-it-or-lose-it one, and supposedly, not a single other person had ever lost it. Apparently, working too hard set a bad example. At least as far as human resources and Sergeant Gray were concerned.

What the hell Lucien was going to do with the mandated week off was a still a mystery, and it was only the first Tuesday. So far, he'd used all his newly freed time to run, eat and repeat. Not at all productive. That didn't mean he was going to let his boss turn it around. The older man could suffer for a bit. Or at least for another sixteen minutes and twenty-nine seconds.

Tap-bounce, tap-bounce. Bounce-tap.

Tap-bounce, tap-bounce. Bounce-tap.

The phone went off yet again, and this time, Lucien pretended not to notice. Still jogging, he grabbed the TV remote from its spot beside the phone, and tried to push the volume button. The sweat on his palm made his finger slip, though, and instead of just turning it up, he accidentally changed the channel, too. The local news blared to life, a serious-sounding anchor speaking over a flashing red bulletin.

"You're hearing it here, on Choice News for the first time," said the unseen woman. "For those who've just tuned in, we're talking about serial killer Georges Hanes, dubbed the Kitsilano Killer because his victims were living or raised in the upscale Vancouver neighborhood. Most people are familiar with the man, who murdered four families over the course of just a single year. Only one victim out of the sixteen targeted individuals survived."

For a second, Lucien tuned out the announcer's voice. The Kitsilano Killer's story was notorious. As highly publicized as it was gruesome. And there were few who knew the story as well as Lucien did. He'd been on the inside of it, and had even testified in Georges Hanes's trial. Helping to put the man behind bars was one of the most satisfying moments of his seventeen-year career. He doubted—and *hoped*—that he would never experience another case like that one.

It wasn't all of that, though, that made Lucien need a moment. It was the living victim, whom he knew even better than he knew the case.

Lucien breathed out. Then in. Then forced his eyes back up to the TV. The screen now housed a familiar mug shot.

Georges Hanes.

Average height, average build. Light brown hair, light blue eyes. No one would look twice if they passed him in the street. Yet there was still something in his face that made Lucien grit his teeth together uncomfortably. Maybe it was his cop gut, or maybe it was just knowing what he knew. Either way, his hands tightened into fists as he focused once more on the newscaster's ongoing chatter.

"Today marks the three-year anniversary of Georges Hanes's guilty verdict," she was saying now. "So his escape early this morning during a routine drill is an even bigger blow."

The statement finally broke Lucien's rhythm.

Tap-bounce, tap-bounce. Bounce-tap. Stumble, thump.

His big body went flying, and so did everything else. At the same moment his elbow smashed the bottom edge of the treadmill, his water bottle hit the ground, spraying liquid from its abruptly popped top. The TV remote smacked against the fast-moving rubber three times, then sailed off and disappeared under the couch. His cell phone, which had just started to buzz another time, came out of nowhere and thudded against his forehead. Snarling under his breath at the debacle, Lucien snatched the cell up and tapped the answer icon with entirely more force than necessary.

"Where is she?" he demanded without preamble.

His boss replied with equally little pretense at small talk. "Damn well wish I knew. Why the hell haven't you been answering your phone, Match?"

"Busy with vacation," Lucien snapped. "Did you send anyone to her place?"

There was the briefest pause. "She moved, Lucien, and didn't leave a forwarding address."

Worry hit him like a baseball to the gut. "How long ago? Weren't we keeping tabs on her?"

"We were. Minimally."

"What does that mean?"

"That six months ago, our family liaison officer checked in on her and everything seemed copasetic."

"So why would she suddenly—" He cut himself off, knowing it was a waste of time to ask rhetorical questions. It was far better to come at the situation like a police officer than like a man. He switched to a curt, professional tone. "What about the neighbors? Friends? Place of employment? Someone will have a hint."

"Don't go all detective on *me*, Match. I wrote the damned book on it while you were still playing cops and robbers. You know the uniforms are already out canvassing her old neighborhood, and we're trying to track down where she's working at the moment, but it seems a bit like she might've gone AWOL on purpose." There was another pause, and then his boss spoke again, sounding far less irritated. "I figured you, of all people, would have the best idea about where she was."

"Yeah, well…you figured wrong." His own tone was almost bitter, and barely scraped by with not being childish, too.

"Okay," his boss replied. "Guess this was just a courtesy call, then. I know you'll want to be looped in, so if you feel a need to come down to the station…"

"I'll be there." He said it quickly, then closed his eyes and added, "Sergeant?"

"Yes, Detective?"

"How the hell did he get out?"

"Not entirely clear on that yet."

It wasn't even close to a good enough answer, and

he had to loosen his jaw to answer. "All right. I'm on my way."

The stone-heavy feeling in Lucien's gut intensified as he hung up, and he cursed himself for the fact that he *hadn't* kept proper tabs on her. Three years ago, she'd been his responsibility. For two months straight, he'd been directly in charge of her safety, more bodyguard than cop at that point.

Maybe because you would've liked it to be more than that?

As quickly as the question came, he shoved it off. Not because it wasn't true. It definitely was. Not a day had gone by over the last three years that Lucien hadn't thought of her. Even when he was trying to avoid it, his mind would always slip in a little bit of Raven right before he fell asleep. The soft, dark waves of her hair. Those deep blue eyes that looked almost indigo in the dark. The rare sound of her laugh, or the clean, soapy scent that hung in the air when she stood close enough. Yeah, there was no denying that Lucien would've chosen something more.

The problem was that he couldn't acknowledge any of that to his boss. Even if he'd been the type to regularly expound upon his feelings, there was zero chance he'd just come out and say, *Sorry, Sergeant. I didn't follow up on her life because it was what I actually* wanted *to do, and that sure as hell wasn't okay.*

"Backfired in the worse way possible, didn't it?" he muttered, finally opening his eyes again. "How am I going to find her, if she doesn't want to be found?"

As the words left his mouth, the TV caught his eye once more, and he realized he didn't even need an answer to the questions. The three-year anniversary date told him exactly where Raven Elliot would be, regardless as to her current address.

The morning breeze had the tiniest bit of a chill. It ruffled Raven Elliot's long ponytail, reminding her that even though she had her jacket tied around her waist as she jogged through the streets, it wasn't quite spring. Her step counter had buzzed a while back, telling her she'd hit the seven-kilometer mark. It was her target, four days a week. But today was different. She wasn't out for exercise. She wasn't out for fresh air. She wasn't *really* even out to clear her head, though the clarity offered by the rush of oxygen was a bonus. But no. Today wasn't about that. It was about a destination. And remembering.

One thousand and ninety-five, Raven thought as she hit a corner, then bounced on the spot as she waited for a car to go by before crossing.

That was how many days had passed since the bars slid shut on the man who'd destroyed her life by taking away everyone who mattered. And of those days, Raven had spent one thousand and—give or take—avoiding thinking about it. The solitary weeks after had been the hardest. She'd spent too *much* time thinking about it. Every waking second, it'd felt like. And there were still moments when she couldn't help but let it overwhelm in. Birthdays. Holidays. Dates that should've been celebratory, but were instead nothing but tragic. But as soon as the thoughts reared up, she stuffed them back down again.

It wasn't a particularly healthy coping mechanism. As a grief counselor, she knew that better than most. But it was her *only* coping mechanism. And if she was being honest, it worked better than any of the techniques she taught to her clients. Temporarily, anyway.

One day, she told herself. *One day I'll figure out how to confront it.*

But for now, avoidance was what she stuck with. Except today, on the anniversary of Georges Hanes's incarceration. It was the only time she consciously mulled things over. She thought about her parents and her brother, and she cursed the man who killed them. She remembered his complete lack of remorse and his final official statement, where he at last confessed, then admitted that if he were set free, he'd do it all over again. Raven also let herself consider whether or not there was anything she could've done differently, while it was happening. Some clue. Some missed hint. A move that would've saved a life. And on top of all of that, she thought about Detective Lucien Match—which was slightly more self-centered than the rest—and she let herself be painfully sad.

What's he doing now? Raven wondered.

It was Tuesday, so probably working. She could easily picture his large frame straining against the crisp white shirt he preferred to wear while on official police business. His fingers would be tugging at his tie, perpetually loosening and tightening it until the very second his shift ended. Then he'd take it off, toss it aside and let out a dramatic sigh he wasn't even conscious of. Raven, on the other hand, was conscious of every move he made. It was an unavoidable consequence of spending twenty-four hours a day together for two months straight.

She knew that when he was having a hard time expressing himself, he tugged on his right ear.

She knew that he laughed out loud when he read the

comics in the newspaper, which he did every morning as a way of easing some of the pressure of his very *non*funny job.

She knew that when he got a cold, he snored, and that it embarrassed him, and that he bought funny little nasal strips to combat the issue.

In short, she knew him as well as a wife knew a husband—the good, the bad, the meaningless and the meaningful details of his existence—and there was a time when she'd thought that would become a reality.

Transference.

It was the word she repeated to herself each time she woke up from a dream full of brown eyes and salt-and-pepper hair. The concept she clung to, in order to excuse the way she felt about Lucien. She didn't love him. She just thought she did. But the fact that he hadn't felt the same still made her eyes sting, even three years later. Her chest ached longingly anyway. The time and the space between them had done nothing to ease the way she wanted him. It was like fresh heartbreak, every time his face crept up on her.

Transference, she repeated silently.

It would've been a little pathetic if it were anything but that.

She hit another corner, tossed a glance back and forth, then darted across the road. She was getting closer now. And instead of being slowed by reluctance, she pushed on a little harder, a little faster. Her feet smacked the pavement, sending a roughly pleasant vibration through her feet and up her calves. The motion made her feel more powerful than she did in day-to-day life, and she liked it.

She picked up the pace again. The houses gave way to trees, which blurred by in a green-and-brown haze.

A slight hill loomed ahead, and Raven's lungs already burned in anticipation. She dropped her body a little lower, made her stride a little shorter and pushed on.

Halfway up, she thought her legs might give out. Her thighs and calves burned simultaneously, protesting against the effort. Raven would pay for it, when the day was over. She'd probably be sore for a week, actually. But even if she'd been thinking about that ahead of time—and had factored in the extra three kilometers added because of her relocation, five months earlier— she still wouldn't have altered her plan.

The burn was good. Earned. Needed. And when she reached the top of the hill, she was smiling through the pain. She had a crazy urge to lift both her hands over her head and let out a self-directed cheer. But a dark-colored car passed her on the road just then, and through its window she could see the driver. He wore a dark hood and sunglasses, and his mouth was set in a down-turned line. It solidly reminded her that this wasn't the place for a celebration.

Breathing heavily, Raven lifted her gaze and found the familiar wrought iron fence. Its rose accents and curling letters were taken straight from the how-to-decorate-a-cemetery handbook. Black. Pretty. But not what could be accurately described as inviting.

Pushing off an unreasonable prickle of the hairs on the back of her neck, Raven rolled her shoulders, then stepped forward. She made her way through the gate and followed the winding road down the other side of the hill. At the bottom, she could see a row of small but ornate buildings. They were all old mausoleums, and were still used as such. But one building stood apart from the rest, and even though its exterior was much the same as the others, it was actually home to the resident caretaker and his wife. Jim and Juanita Rickson. The kindly couple—who were roughly the same age as Raven's parents had been, and whom Raven had come to know quite well in those first, hard months by herself—would be expecting her today, so she aimed herself in that direction first.

But when she got to the door and gave it a light tap, there was no answer. It was a little unusual for neither of them to be there. Obviously, there were outside things to be done. Lawns and pruning. Plots to be maintained or prepared. *Still.* One or the other usually stuck around in case visitors had questions, or in case the phone rang.

"Jim!" Raven called, knocking again just in case. "Juanita?"

She waited for another few moments, then decided to try a second time after her visit to her family. Brushing off another tickle of unease, she headed back up the path away from the buildings, then rerouted to the main part of the cemetery. It was a few minutes' walk to the spot where she was headed, and the temperature seemed to be dropping and the cool breeze was fast becoming an actual win. It felt extra cold on Raven's sweat-drenched skin. But it wasn't the declining weather that made her shiver as her family's three headstones came into view. It was what sat at their bases.

Flowers.

A mistake, maybe? But what were the chances that some person had come by with three identical bouquets and placed them against the wrong stones without noticing? They were bright and fresh, too. No wilting whatsoever. Like they hadn't been there long at all. And the closer Raven got, the more warning bells went off in her head.

She stole a surreptitious look back and fore, trying

to subtly search for who might've left them. She took another few steps forward because she was afraid that if she stopped, it would draw attention to the fact that she'd noticed the oddity. Then a branch cracked from somewhere behind her, and her resolve to look normal evaporated.

She spun and crouched at the same time. Her plan was to launch herself into a run. To take off as fast and hard as she could. But she only made it as far as the turn before she crashed straight into a terrifyingly solid, undeniably male form. And all she could do to save herself as a set of too-strong arms closed around her shoulders was let out a bloodcurdling scream, aim her knee at her assailant's groin and pray for the best.

Chapter 2

The only reason Lucien was able to stop himself from taking a blow to the most unpleasant place possible was that he'd taught her the trick himself.

Eyes or baby-maker, he thought as he stepped back to avoid her attack on the latter.

That's the choice that he'd teasingly given her during an impromptu self-defense lesson. He'd actually *enjoyed* teaching her how to take down a man twice her size. Not just because it would potentially save her from ever succumbing to the same fate she'd endured when Hanes grabbed her, but also because Lucien got to play the bad guy, and the bad guy got to put his hands on Raven. A lot. He couldn't even regret it now as he automatically defended himself from her next move— a jab at his eyes, just like he'd shown her.

Hands up, thumbs out.

Lucien split the intended attack wide by driving his

own arms up between hers, then pushing her hands apart. He said her name at the same time.

"Raven."

She didn't seem to hear him. It wasn't surprising, considering the wild, terrified look on her face. Her eyes were wide and unseeing, her mouth trembling with sharp breaths.

"Raven," he repeated, a little louder.

It didn't do any good. She was already on the attack again, this time in a move that was sheer desperation. Her palms drove forward and smacked hard into his chest, and in spite of his greater size and strength, the impact threw Lucian off-balance. His feet fought to stay stable, but a divot in the ground made it impossible. With arms flailing, he started to topple backward. Automatically, he grasped for something to keep himself upright. Except the only thing in reaching distance was Raven, who hadn't quite backed off after her lunge. So his fingers closed on her. She wasn't stable, either. His sudden grab yanked her forward, and together, they hit the ground.

Her compact frame splayed over him, and for a moment, the pose was actually blissful. In spite of the way Lucien's back smacked to the grass and in spite of the fact that his elbow hit a rock, it still felt damn good to have her close. The smell he remembered was the same. Her skin was as soft as it'd always been. And when her eyes at last cleared enough that she was really seeing him, the sun lost its struggle with the clouds overhead, and her irises took on that unusual shade he'd always found so mesmerizing.

"Lucien!"

Her gasp made him want to groan, and not just because the first thing she'd said was his name. Hearing her familiar voice brought him right back to the last time they'd been this close. It'd been the moment Georges Hanes had received his verdict. The relief had been palpable. Almost joyful. Raven had thrown herself into his arms. Purposely, that time. Her slim arms had found purchase around his neck, her subtle curves had pressed to his body and she'd murmured how glad she was it was all over. Finally. Then she'd leaned back— but not too far back—and stared up at him, her eyes soft and expectant.

Lucien had wanted to kiss her. To channel two months of pent-up desire into a heated meshing of mouths. To drag her to the bed. To turn the time they'd shared out of obligation and necessity into a second two months, this time out of passion and choice.

He'd waited a heartbeat too long. Just enough time for reason and truth to step in and remind him that not only would it be crossing every professional boundary in existence, but it would also end in disaster. Lucien couldn't give her the love and tenderness she deserved. He was capable of so much—chasing down impossible clues, putting criminals behind bars—but he wasn't the right man for softness. Hell. He couldn't even say the words, let alone put them into action. Yet right here, right now, it seemed like insanity not to have tried.

Three years, he thought. *What was I thinking, letting her go?*

The truth was, though, that she was never really his *to* let go.

Stupid, he chastised. *So stupid.*

Unconsciously, he reached up and placed his palm on the side of her face, then dropped it again before he touched her. He wished he'd been able to take a different path. So badly that it was an ache through his whole body. What would happen if he kissed her now? Would she kiss him back? Smack his face instead? Confirm what he already knew and tell him he could never be that particular brand of man for her?

"Lucien." She breathed again. "Is that really you?"

He made himself focus on the present. On reality.

"It's me." His voice was gruffer than he would've liked. "You all right?"

"I'm—oh. Yes. Hang on." Her face had already turned pink, and she quickly slid off him to sit back on the grass. "Sorry."

The loss of contact brought a rush of cold, unpleasant air. Lucien fought an urge to simply grab her and pull her back so that she was flush against him once more.

"Don't be sorry," he made himself say instead, sitting up as he spoke. "Didn't mean to the scare the crap out of you."

"You didn't." She paused. "Well, you did. But not on purpose, I assume. Or I hope. Because I don't like to assume. But you know that."

In spite of the oddity of the circumstances—and in spite of the news he'd come to impart, too—Lucien chuckled. Raven's quirky awkwardness always made him laugh. She had a knack for saying whatever random thing popped into her head. It was the exact opposite of his own conversation style, which was far more minimalist.

"Did I hurt you?" she asked, and he swore there was a hint of hopefulness in the question.

He lifted his eyebrows. "You missed the important bits, if that's what you're asking."

The pink in her cheeks deepened. "I was just trying to do what you taught me."

"Yes, you were."

His statement was followed by a moment of silence. Somehow, the somewhat meaningless conversation and the brief interlude after carried all the weight of three years of separation. All the questions. It was hard to bear.

Trying to shake it off, Lucien pressed his knee to the ground, then stood and held out his hand. She eyed his palm for a second before bypassing his unspoken offer of help. She came to her feet without assistance and took a tiny step back and lifted a guarded look in his direction.

"Lucien…" she said. "What are you *doing* here?"

He opened his mouth to explain. He knew there wasn't any point in sugarcoating it, and words weren't his forte anyway.

But how do I say it? How do I tell her that her nightmare is on the loose?

He tried again, but then spied the way Raven's eyes flicked toward her parents' and brother's gravesites, and he used it as a temporary stay on his explanation.

"Something the matter?" he asked.

She drew in a nervous breath. "Someone left flowers. Was it you?"

"Me? No."

"Oh."

Lucien frowned. He knew Raven's family history well enough to understand why she found it disconcerting to see the flowers there. Mr. and Mrs. Elliot had both been only children, and any relatives they had were far too distant to come bearing flowers. They were well liked in their little neighborhood, but the cemetery was almost a hundred kilometers from where they'd spent their last days. Raven's brother, Ryan, had been a solitary guy. No wife, no girlfriend, and only a few people in his life close enough to be called friends. The flowers were definitely unusual.

All of that...plus the fact that Georges Hanes is on the loose... It gave Lucien an icy feeling in the pit of his stomach. *Dammit. You have to tell her.*

For the second time, he started to speak. This time, it wasn't a look that stopped him. It was a God-awful, terror-filled scream.

Lucien made a split-second decision. His job compelled him to act on the scream, but his heart wouldn't let him abandon Raven. So he did the only thing he could. He grabbed her hand and tugged her to the source of the noise.

Raven's heart had whiplash. It went from beating frantically in fear because of the flowers to slowing with relief when she realized her "attacker" was actually Detective Lucien Match, to skipping a beat when she realized it *really was* Lucien. And now, as they ran hurriedly down the path toward the scream, it was back to fear.

But even with the scream, Raven was infused with a strange undercurrent of coming home. Because as inappropriate as the timing might be, her pulse surged with familiarity. With safety. With the fact that she'd *missed* him for the last three years. Even when she'd been blotting him away from the prominent parts of her mind, he'd still been there, just waiting for a moment like this one. One where he could pop back into her life and remind her solidly that he wasn't gone at all.

In the two minutes they'd been pressed together, Raven noted every detail, new and old. His silver-flecked hair was a little longer than it had been before, but it suited him. It added just a hint of wildness that she liked. He had a few more lines around his eyes, too. A hazard of the job, he'd once told her. Cops aged more quickly than the average population, he'd joked.

But other things were the same. His mouth, for example, hadn't changed a bit. Curved and full, and imbued with something she'd always thought of as strength. Perfect for kissing. Or so she assumed, because she'd never done more than dream about it.

She'd also dreamed about running her fingers over his ruggedly square jaw, which was currently lined with about two days' worth of stubble. The partial beard made her wonder what he was working on, because his shaving habits were like clockwork. He only deviated from them when he was under enormous pressure. So seeing it had filled her with an urge to ask. Which in turn made her want to ask a hundred other things.

God, how I missed him.

The silent admission was more an ache than anything else. Deeper than the one in her body, more biting than the cool air.

Then a second scream cut through the air, and any good thoughts were swept away by the intensity of the sound. Lucien's fingers tightened on hers, and their pace intensified. They were almost back to the row of mausoleums now—their roofs were just visible—and it made Raven want to stop short. Because in her head, she knew it meant something terrible. A horrible explanation for why neither Jim nor Juanita had answered the door. As much as she tried to tell herself it could be unrelated, or something not as bad as what flashed through her mind, Raven couldn't sweep it away.

And it was suddenly *her* pushing them to move faster. Her feet hit the ground so hard that her eyes watered. She was in front of Lucien, straining to pull him along. He was saying something. Arguing. Ordering her to stop. Logically, she knew she was headed straight into potential danger. But she couldn't stop herself. She broke free and pushed on, nearly falling more than once as she tore down the hill.

Her thoughts—a frightened plea—bounced in time with her feet.

Please, no. Please, no. Please, no.

She made it all the way to the door—and even placed her hand on the knob—before Lucien caught up to her. And he wasn't messing around. His arms slammed into a vice around Raven's body, and he actually lifted her up and physically moved her away from the front step. She struggled to get free, but he didn't let go, even when she drove an elbow into his stomach.

"Let me go!" she hollered.

"Raven," he said into her ear, his voice as calm as ever. "You *need* to let me go in first."

Her near-hysterical reply contrasted sharply with his tone. "But you don't even *know* them!"

"No. I don't. But I know *you*. So I know you're not armed. I know you're scared and worried. And I know you don't have a death wish."

"And you do have one?" It was a ridiculous question, and she knew it before he even answered.

"You know that I don't," he said gently. "But this is my job, Raven."

"I know that."

"So let me do it, then. Tell me their names."

She stopped fighting and sagged against him. "Jim and Juanita."

"Thank you."

He gave her a quick squeeze—less restraining and more comforting this time—then let her go and stepped toward the door. He reached up and gave the wood two sharp taps, then immediately went for the handle, calling out in an authoritative way as he did it.

"This is Detective Lucien Match with the VPD," he announced as he gave the knob a light twist. "I'm coming in slowly. Jim or Juanita, if you're here, now would be a good time to say so."

Raven waited for him to add that he was armed, or something to that effect. But he said nothing about a weapon, and she realized belatedly that it was probably because he wasn't carrying one. Not unless he had it magically stowed inside his jogging gear. And why was he there in athletic apparel, anyway? He wasn't exactly dressed for police work. It was another belated realization. And possibly an important one.

Raven's concern spiked, and she started to comment, but Lucien spoke first.

"Stick close behind me," he said over his shoulder.

Her relief at not being left behind overrode her worry for a second, silencing her. And the pause was just long enough that Lucien had time to swing the door open. But the alleviation only lasted as long as it took for Raven to catch a glimpse of the entryway. Signs of a struggle were obvious. An umbrella stand lay on its side, the contents strewn over the floor. A coat tree had met the same fate, and its base was actually cracked, leaving several jagged edges sticking up. Glass littered the tile, but it was impossible to say what, exactly, had broken. It could've come partially from the shattered French doors on the opposite side of the foyer. But the larger, glittery pieces looked like something else. Whatever it was, nothing about the scene was good.

Lucien's posture grew stiffer, and he put his arms out—as though Raven was going to attempt to run past.

Or maybe like he's going to use his body as a shield, she thought with a shiver.

She hated the idea. But she wouldn't put it past him to try. He was doggedly heroic like that. No one knew it better than Raven. And she wouldn't forgive herself if he sacrificed himself.

"Lucien," she whispered. "I think—"

Her words cut off as a small, barely discernible cry lifted from somewhere ahead. Lucien—who'd turned his head her way when she'd said his name—jerked his attention forward again.

"It's her!" Raven said, grabbing at his arm. "It's Juanita."

"We can't be sure," he replied.

"I *am* sure. And if you don't yell for her, I will," she warned.

"That's not how this works," he said. "I'm not just urging caution for fun. You think I *wanted* to come out here like this? I'm supposedly on a vacation, but this morning I got called out because—"

"Because *what*?"

But there was another muted sob, and Raven cared less about an answer and more about action. She was a-hundred-percent sure the sound had come from the caretaker's wife. The fear of not being able to help— *please, God, don't let it happen like that again*—overwhelmed her common sense, and now she *did* rush ahead. Lucien tried to stop her, but she ducked under his arm and darted forward to push through the broken French doors on the other side of the small space. The big man hissed out a curse, and his feet thumped on the floor as he gave chase. But Raven was quick, and she knew where she was headed.

The layout was a touch unusual. A hazard of the

building conversion and the addition. But Raven moved without hesitation. She took a left in the T-shaped hall—going to the right would've led to the attached greenhouse—and slammed through the swinging door. On the other side of it were two more doors. The first—the one that led directly into the caretaker's living quarters—was closed. The second—which led to the main office—was not only open, but also hung awkwardly from its hinges.

Heart thumping, she paused. "Juanita?"

"Raven? Is that you?" came the wobbly-voiced reply. "I'm in here."

Both relieved to hear Juanita answer and also worried about what she'd else find, Raven stepped forward. But she didn't make it all the way to the door before Lucien appeared at the end of the hall, his expression dark.

"Are you trying to get yourself killed?" he growled. "I don't remember you being this reckless."

In spite of the circumstances—and in spite of the fact that he was right, too—his tone made Raven bristle. Three years ago, he might've known her better than anyone else on the planet. But he'd left. And she'd had to pick up the rest of the pieces on her own.

"People change," she replied stiffly, spinning toward the broken door.

Ignoring Lucien's continued protest, she stepped into the room. And what she found was both better and worse than what she'd anticipated. There was no evidence of a body, which flooded her with a relief so strong that her eyes watered. But the state of the room was frighteningly disastrous. Books and papers were scattered everywhere. The desk had been flipped. And an ominously crimson substance was slashed across the wall.

She heard Lucien's indrawn breath, and then she heard the beep of his phone, followed by a reel-off of official sounding numbers and letters. But Raven's primary focus was the woman who sat in wide office chair in the corner of the room. She had a shell-shocked expression on her lined face, her gray hair was a wild mess, her hands were wringing in her lap. There were streaks of red on the front of her cream-colored blouse, and she wore only one shoe.

Raven hurried to her side and knelt to take her hand. "Juanita. Are you hurt? Tell me where."

The older woman shook her head. "No. It's not me. It's—"

Her voice broke, and Raven knew it was about her husband. Before she could stop it, her gaze flicked toward the red walls. An all-over body chill made her shake.

Oh, God. It's blood.

It had to be. There was nothing else with quite than hue. But there was so much of it. How could there *possibly* be that much? She could only think of one way to get it, and her stomach churned to even consider it.

She had to force herself to speak in a calm voice.

"Where is he, Juanita? Where's Jim?" she asked softly.

Juanita blinked, her dark eyes filling with tears. "That's the thing. I don't know. He's just…gone."

Raven breathed out. The other woman went on, describing how she'd stepped out for a few minutes and come back to find the place like this. Raven tried to listen. She tried to focus. It was harder than she wanted it to be, because a dozen bad memories kept trying to float to the surface, and it took real concentration to shove them all down. And even with all the effort, she couldn't quite shake the feeling that this moment had something to do with her and her past.

People get broken into all the time, she told herself. *It's unreasonable to think this is about you.*

The reassurance might've helped a little if not for three things. The first being the flowers on her parents' gravesite. The second being the poorly disguised worry in Lucien's voice as he suggested they find a more secure space to wait for backup. And the third being that when she lifted her eyes again, the crimson on the wall finally came into focus, and she realized it wasn't just random slashes…it was words, too. Small and far more precise than their suspected medium should've allowed. Disturbingly, it looked almost like they'd been painted with a brush, and the lettering spelled out a sinister message.

A LIFE IS OWED TO ME. SO I'LL TAKE ONE EVERY DAY UNTIL YOU GIVE ME YOURS.

And she knew that it was intended for her.

Chapter 3

As Lucien paced the length of the small kitchen yet again, he cursed himself for not spitting out the truth when he'd had a moment to earlier. It should've been the first thing he'd said, regardless as how his and Raven's reunion had gone.

Should've taken one look into her eyes and announced it. Be a hell of a lot better than this crap.

She hadn't had much to say as he'd done a fast perimeter check. She'd been quiet during his statement retrieval from Juanita Rickson, too. Even when he'd quickly explained that it was best to write it down while it was still fresh in the older woman's mind, all Raven had done was nod. She was silent now, too, except for the soothing things she murmured to Juanita.

So she's not really silent at all, he thought. *She's just giving* you *the silent treatment.*

Neither of them had brought up the message scrawled

on the wall, and what it likely meant. What he didn't want it to mean, but what would undoubtedly turn out to be the truth. Lucien's mind wavered between wanting to think about it, and not wanting to acknowledge it at all.

Focus on getting through these moments, he told himself. *Deal with the rest—the message included—later.*

Except that if he could've done anything he wanted to, he would've chosen to pull Raven outside to confess the truth right that second. He would've taken her away and hidden her from sight. Of course, even if there'd been a chance that she'd leave Juanita's side, Lucien's police training wouldn't have allowed him to leave the caretaker's wife unattended. Not only was she visibly— and understandably—on edge, but there was also no way to know if the culprit—yes, he was sticking with that generic term until he had proof positive that it was Georges Hanes—was still lurking nearby.

"Lucien."

Raven's voice almost made him jump. He paused in his pacing and turned his attention her way, glad that she was addressing him directly.

"Yes?" he said.

She nodded pointedly at the empty chair at the table. "Sit down. Have some tea."

He eyed the mug that already sat in front of Juanita, then started to open his mouth to remind Raven that he was a coffee man. Which she knew. Then he realized her intention was to get him to cease his pacing.

He cursed himself again, this time for his lack of professionalism. He was generally even tempered. He'd even heard himself called implacable on more than one occasion.

But this is different.

Georges Hanes and Raven herself *made* it different.

The first few weeks they'd spent together had been hell. What Hanes had done to her…what he'd left her with…with*out*…it had nearly broken her. It was Lucien who dragged her out of it. He listened to her cry in her sleep. Comforted her when she was inconsolable. Held her. Cooked her meals, for God's sake. Plus, a hundred other things that he'd never—as a cop or as man—thought he'd be doing for someone. The idea of seeing her go through it all again filled him with teeth-gnashing anger. She'd made it once, but a second? He didn't see it happening.

"Lucien." Raven's tone was just barely shy of sharp this time.

He realized he'd started pacing again, and when he looked toward the two women, he saw that Juanita's face had a hint of concern on it, and it was definitely for him. It would've been funny if it weren't so wrong. Muttering an apology, he sank down into the empty chair. He told himself to relax, at least a little, and dragged the mug of tea closer. If nothing else, the heat provided a focal point. He flexed his fingers on the ceramic.

"Shouldn't be too much longer until the backup arrives," he said a little lamely.

Unexpectedly, Raven's hand came up to rest on his for a moment. The touch—gentle but deliberate—was soothing, and a bit of his tension eased. Ironic, considering that *he* was so damn worried about *her*.

He wondered if she had any idea about the feelings he'd buried. They seemed very, very close to the surface now. Maybe they were even on his face. God, he hoped not.

Thankfully, he was saved from dwelling on it any more. At least for the moment. Sirens came to life in the distance, and got rapidly closer. From there, things moved quickly. The small house came to life in the busy, crime-solving way that Lucien was accustomed to.

As the work got underway, he made sure not to insinuate himself into his colleagues' investigation. Though he stayed close—available to assist with their questions about what he'd seen—he was careful to play the role of witness rather than cop. He pretended not to tense as they paid extra care in photographing the crimson letters, and blocked out their whispered suppositions about the words. The only bit of interference he ran was when he pulled his boss aside to ask that Raven not be told about Georges Hanes. He still wanted to be the one to do it. Sergeant Gray agreed, so Lucien simply rode through as an observer, watching the team work through the scene.

An on-duty detective came in and took over where he'd left off, questioning Juanita more thoroughly than he'd done, using his notes as reference.

A couple of uniformed officers and a scent-tracking dog explored the interior and the exterior. Unsurprisingly, they found nothing and everything at the same time. The whole area was marked with Jim Rickson's scent. Yet there was no specific path leading anywhere.

An ambulance arrived on scene with the others, and the paramedics examined the caretaker's wife. She had a meltdown while they were taking her blood pressure, and they administered a sedative. The medical professionals decided it would be in her best interest to speak to someone at the hospital. They took her away, lights on, sirens off.

Two forensics officials got there shortly after that, and they began their process. Photographing. Sampling.

Note taking. They were methodical in their technical, all-important, scientific realm.

Through it all, Lucien kept up his calm front. But all he really wanted to do was stick by Raven's side. Or to be more accurate, he just wanted to remove her from the whole thing. So when his boss made the suggestion that he take her away from the scene for a break, he jumped on the chance.

Once they were moving along in his car, though, he found himself wanting another few minutes of non-Hanes-related conversation. His earlier need to just spring the truth on her seemed needlessly abrupt.

Better to ease into it.

"Doing okay over there?" He paused, realized it was a bit of a ridiculous question considering the circumstances, then added, "Relatively speaking, I mean."

She exhaled, then nodded. "I'm in one piece."

"The team will take good care of Juanita," he promised. "The VPD has some of the best officials around."

"I know."

The two-word reply was loaded with something heavier, but Lucien couldn't pinpoint quite what it was. He wasn't sure he wanted to. Not right at that moment, anyway.

He cleared his throat and tried to change the subject. "So…the records say that you moved recently."

There was a brief hesitation before she answered, and he sneaked a look her way. Her expression was puzzled. Like she was thinking, *Small talk? Really?* After another second, though, she shook her head and let out a tiny sigh, accepting it.

"Yes," she said. "I got a cat."

It wasn't what he was expecting to hear. "What?"

"A cat."

"A cat?"

"Yes," she said again, this time with a little smile. "Goes meow, is covered in fluff. Purrs and knocks over my flowers on purpose. Actually, he's kind of a jerk, now that I think about it."

He couldn't fight a chuckle. "Glad he was worth a complete move."

"He kind of was, though," she replied. "He finally got me out my co-op lease. And you know I hated that place more than a little."

He *did* know. She disliked the high-density housing location. Her property-management company was terrible at staying on top of maintenance. The only thing that had kept her there was the five-year buy-in she'd taken just before everything in her life got turned upside down. Moving early would've forfeited the investment. But admitting just how well Lucien remembered every detail would only draw unnecessary attention to his feelings, and probably also bring things back to the topic he was currently avoiding.

So he cleared his throat again. "And work? You quit the reception job, I heard."

It was actually the last thing he'd found out before realizing that the tabs he kept on her were always going to be more than professional.

"That's right," she said. "I went back to school. Grief counseling."

"Interesting work?"

"I like it, and I think I'm pretty good at it."

He could picture it, actually. She'd be able to use her own experience as a solid foundation for helping others. He liked the idea that she could do that. Bring some good out of the bad.

They talked like that for a few more minutes, all of

the conversation basic. Steered toward keeping things on the surface. He told her a few anecdotes about recent arrests—the same ones he saved for entertaining strangers at parties. She chatted about school, and said how she was surprised to find out she enjoyed learning, then asked about his career. He admitted to passing on an opportunity for promotion because it would've taken him out of the province, and he didn't want to leave the West Coast. It was a good conversation. One that felt nearly normal. He even enjoyed it a little, even as he acknowledged just how badly he'd missed the simple sound of her voice. And every time things threatened to get more serious, or skirted around the past—which would inevitably lead to the Kitsilano Killer—Lucien very carefully turned things light again. Except when a slight lull hung in the exchange, Raven let out a small sigh, and her eyes fixed out the front of the car, and he realized he hadn't been fooling her at all. Her next words confirmed it.

"You kind of suck at this, Lucien." In spite of its content, the statement held no rancor. "Even if all that back there hadn't just happened, and even if I couldn't tell that we're headed toward our old safe house, you still wouldn't be able to just pretend we're two old friends, catching up."

His hands tightened on the wheel. He thought about arguing with her. Or pleading ignorance. The he thought better of it, and shook his head instead.

"I know," he replied. "Never been very good at that fake it till you make it stuff."

"Don't say that like it's a bad thing."

"Isn't it?"

He didn't mean the question to sound so loaded, and her gaze flicked his way. He didn't look toward her, but he could feel the curiosity in her stare. His fingers squeezed a bit harder. He *did* suck at surface stuff. At small talk.

But you're way worse at the important stuff, aren't you? he said to himself. *If you weren't, maybe things wouldn't have turned out the way they did.*

"Lucien…"

His name wasn't much louder than an exhale, and it was tinged with emotion. She paused after she said it, and he braced himself for something. A confrontation, maybe. An accusation. For her to echo his own sour thoughts on his inability to express himself. None of it came. A moment later, she spoke again, her voice firmer.

"Why don't you just tell me why you really came out and found me today?" she asked.

He worked to relax his hands. "I think we should wait until we get to the safe house."

"No." She said it sharply, and before Lucien could react to the surprising vehemence, her hand was beside his on the wheel.

"What are you doing?"

"If you don't tell me, I'm pulling us over and I'm getting out."

"Pulling us over? You're not—"

Her hand gave a yank, and in spite of his own, stiff grip—or maybe because of it—the steering wheel turned an inch in her direction, then bounced back in his. The car shuddered. Lucien tried to adjust, but Raven pulled again. This time, the vehicle veered hard to the right.

"Raven!"

She tugged a third time, and the tires crossed the line, and sent gravel flying up. A horn honked from behind them, and even though Lucien didn't believe she actually wanted to cause an accident, he slammed on the brakes and brought the vehicle to an abrupt stop. The moment they stopped moving. Raven slammed her seat belt off, flung open the door and jumped out. Cursing under his breath, Lucien followed.

"Raven!" he said again.

She flashed a look his way. It was angry and scared and hurt at the same time. Lucien took a step toward her, wanting to sooth it all away. As usual, words failed him. When he said nothing, she spun away, and the sight of her back brought a rush of memory in. The pale pink T-shirt she'd been wearing when he last saw her. The nagging surety that he was making the biggest mistake of his life by letting her go, battling with the knowledge that he wasn't the right man for her.

I don't want to go through that again.

"It's Hanes," he blurted.

She paused. "*What* is?"

"He escaped this morning during a transfer from one cell block to another."

She turned back. Her expression was shocked, and she shook her head disbelievingly. For a second, he thought she was going to deny his claim. Instead, her eyes rolled back, and with a heartbeat to spare, Lucien realized she was in the process of passing out. He rushed forward and closed his arms around her just before she hit the ground.

Raven was having the most pleasant dream. But it wasn't new. It was actually a variation of one of her favorite recurring ones.

In it, she and Lucien hadn't gone their separate ways. He'd confessed his love to her in a gruff but meaningful way that suited him perfectly. They'd stuck it out, and were entering into blissful, wedded life.

It was cheesy as anything. But she didn't care. It was a dream, and that's what dreams were for. And this particular time, it felt extra real. She could smell the deep, musky scent that was uniquely Lucien. His arms cradled her close to his chest, and the warmth he exuded was much more enjoyable than her flannel sheets. She wriggled a little, trying to get closer. His grip tightened, and she sighed contentedly, her eyelids fluttering. She could even *see* him in this dream. And not vaguely. She smiled at the line of his chin. How could one man have such a perfect chin? And what even constituted a perfect chin?

Doesn't matter, said Raven's groggy brain. *Whatever it is, Lucien has it.*

"I'm so glad we did this," she murmured.

"Did what?" he replied, his voice rumbling close to her ear.

"Got married."

Under her, Lucien did a very non-romantic-dream thing. He let out a choked cough, then stumbled forward. His momentum drove them straight into a wall, crushing Raven between his big body and cedar paneling. The sharp pain in her shoulder made her eyes fly the rest of the way open, and too late, she clued in that it wasn't a dream this time.

The last thing she remembered was standing across from Lucien on the side of the road as he delivered his shocking news. Now they were inside the front entryway of the safe house the two of them had called home for nearly nine weeks. And Lucien was carrying her for real. He'd probably carried her to the car, too. And now he was staring down at her, his chocolate colored gaze full of surprise.

Yeah, because you just told him you were glad you got married.

Embarrassment flooded through Raven, heating her face and making her stomach churn. The only good thing about the abject humiliation was that it temporarily distracted her from the terror that had gripped her when he'd revealed the truth about Georges Hanes.

Georges Hanes. Oh, God.

Her vision swam, and she had to work to keep from slipping away again. The man was free. And she was sure that whatever had happened to Jim and Juanita was intended to hurt her.

"Raven?" Lucien's voice pulled her back to the moment, and she took a breath.

"I'm okay."

"You sure?"

"Yeah, I was just—" She cut herself off before the word *dreaming* could escape from her lips, and tried again, hoping Lucien either hadn't noticed, or would simply let it go. "I'm fine. It was just a shock. You can put me down."

He didn't comply right away, though. Instead his mouth opened like he had something to say. She tensed, waiting for a statement that would add to her already heightened awkwardness. But after a moment, his jaw snapped shut again, and he stepped back and eased her to the floor.

"Here we are," he said. "Should we go in?"

"Sure."

She let him lead her up the hall to the open-concept living space. She knew the way, but stepping in behind Lucien gave her a minute to process their environment without his always observant eyes on her. And maybe he needed the time, too, because when they reached the attached kitchen and great room, he flicked on the gas fireplace, then gestured to the couch and suggested she sit down while he made some of their favorite hot chocolate.

We're really here, she thought as she sank down into the familiar spot.

Her eyes roamed over the adjoined rooms, looking everywhere but right at Lucien.

It was the same as she remembered. Neutral but homey colors. Wide windows covered in beige curtains. Classy but durable furniture. Raven knew as much about it as if it had really been her home. If her own place had been designed with police-witness safety in mind, that is. Late one evening when neither she nor Lucien could sleep, he'd told her a rash of details. Like the fact that every piece of glass was the shatterproof kind. And that the bookcase across the room had a false back for storing weapons. Maybe it was weird to think of a living space like that as home. But Raven had felt secure. She'd liked it. She'd *missed* it when she'd moved back to her real apartment.

A hundred times, she'd considered driving by, just to get a look at the house. But the police had cautioned her against the idea. It could put some other, under-the-radar victim in jeopardy.

It was strange to her, to think that the moment she and Lucien walked out, someone else might've walked in. How many people had stayed there in the last three years? Had any of them felt like she had, and wished they never needed to leave, even when their ordeal was over?

Her gaze made another pass over the space. This

time, something caught her eye. A small notepad jutted out from the edge of the fireplace mantel.

Raven pushed to her feet. She knew what it was before she even got close enough to snag it.

Country Kitchen.

Those were the words stamped onto the top of every page. And every three-inch-by-four-inch sheet was lined, and each row had a miniature cow on one side and a tiny rooster on the other.

When she lifted it up to take a look, she was expecting all of that. But what she wasn't anticipating was to see a shopping list in her own, familiar handwriting.

Chapter 4

A moment of surrealism overtook Raven. It was as though she was right there writing the list all over again.

Eggs.

Coffee filters.

Bread (no seeds, please).

Sparkling water.

Her fingers were just forming the next word—*mozzarella*—when the call had come through. She'd stopped, midscrawl, when Lucien let out an out-of-character cheer, then hurried toward her. She'd hugged him impulsively, then realized what she'd done and started to pull away. But even *more* atypically, he'd scooped her off the ground, practically crowing about the guilty verdict that had come in way sooner than anticipated.

It'd been an incredible moment. Georges Hanes, getting life behind bars. Lucien holding her close like she'd wanted him to for the last two months. She'd laughed. Met his eyes. Anticipated a kiss. Her whole body had tingled with need, and she'd sworn the responding desire was evident in Lucien's eyes. He wasn't prone to overblown emotional outbursts or long speeches about his feelings, but Raven had thought that she'd known him well enough to see what was under the surface. He wasn't just a good man; he was the best kind of man. Hardworking and patient and morally upstanding. She'd believed all of that was the reason he'd held back. How she'd been so wrong was a painful mystery. Because just a heartbeat after he'd picked her up, he'd set her down again, murmuring about being glad the case was over. And she'd definitely had no problem understanding that what he was really saying was goodbye.

The remembered disappointment was a sharp ache in her chest. One that made her have to blink away threatening tears. It'd hurt then and it still hurt now.

You need to let it go.

Forcing a few calming breaths, Raven brought her attention back to the moment. She frowned down at the list, seeing that it had a not-too-light coating of dust on it. Like it had been sitting there for all of the three years. Except it seemed impossible that it might actually be true. The little notepad had been resting in plain sight, exactly where she'd set it right before Lucien had told her the news. Surely, someone would've seen it and put it away somewhere? Or if they'd assumed it belonged on the mantel, wouldn't they have ripped off her list and thrown it away to make their own? Or dusted it?

She frowned and lifted her gaze, a puzzled question on her lips. But she stopped without uttering it. Because Lucien stood right on the transition board between the tile in the kitchen and the carpet in the living room, a mug in each of his hands, and a strange look on his face. It almost looked like…guilt. Maybe mixed with a bit of embarrassment. And his eyes were definitely trained on the list that Raven held.

She cleared her throat, and his head jerked up. And if she didn't know better, she'd have said his cheeks were flushed.

"Hey," he said, his voice laced with awkwardness as he stepped closer. "Best-before date on the hot chocolate says next month. Cutting it close, but we should still be good, right?"

"If not… I guess there are worse ways to go." The joke fell flat under the current circumstances, and Raven felt her cheeks warm.

But if Lucien noticed or cared, he didn't say anything. He just held out the cup, handle first. Grateful for the lack of comment, Raven started to reach for it. But she stopped abruptly when she saw the logo on the side. It was a picture of a Boston terrier. Innocuous to most. But personal to her. To *them*.

When they'd first settled into the safe house, Raven had noticed that every dish in the cupboards was the same as the others—plain white ceramic. She'd commented on it. She'd told Lucien that it made the place seem less real because she'd never met a person who didn't have at least a mismatched mug or two. The very next day, the Boston terrier mug arrived. He refused to tell her where it had come from. But more mugs came, too. One each week, even though the cupboard was overcrowded after just three had been added. Lucien had gotten rid of some of the white ones to make room, but laughingly told Raven that the moment the place was swept for new residents, the out-of-place mugs would be tossed and replaced again.

So why is this one still here?

Fighting an urge to go and fling open the cupboards to check for the others, she took the proffered mug, then sat down.

"Lucien…" she said. "Has no one used the house since we were here?"

He seated himself on the other end of the couch. "No."

"But didn't you tell me it was one of the most popular choices?"

"Yes. That's right."

He took a sip of from his own mug, and she was absolutely sure he was trying to sidestep an explanation. It was odd. As reticent as Lucien could be, he was never evasive.

And why bring me this particular cup if he doesn't want to talk about it?

She brought her gaze up from the Boston terrier to Lucien, and she saw that he was looking at the mug, too. And when she spotted the slight widening of his eyes, she realized it'd been a mistake. He'd probably grabbed the stupid thing by mistake. Habit.

Raven almost laughed. If she'd ever had a reason to stop and think about it, she would definitely have assumed Lucien would be a little better at covering his tracks.

Apparently not.

She made herself keep a completely straight face as she took her own sip, then said, "It's good. Thank you."

"Too bad we don't have any whipped cream," he replied. "I know you love it."

She started to agree, but the words wouldn't quite come out. Her moment of levity fell away. The fact that he *did* know was nothing but another reminder of her past heartbreak. In fact, every moment was the same, and Raven couldn't help but wonder just how much longer it was going to go on. And how much more of it she could handle.

She looked down at her hands. "Are we going to have to go through all of this again?"

Lucien immediately set down his mug and slid over to clasp her fingers in his own. "It's different this time. We know who he is. The public knows his face."

Raven couldn't muster up the courage to tell him that she hadn't just meant Georges Hanes. She switched to discussing the case. It was a necessary conversation anyway.

"How did he get away in the first place?" she asked. "You said it was a transfer?"

"Only within the same prison," he explained. "Some kind of structural upgrade being done. I didn't get all the details from Sergeant Gray, but I can if you want them."

"No. It's fine. None of that changes that he's out there. Out *here*."

"The guys'll catch him, Raven. I promise." He gave her hand a reassuring squeeze, then let her go.

"I know they will," she conceded, trying not to notice how her heart dipped low when he released her fingers. "Or I have to believe it, anyway. But how long will that take? They only caught him the first time by accident."

"There was a sprinkling of shrewdness in there, too," he reminded her.

She didn't argue. It was true. The rookie cop who'd been responsible for Hanes's capture had stopped the evil man for jaywalking, of all things. He'd spied the corner of a piece of pale pink, polka-dotted fabric sticking out of the murderer's back pocket, and recalled that one of the unaccounted-for items in the Kitsilano Killer case was a scarf matching that description. He'd slapped on a pair of cuffs—not really following any kind of protocol at all—and brought Hanes in. *Thank God for probable cause* was what every VPD cop had said at the time. And Raven knew the story well because it had been *her* scarf in the killer's pocket.

"We've talked about my theory on this before, right?" Lucien said.

Raven sighed and nodded. "One part genius, one part happy accident."

"Exactly."

They really had talked about it plenty over the course of their two months together. Criminals—even the ones labeled as masterminds—were human. They were fallible. And the world was full of fortuitous coincidences. The police worked to create more of them. Lucien believed that fate and hard work lined up, and that that was ultimately how crimes got solved. It was a little romantic and a little fantastical. But Raven liked it anyway. It was a colorful chink in the otherwise prosaic detective's armor. But it didn't change the fact that at the moment, a serial killer—one who'd been after her personally—was on the loose.

"I'm scared," she admitted softly, her eyes on the swirling hot chocolate in her mug.

In a rare moment of explicit emotion, he replied, "I know. And I am, too."

Raven looked up, unable to conceal her surprise. Lucien seemed closer than he had just a moment earlier. She could feel the heat from his body more than she could feel the heat from the steaming liquid in her cup.

"This is the last thing I wanted," Lucien added, his

voice rawer than usual. "The last way I wanted us to meet up again."

"It is?"

He really *was* closer. She was sure of it. His subtle, masculine scent permeated the air, and she couldn't help but draw in a breath of it. The inhale seemed to draw him nearer still. And unexpectedly, one of his hands came up to touch her cheek. It was the most deliberately intimate contact he'd ever initiated between them. It was heady and electrifying, and Raven wanted more. She even tipped her face up, expecting it.

But just as the moment she'd waited for—the moment she'd literally dreamed of on repeat for the last three years—came, it was ripped away by the sudden buzz of Lucien's cell phone. The noise jarred reality back into place. And as the brown-eyed detective pulled away and stood up, then dragged the slim electronic device from his pocket, Raven wondered if she'd been holding on to the fantasy a little too long.

Silently, Lucien cursed his boss. Out loud, he greeted the man with a growly hello.

Although I should probably be thanking him, he acknowledged as the other man told him the forensics team had made a little bit of headway at the crime scene.

He'd been the barest heartbeat away from saying screw it to all the reasons why he couldn't follow through on the need to kiss her. Another breath, and he would've dropped his lips to hers. Three years' worth of missing her would've poured into it. All the regret. All the wishing things were different. And the phone call had very effectively ruined it.

Yeah. So I'm not exactly thankful, am I?

His boss's voice cut through his battling thoughts. "You hear what I just said, Match?"

"Maybe repeat that last bit," Lucien replied.

"Pig's blood," stated the other man. "That was what was on the walls. Forensics did a precipitin test, came back as good old-fashioned pork."

"Not bad news."

"Glad is wasn't blood that should've been inside Jim Rickson, that's for sure."

Lucien glanced toward Raven, hoping she hadn't heard the macabre statement. Thankfully, her attention was on her hot chocolate.

That damn mug, Lucien thought.

He'd grabbed it automatically because he knew she liked it, and because it brought back a few of his own fond memories. He hadn't been considering the fact that it would draw attention to the little secret he was holding on to.

If an entire house can be called little.

Once again, Sergeant Gray's voice cut in. "Lucien. Seriously, man."

"I'm listening," he lied.

"Then repeat it back to me."

Lucien complied, more on autopilot than as proof that he'd comprehended what his boss had just said. "Pig's blood, no fingerprint hits. Clean scene. Perp was careful."

"That. And now we can't find Mrs. Rickson."

Lucien's attention was abruptly hyperfocused. Why hadn't the other man *led* with that particular revelation? If Jim was missing rather than dead, and his wife was AWOL, too...

Maybe I heard wrong.

"Say that again," he ordered brusquely.

"Think you *did* hear me this time." His boss's tone was grim.

"Where the hell is she?"

"Nature of not being able to find someone is that you don't know where they are."

Lucien dropped an expletive, then asked, "How'd it happen?"

"One minute she was in the hospital bed with two armed guards, the next she was gone without a whisper," said Gray, then added the suggestion that Lucien was dreading. "Sounds like it fits the pattern, doesn't it?"

Lucien told himself it was too quick of a turnaround. The Kitsilano Killer had been meticulous in his ritual, perfect in his timing. First the husband, then the wife. Next the daughter, and finally the son. The pattern was spread out over days. Three weeks, to be exact. It included specifics. Details to the point of obsession. Hanes never strayed.

Unless he's become impatient, said a little voice in his head. *Serial killers escalate. That's a fact. And who knows how desperate he's become over the last three years? Behind bars...no outlet in sight.*

There was another small thing, though. One the sergeant hadn't mentioned and that gave him a modicum of hope that his conclusion might be off.

"What about the riddle?" Lucien asked, keeping his voice low. "Did forensics find one?"

"Find one? Not to try to make it sound remotely funny...but I know you saw the writing up there on the wall."

The silence on the other end might as well have been a holler, but Lucien refused to break it. His mind insisted that the Kitsilano Killer's notes were consistent.

Utterly. Each one, two lines long, scrawled in crooked block letters across identical slips of yellow paper. They were hints—though sometimes so obscure that they were utterly indecipherable until after the fact—as to the locations of the kidnapped victims. The words written in blood were too on-the-nose to line up with Hanes's MO.

At last, the sergeant sighed. "C'mon, Match. You're not in the habit of glossing things over. You're better than that. And—"

"The lack of paper is a consideration. But I'm more concerned about the words themselves."

"Lucien."

"Just a consideration, boss."

"What consideration? That because it's not on a yellow slip of paper, it can't be what we both know it is?" The other man paused. "Why are you fighting me on this, Detective?"

Lucien closed his eyes. Why *was* he fighting? He knew what the truth was. He'd known it the moment he'd heard Juanita's scream. Every subsequent detail added to that surety. Yet here he was, in total denial.

He opened his eyes and fixed them on Raven, who still seemed to be staring into her hot chocolate. There was the answer to the sergeant's question, right there. He was fighting the logical explanation because he didn't *want* it to be true. The detective in him knew the clues lined up, but the man in him was loathe to admit the danger.

There was a throat clear on the other end of the line, and his boss almost—but not quite—changed the subject.

"Anyway," Gray said, "I figured you'd want the details. Didn't know how involved you'd want to be, but

I'll leave it with you to decide. You know the case as well as anyone. Better, probably. So if you want in on the task force, you're welcome. But if you'd rather stay with Ms. Elliot again, that's no problem either."

Relief made Lucien's shoulders sag. "That's what I'll do, then. Keep me updated, boss?"

"You got it."

He clicked the phone off and turned to find that Raven wasn't so focused in her beverage anymore. She'd come to her feet, and now stood near the bullet-proof window. Her face was pointed his way, though, and he could see that her already fair skin had paled to the point of sickly. Her eyes had a pinched, trying-not-cry look to them, too, and it made Lucien's heart squeeze. The need to soothe away her suffering was intrinsic. He *had* to reach for her. He stepped closer, put a hand on each of her shoulders and rubbed his palms up and down.

"There was some good news in there," he said.

She shook her head. "But it's him, isn't it?"

"We can't be sure," he said with as much diplomacy as he could muster up.

"But I *am* sure. I can feel it. I think I felt it before I even knew he'd escaped. I saw those flowers, and—" She cut herself off, and Lucien was sure it was because the unshed tears were getting closer and closer to the surface.

He wanted to pull her into an embrace, but with the almost kiss still fresh in his mind, he didn't trust himself to keep a hug as platonic as it ought to be. He guided her to the couch instead, careful to put a space between them when they sat down. Her eyes found him anyway, holding him just as firmly as her hands might have.

"You don't have to stay with me," she said.

It wasn't what he was expecting to hear. "What?"

"I wasn't eavesdropping," she told him firmly. "But your boss said the last bit a little loud. If you need to go and work on the case, I'll be fine."

It cut at him, that she thought he'd leave.

"You'd be *fine*?" he repeated back to her.

She just nodded.

He scrubbed a hand over his chin. "Even if I believed that, I wouldn't go."

She shuffled, and her knees were suddenly pressed to his. A hundred sparks ignited at the touch. Lucien didn't pull away. He wasn't sure if he *could* pull away. Especially when her hand snaked over to grab his. The hundred sparks became a thousand.

"I know you want to be a part of catching him," she said. "I remember how frustrated you were three years ago when you couldn't be the one to solve it."

He couldn't really disagree with her. No bigger case had come before or since. He'd been the one who'd put the clues together to save Raven. He'd believed that his expertise would help the case along.

But then came Raven.

He swallowed a lump of thick emotion and answered her in an even voice. "That was before I dedicated the time to keeping you out of harm's way."

"I don't want to box you in, Lucien."

"Trust me. You don't. You won't."

"And I don't want to hold you back from doing your job."

"Not possible. Taking care of you *is* my job."

She met his eyes and leaned forward a little. The hand that held his freed itself, then crept to his forearm. Then his elbow. It slipped up to his shoulder. Her gaze never left his face. Like she was gauging his reaction.

Assessing, to see if she should stop. Lucien held still. He was paralyzed by the contact, but in the most pleasant way possible. When her fingers at last reached the back of his neck, then slid to his hair, his breath came out in a near groan.

The thousand sparks buzzed into a hundred thousand. More, maybe.

How many nights had he lain awake, wishing she was there? How many times had he thought about being this close to her lips? Even just speaking to her again had been a part of his richly imagined world. He and Raven, together.

Her hand came around now to his jaw. Her thumb stroked across the two-day old stubble, and her face tipped up, full of intention. But achingly slow.

God, he wanted this. Wanted her.

He tilted his mouth, and though the touch was minimal—*too minimal*—the heat of her lips slammed into him. Those ten thousand sparks ignited. More than that. They exploded, lighting up every inch of skin. It was almost distracting—taking away from the feel of her soft, warm lips, which pressed a little harder now. Still tentative, still waiting.

Waiting.

He didn't want to do any more of that.

He dipped his face down, preparing to deepen the kiss in a way that would matter. As he did, he spoke without meaning to, his lips vibrating against her.

"I'm sorry," he murmured.

His words made her pause, and he couldn't blame her for stopping. Who the hell said "sorry" in the middle of a first kiss?

Isn't the answer to that obvious? He thought. *Someone who knows he shouldn't be* having *that first kiss.*

"Raven."

He didn't get a chance to say anything else. She ripped herself away, shot to her feet and—muttering something so breathless that he could barely understand a word of it—she spun and strode toward the hall so fast it was nearly a run.

Lucien stared after her. He knew he should give chase. Offer some excuse for the apology.

Apologize for the apology?

He couldn't do it anyway. Following her would just fuel the situation into something worse. An awkward one, where he'd be compelled to confess his lack of professionalism and be forced to relinquish her care to a colleague.

He was angry at himself for letting the kiss—however quick and minimal it might've been—happen in the first place. For not stopping it the moment she tipped her face up, and he'd become sure of her intentions. And anger wasn't even the presiding emotion. That role belonged to a different feeling. *Disappointment.* Not so much in himself, but more in the fact that this moment had turned out how he'd always known it would. He'd wanted it to be different. To be some kind of miracle, where the line blurred and the not-right become not-wrong, and it didn't matter that she was a witness and that he was the cop responsible for guarding her. Instead, it was the same as it had always been. Raven was still everything he wanted, and he was still the man incapable of deserving her.

Chapter 5

The splash of cold water on to her face did nothing to ease the heat of Raven's embarrassment. She'd been so sure that she was reading Lucien right. And even with that certainty, she'd exercised caution. She'd looked for some indication that he didn't want to kiss her as badly as she wanted to kiss him. She hadn't found one. And for an instant, perfection had reigned.

Their lips had met.

A tether had formed.

Her heart had been full.

Then he tore it away.

"With an apology," Raven muttered, staring at her reflection in the mirror.

What was he sorry for? Letting her just barely kiss him? That had to be it. But why, then, had he allowed it to get to the point of their lips actually touching?

Maybe it was less of an apology and more of a reminder. What did he say? Oh. Right.

"'Taking care of you *is* my job,'" she said it aloud, solidifying the words.

In the heat of the moment, Raven had taken the statement to mean something good. But without their bodies close and their mouths almost touching, she could see it for what it was—a statement of fact. She was his job. Nothing more. And even if he was attracted to her—because she didn't think she was that far off in her assessment of the physical signs—it could never mean anything. No matter how badly she wanted it. Lucien wouldn't risk his job over some fling.

Her cheeks tried to warm even more, and she lifted another cupped handful of water up to her face. But she somehow doubted that even the biggest, iciest bucket of water would cool her humiliation.

For three years, she'd been holding on to some fantasy. One that fit with romantic reunions and sweeping declarations of emotion.

She eyed the closed door. She knew Lucien wasn't going to come rushing at it, banging and begging to be let in. It wasn't who he was. And she *liked* that about him.

Liked? prodded a voice in her head. *That's as far as you're going to go?*

She forced the thought aside. Because she *did* like Lucien just the way he was. His personality was what had helped drag her up from the abyss of loss. If he'd been the kind of man who wanted to talk every feeling through, she wouldn't have made it through. She'd needed his quiet strength. She'd fed off it and used it to help herself become whole. And in the process, she'd grown to see that underneath his reserved demeanor was a passion for doing things right. People mattered to him. Goodness did, too. She knew where the gruffness came from. She respected it. Admired it. And even thinking about those qualities and what he overcame to become the strong person he was…it made Raven ache to be with him.

So, no…like is definitely not a strong enough word.

She let out a breath and shut the water off. For the last three years, she'd been able to keep her feelings at bay. A large part of that probably had to do with space. But clearly, now that they were back in close quarters, it was going to be an even bigger issue than before.

"And you can't just keep throwing yourself at him," she said aloud.

Not that she was going to. She wasn't exactly a gushing teenager. And she had enough self-control to assume she'd be able to hold it in. But the problem was that she didn't want to have to try. She didn't want to have to consciously not touch him or force herself *not* to feel her breath catch every time she saw the warm brown of his eyes. She didn't want to *hope*. And the emotions she'd pushed down obviously weren't just going to go away.

"Self-respect," she added, adjusting her ponytail in a smoother, tidier position.

She straightened her shirt and met her own gaze, willing herself to see some resolve there. She was going to need it in order to do what she was about to do. Lucien wouldn't like it, either. He'd made it clear that her safety was a priority.

Too bad he doesn't want to make my heart a priority instead.

"And thoughts like that are *exactly* why I'm going to march out there and demand a new bodyguard," she said firmly.

She cast a final once-over at her reflection, then spun

back to the hall. But she didn't make it back to the living room before she got distracted. It was the quick glance to her left that did it. She spotted her old bedroom door, and curiosity got the better of her. Had it changed at all? Or was it as untouched as the rest of the house? And why had Lucien avoided telling her why it hadn't been used? Feeling compelled to take a look, Raven changed direction and headed there instead.

She drew in a breath, opened the door and flicked on the light. And she found things exactly as she'd left them. The same ivory duvet, flecked with blue flowers. The same cobalt bed sheets and pillowcases. On the nightstand sat the book she'd been reading before she left. She hadn't thought of it in years, but at the time, she'd bought a replacement copy so she could finish it.

She stepped a little farther into the room, her gaze sweeping the space for more evidence. It was all there, out in the open. A little tube of her favorite moisturizer on the dresser. A sweater and a pair of pants visible in the partially opened closet. And Raven had a feeling that if she walked over to the en suite bathroom, she'd also find the toothbrush and paste she'd forgotten.

Maybe it should've been a little weird. Or more than a little, even. But it wasn't. It just made Raven sad, and even more interested in knowing *why* nothing had been cleared away. Shaking her head, she started to move back to the door. But as she did, she bumped straight into Lucien, who stood in the frame. He brought a hand out to steady her, then stood back and looked around the room with an oddly sheepish expression on his face.

Raven stared at him. "Lucien…what's going on?"

"I bought it."

His answer startled her so badly that she thought she'd misheard, or at least misunderstood.

"You what?" she said.

"Bought it," he confirmed.

"The…house?"

"Yeah."

"But…*why*?"

His uncharacteristic sheepishness grew, and he lifted his hand to the back of his neck, rubbing it like he could rid himself of the visible embarrassment that way, and then he gave his right ear a quick tug. "The PD were decommissioning it as a safe house. Said they might demolish it."

A little stab of sentimental anxiety poked at Raven's gut. What if they *had* demolished it? She hated the idea. As much as she wanted to close off everything that had to do with Georges Hanes, she wanted to hold on to the only good thing to come out of it all. Meeting Lucien. Even if he didn't share her feelings, she could never regret knowing him. Tearing down the house would've been almost devastating.

Yeah, okay. So you *hate the thought of a demolition*, said a voice in her head. *But Lucien isn't exactly the nostalgic type.*

But studying him at that moment, Raven might've argued otherwise. The way he shifted from foot to foot awkwardly. How his eyes darted around the room like he was trying *not* to look. The stilted explanation about the fact that he didn't actually live there, but just held on to the property for the future. And that ear tug. But still. It didn't add up to what she knew about him. And it certainly didn't match up with the man who'd broken off their first-ever, could've-been-perfect kiss with an apology. Which brought her back to the plan.

She exhaled and straightened her shoulders. "I want you to take me home."

It was his turn to look startled. "What?"

"Home," she repeated. "If I remember correctly, you can't keep me in the safe house against my will. And since this *isn't* even a safe house…"

She waited for him to argue. To point out that Georges Hanes knew exactly where she lived, and it would be that much easier to find her. And she steeled herself to argue back. To tell him that the first time around, she'd been told it was her choice whether or not she left herself exposed. But instead of fighting with her about it, Lucien just shifted a little, then spoke in a stiff voice.

"I would never keep you anywhere against your will, Raven. You know that."

"A little reminder doesn't hurt."

But for a second it *did* seem to hurt. He flinched, and for a moment she thought he might argue. Instead, he just nodded.

"I'd like your permission to place a watch on your house," he said, his voice only marginally stiffer than usual.

She nodded, too. "Yes. Okay. But outside. And I think it should be someone else who does it."

Lucien's jaw tightened. "Did I fail you the last time?"

The question made Raven blink. "Fail me?"

"Did I let Hanes get to you? Make you feel unsafe? Do anything that would lead you to believe that I'm not the best person for the job?"

"It's not that."

"Do you think I'd do it now?"

"No. This isn't about you."

His chin was so stiff it looked like it might crack. "If it's about what happened out there a few minutes ago, I promise you it won't happen again."

Raven fought against a sudden ache in her throat. She wished she could tell him she wanted the opposite, and that his guarantee of no repeats was the very thing that made her need the space she was asking for.

Self-control and self-respect, she reminded herself fiercely.

Aloud, she said, "I'd be more comfortable knowing that you weren't sitting outside my house."

It was true. Though probably not in the way it sounded. Lucien's thumb flicked once against his thigh, lifted to his ear, then stopped.

He nodded again. "All right. Any objections to me driving you home?"

Raven shook her head, mostly because she didn't really trust herself to speak.

Lucien's jaw ached from keeping it rigid. His shoulders and back were starting to hurt, too. Every bit of his body was tense with a need to speak. A desire to apologize again, and to ask Raven to forgive his shortcomings. He knew he was a complete idiot for not declaring his feelings and letting things fall where they might. If ever there'd been a moment to do it, then this was it. In fact, the last few hours had been nothing but perfect moments for a heartfelt outburst.

When she'd turned and run into him at the cemetery, it would've been a good opportunity.

Or the kiss. Instead of saying sorry, he could've gone with three other little words.

Chasing after her might've been an option. Taking her in his arms. Kissing away the tears instead of letting her wash them off as he knew she'd done.

Even after that. When he'd told her he bought the safe house, he could've admitted that it was because the place was tied up with his memories of her. She'd somehow turned the generic environment into something meaningful. Something he couldn't let go of.

At any of those points, he could've told her. He could've suggested recusing himself from the case, if that's what it took. Yet Lucien had let each one of the moments pass by.

There's right now.

Just the two of them in the quiet of his car. On the precipice of losing her for good. Nowhere for either of them to go.

He couldn't do it. His mouth remained stiff, the words sticking in his brain. Further proof that he wasn't the right man for this particular job. As soon as he had the thought, he cringed. Raven was so much more than a job. And that right there was the problem. He couldn't make himself see her as work. It took away his ability to think critically, and more important, weakened his objectivity. In Lucien's mind, those things were the biggest elements of working effectively in law enforcement. Having them compromised was no good. Which is why her asking him to leave was actually a positive thing. Or it should've been. In actuality, it just stung.

Was he really going to let her go all over again? The idea made his throat tighten.

He wouldn't just walk cleanly away. Sure, he'd obey her wishes and have a couple of experienced, trustworthy uniforms set up on her block rather than sitting there himself. He'd already placed the call and requested specific officers. But he had to ensure that Georges Hanes was behind bars again for good, and there was no chance he'd allow that to go to someone else. Raven might not be his—not the way he wanted—but he would never, ever leave her unprotected.

He sneaked a glance toward her. She was buckled tightly into the passenger seat, her already-diminutive frame looking even more petite in his oversize SUV. Her eyes were closed. Lucien knew she wasn't asleep, or even close to it. The pinch of her forehead gave her away, as did the clench of her fingers on the nylon seat belt.

You deserve more than I can give, he thought for what had to be the millionth time.

He forced his gaze back to the front windshield, but he no sooner swiveled his head than she spoke, her voice drawing him back for another second. Her eyes were open now, the frown on her forehead even more pronounced.

"Can I ask you something?" she said.

It was the first thing she'd said since giving him her new address, and the abruptness of it echoed heavily in the otherwise silent car.

Nothing good ever comes of a question like that, Lucien thought, looking away before answering in a carefully neutral tone. "Sure. Ask away."

"What do you think Hanes's message meant?"

The inquiry surprised him. Not because Raven wasn't well aware of the details of the first Hanes case, but simply because it was work related. And—even though he knew it wasn't fair—it dug at him a little. His own tumble of emotions was so close to the surface that he'd really expected something personal.

He squeezed the steering wheel, redirected his thoughts and made himself answer casually. "What message?"

"The one at the Jim and Juanita's place."

"Sergeant told me there was no note."

Her swallow was audible, and her voice quavered

as she said, "I know you know what I mean, Lucien. The message in the blood. About owing a life and taking one."

He considered downplaying it a bit more, but realized he would be doing Raven a disservice if he lied to her.

"I *do* think it could be from Hanes," Lucien admitted, flicking on his signal and turning up the street that would lead to her new neighborhood.

"But?" she prodded.

"It doesn't fully fit with his usual style. Hanes was always subtle. He thought of his little notes as clever games, didn't he? Trying to see if the police could outsmart him."

"Yes." The word cracked a little as Raven said it, and her next statement was tinged with sorrow. "Only the loser in Hanes's game winds up dead."

Lucien cursed himself again, this time for his obtuseness. He knew better than anyone what she'd lost. *Who* she'd lost. Every member of her family had died at Hanes's hands, and there was nothing gamelike about it on her end.

"Sorry," he said gruffly. "Didn't mean to come across like I'm taking this lightly, Raven."

"I know you didn't. And I know you aren't, too." The reply sounded tight, though, and a glance her way told him that her eyes were fixed out the front windshield. Her hands twisted in her lap, and she spoke again, this time with audible edginess. "What do *you* think it means?"

"I haven't stopped to think about it." It was a true statement, but he didn't bother to say that his lack of thought was directly linked to the fact that he didn't *want* to think about it, and instead added, "The task force is working on decoding it as we speak."

Raven, though, wasn't ready to let it go so easily. "He meant me, didn't he?"

"We don't know that," Lucien told her firmly.

"He said, 'You owe me a life. So I'll take more, until you give me yours.' Or something close to that. It's *my* life he wants. Because I'm the one who got away from him."

"Not a forgone conclusion. Even if Hanes had ever gone for literal with his messages, that doesn't change the fact that he never gave any indication that he was going to come after you again. Not once the entire time he was in custody."

She swallowed. "No. That's true. He seemed... *happy*...that someone had cracked the clue and saved me."

"Because that was his goal. He said as much during his final testimony."

Lucien wished he didn't remember it quite as well as he did. The way Hanes smiled when he talked about a worthy adversary. Even now, the memory was a teeth-gritting one.

"But he's had three years to think about it," Raven pointed out. "He could've changed his mind. Or come up with a new game, or—"

She cut herself off in a strangled gasp, and for a moment Lucien thought it was a physical problem. He started to reach out, a question on his lips. As his head turned toward her, though, something outside caught his eye. He realized immediately that it was the source of her distress.

Just up the street was a small row of town houses. Maybe twenty units, at most. A three-foot fence, painted a brilliant white, lined the edge of the tidy property. Each of the units had its own gate and path. Atop the

one just in front of until number six—Raven's unit—
sat three bouquets of flowers. That by itself would've
been odd. But what shifted the scene from strange to
disturbing was that Lucien was certain that the bouquets were the same ones that had been sitting at the
gravesites of Raven's family.

Chapter 6

Raven's eyes whipped around in futile search of the person who'd placed the flowers there. Who'd *moved* them from the cemetery to her house. Who knew where she lived.

Who? That's not a question without an answer, said her subconscious. *Georges Hanes.*

Her vision swam, and so did her head.

Any and all thoughts of separating herself from Lucien's company flew away. Instead of being a source of stress, he was suddenly the only thing keeping her sane. Just like he had been, three years ago.

"Lucien. Those flowers…" Her throat closed, and she couldn't manage anything else.

His hand came out to clasp hers, and even though the reassuring squeeze was brief, just the simple touch eased the blockage in her airway.

"I see them," he said.

"What do we do?"

"We stay calm. We pull over just up ahead, and we wait for the four officers I called in to get here. It should be anytime now."

For a second, his words distracted her. "*Four* officers?"

"No risks, Raven." His tone was grim. "I'm not willing to let Hanes have even a ghost of a chance of getting through our defenses. If I'm not behind the lines, then I want a visible wall."

In spite of the way she told herself not to, she warmed at little at his protectiveness. She also started to point out that he was *one* man, and he'd done the job himself, but two police cruisers rounded the block just then, stilling her words. Lucien waved to them from behind the wheel, and one pulled over while the other drove up alongside his SUV. The officer in the driver's seat rolled down her window, and Lucien did the same.

"Afternoon, Detective," said the woman. "Everything okay?"

"Not exactly," Lucien replied. "It's Constable Davies, right?"

"Yes, sir."

"Well, Constable Davies, there's been a slight change of plans."

Raven listened as he first explained about the flowers, then gave instructions on approaching the house. She handed over the keys and recited the alarm code when asked, but guilt dug at her when she realized he was passing off what should've been his job. He was the senior officer. The person with the most inside knowledge about the case. Yet he was stuck in the car acting as a glorified babysitter. But she couldn't make herself protest as the other three uniformed officers got out and joined Davies so they could do their thing. She didn't open her mouth as he called his boss and reiterated the story, then posited *her* theory about the note written in blood. It was selfish, but she wanted Lucien by her side.

"Doing okay over there?" he asked as he hung up the phone.

Raven forced a nod and fixed her gaze out the window, watching as the police made their way up her front walk. "I'm fine."

"Don't worry about them," he said, clearly misreading the source of her anxiety. "If this *is* Hanes, I don't think he'd deliberately put up a warning, then sit in your house waiting for you to waltz in."

"No, I guess not." She sighed without any real relief. "He likes that game of his too much."

Lucien's hand came back to hers again, and this time it stayed. "I'm not going to give him any time to enjoy it."

Raven didn't say anything back. In spite of the conviction behind his statement, she was desperately afraid that he was wrong. She had a dozen arguments. But she worried that if she voiced them, he might let her go. And she wanted to hold on to him as long as possible. Thankfully, his warm fingers remained clasped around hers for the entire time it took the other police officers to conduct their search. She didn't even care that his touch was just a platonic offer of comfort. For the moment, she'd take what she could get.

But when the female officer—Constable Davies— appeared at her front door and gave an all-clear sign before she started their way, and Lucien finally slipped his hand free, Raven felt the separation acutely. And belatedly, she realized she'd made a mistake. She didn't *want* someone else as her bodyguard. At all.

She turned to him, her face warm, and blurted, "Please don't leave."

He blinked like he had no idea what she was talking about. "Leave?"

"Me." Her cheeks burned even more. "Stay until Hanes is caught again. Please."

"I have no intention of going anywhere." He said it almost fervently, and then he startled her by reaching out to touch her heated skin with the back of his hand.

Raven was too stunned by the near caress to react quickly. It wasn't that Lucien never extended sympathy or kindness. In fact, he always did. But before she could recover from the surprise, Constable Davies was tapping on the driver's-side window, and Lucien was redirecting his attention to rolling it down.

"Sir," greeted the uniformed woman.

"Constable," said Lucien. "What's the report?"

"The house appears undisturbed. All points of entry were sealed, the alarm intact. No footprints anywhere along the perimeter, and even if the perp somehow ghosted inside, nothing looks to have been overtly tampered with." She paused, and her eyes just barely flicked to Raven before settling back on Lucien. "Detective?"

"You can say whatever needs to be said in front of Ms. Elliot," he replied.

Davies still seemed hesitant. "It truly appears that whoever left those flowers didn't come inside."

"But?" Lucien prodded.

"Just a small thing." The other woman looked toward Raven. "There's a frosted window around the back on the second floor. You leave that open a crack, Ms. Elliot?"

Raven nodded. "My en suite. Yes, I usually leave it open. Why?"

"Ever leave something hanging from the frame?" Davies wanted to know.

Raven frowned. "No."

Lucien cut in. "Whatever it is, Constable, spit it out."

"My partner, Constable Whitmore saw something sparkling up there when we were examining the perimeter. Didn't think much of it, but when we went inside, it caught my eye, too. Found a tiny piece of gold taped to a piece of fishing line, and I thought…" Davies trailed off.

But she didn't have to finish. Raven knew exactly what had gone through the other woman's mind.

"You thought of *me*," she said, meeting the policewoman's eyes.

Davies nodded, her expression apologetic. "I was a rookie when the Kitsilano Killer case broke. Came through training with the guy who ticketed Hanes on the jaywalking, actually. And I followed the whole thing closely. So I know that the gold mine and the fishing line fit."

Raven fought to keep from closing her eyes. Her body wanted—instinctively—to help her slam a mental wall into place. To keep the memory at bay. But she knew that shutting down wouldn't do them any good at the current moment. She made herself look at Lucien, who was studying her with an undisguisedly concerned expression on his face.

"If there was any doubt that this was Hanes, I think it's gone now," she stated, pleased when her voice came out strong.

"I don't disagree," Lucien replied. "And I think *you* won't disagree that staying at your house is no longer an option?"

Raven shook her head. "Definitely not."

"Good." Lucien turned back to Constable Davies. "All right. Change of the already-changed plans. Why don't you and your partner follow us to the Silver Spoon Café, keep us company from a distance? I think Ms. Elliot and I could use a break. Have the other two officers call in Forensics to process the scene. I'll fill the sergeant in, and we'll go from there."

"Yes, sir," the woman agreed, then turned sharply and strode back toward the house.

Lucien rolled up the window again, then swung his attention to Raven, his smile softening his words. "You wanna argue about any of that?"

She couldn't make herself smile back. "No."

He nodded brusquely, then dragged out his phone and placed the promised call to his boss. Raven only half listened to the exchange, and only half noticed when Lucien announced that they were going to get moving. Her mind busy slipping to the past. To the eight days, three hours, and twenty-three minutes she'd been trapped in the bottom of an old mine shift. Bound tightly with fishing line. At Georges Hanes's mercy. But the worst part hadn't been the dark and the damp and the terror of not knowing exactly where she was. The worst part had been *knowing* what was about to happen.

The three previous sets of kidnappings and murders had been leaked to the press and widely publicized. It would've been impossible to live in the surrounding area and not be aware. So when Raven's parents were taken, the police hadn't messed around. They'd brought Raven and her brother in and warned them that they suspected it was the serial killer's work. Raven had accepted a 24/7 guard, but Ryan had balked. Become angry. Refused to face reality. Insisted it was all a mistake. Raven had tried to make him see reason. In fact, she'd been on her way home from pleading with him when she was suddenly grabbed from behind, a cloth shoved over her mouth, and then darkness.

She shivered with the terrible memory of it all.

She'd *known* she was going to die. Without a doubt. Not a single other victim had survived.

But then came Lucien.

His warm hands, reaching for her in the dark. His deep voice, murmuring assurances that she'd be all right. And finally, his solid body, holding her close and pulling her out.

Personal feelings aside, Raven really didn't need to look any further than that recollection to know why she needed him close again now. He'd been able to save her from Hanes the first time around because he'd managed to decode the clue Hanes had left. Lucien was actually the only one who'd successfully waded through one of the convoluted messages. Which made him the best hope to be able to do it again now. And it was the difference between living and dying. For her. But also for Jim and Juanita Rickson, who were currently in Hanes's grasp.

Jim and Juanita.

Raven realized she'd been so wrapped up in her own fears that she'd nearly forgotten that the older couple were in far more pressing danger. Her heart squeezed painfully in her chest, and the message that had been left behind on the wall in the caretaker's office popped to the front of her mind.

A life is owed to me. So I'll take one every day until you give me yours.

Then a horrible thought occurred to Raven, and her eyes—which she hadn't even realized she'd closed—flew open.

"Lucien," she said. "What if he *did* mean it literally?"

"What?"

"What if Hanes *literally* meant that he'd take a life every day?"

And Lucien's silence told her that the idea had already been on the big man's mind.

Lucien racked his brain for some soothing words that wouldn't sound like a lie. Or like a put-off. Since the moment Raven suggested that the words were a new kind of clue, taking the place of Georges Hanes's standard notes, he'd had an uneasy feeling in the pit of his stomach. In a way he knew was uncharacteristic, he'd avoided digging in to figure out what it was his gut was screaming about. Raven's fear-filled question slammed it home.

Maybe Hanes did mean it literally. The clue written in blood was a classic escalation. The man could have spent the last three years plotting newer and sicker things. And who knew how far he'd go?

He'd confessed his crimes, but his motivations had never been truly clear. The man targeted families, but little was known about his own. The psych evals had concluded that his victims were chosen because of family-related trauma, but if it was true, Hanes had never admitted it. Background checks and research had led nowhere. His backstory was concluded to be a lie, and though he had a steady stream of short-term employment and had traceable living arrangements—late rent and irritated landlords galore—no one laid claim to him as friend or relative. There was an assumption that he'd either masterfully stolen an identity at a young age or created one with great skill. Either way, it was impenetrable. A frustrating wall between law enforcement and Hanes himself.

None of that matters right now, Lucien thought, mentally gritting his teeth.

What *did* matter was that if Hanes wasn't providing a clue—if he was just stating his plan—then it wouldn't take Raven long to figure out how she could stop a rampage.

Like she'd been following his silent train of thought, she spoke up just as Lucien pulled the vehicle to a stop in the Silver Spoon Café parking lot.

"If I turn myself over to him," she said softly, "he'll let them go."

Lucien cut the engine, swung her way and uttered a one-word reply. "No."

His sharp tone made her flinch, and he felt bad about it, but no way was he going to let her think he'd even consider the option. Without waiting for a protest, he slammed his finger to his seat belt. Then he hit hers for good measure, too. He ignored her audible inhale, pushed his door open, then hopped out and strode to her side of the SUV. Her blue eyes were wide, but he ignored that, as well. When he took her elbow to help her out, he was careful not to do it roughly, but he didn't give her a chance to pull back, either.

"Lucien…" she said as her feet hit the ground.

"No," he repeated.

He guided her up to the little restaurant, dropped her elbow long enough to open the door for her, then took a hold of her again. He led her to a corner table, sat down across from her and met her eyes. And for good measure, said it once more.

"No."

She made an impossible-to-describe face. One part

amused. One part frustrated. One part worried. And a final part that looked too much like determination.

"You didn't let me say anything," she told him.

"Does the *anything* you'd *like* to say involve trading your life for someone else's?" he countered.

"I can't let Hanes kill people."

"*I* can't let Hanes kill *you*."

She winced. "My life doesn't outweigh theirs."

Lucien fought a growl and reached across the table to take her hands in his. "And your life isn't something to throw away, either."

"I'm not throwing it away."

"Trading it and throwing at away are the same thing."

Her mouth opened like she was going to argue, but the server's greeting cut her off. "Afternoon, folks. I'm Lauren. Our lunch special today is grilled cheese and tomato soup, but can I start you off with some coffee or some water?"

Lucien was grateful for the momentary distraction from their discussion. He turned a smile toward their very fresh-faced server and quickly ordered a coffee while Raven went with her usual tea. For about ninety seconds, things seemed normal. It didn't last.

Lauren-the-server snapped her notebook shut, smiled back at Lucien, revealing a row of braces, and said, "Thanks very much. I'll bring you and your wife your beverages in just a minute."

Raven was quick to correct her. "We're not married."

"Oh!" said the server, looking from their still-clasped hands to their faces with a genuinely surprised expression, and then she groaned. "I'm *so* sorry. My boss, Joanna, keeps telling me I need to be more careful when I'm talking to customers. But when I walked up, you just sounded like…you know what? Never mind. I'll get your drinks for you. On the house."

When she turned and scurried away, Raven extricated her fingers from his, and said, "We can't do this. We can't just sit here and eat soup and let people think we're a couple while we pretend that an easier way will come up."

"You know me better than that," Lucien replied.

"Do I?" She shook her head. "It's been three years. A lot can change in that amount of time. A lot *has* changed. I went to school and I got a new job. You turned down a promotion, which I think the 'you' I knew wouldn't have done. There's my cat. Who I'm going to need to ask my neighbor to feed, by the way. And maybe you got a pet, too. Maybe you got married. You could literally have had three kids in that space of time."

The more she said, the shakier her voice got, and Lucien realized she was close to the edge. Her self-sacrifice was sheer bravery, but under that, she was terrified. And trying not to show it.

"Raven, listen to me," he said. "I know you feel like you're responsible for Jim and Juanita being taken, but what Hanes does or doesn't do *isn't* under your control. Think about this for a second. You were alone at the cemetery. He could've tried to take you then. He left the flowers and took Jim Rickson instead."

"Because of his game."

"But that's *not* his game, is it? He doesn't bargain. He leaves bread crumbs."

Raven closed her eyes, exhaled heavily, then opened them again and met his gaze. "Can you tell me—in all honesty—that you don't think there's a chance that Hanes is just trying to finish the job?"

"I can tell you that it doesn't fit with his profile. He likes to win, but he wouldn't do what he would see as cheating in order to do it."

"And you think he'd see this as cheating?"

"It couldn't be anything else. You won his game. He wouldn't just waltz in and change that."

"Unless he changed the rules."

"He might do that, Raven," he admitted. "But I can say with a-hundred-percent certainty that it wouldn't be like this."

Her body sagged. "Then how do I help Jim and Juanita?"

He paused in answering as their server dropped off their drinks and took their order. Her eyes only lingered on their hands—which, Lucien noted, had become unconsciously tangled together—before she slipped away again. It was a good moment to try to redirect the conversation. Or to point out that it wasn't Raven's job to help the middle-aged couple. Lucien opted for something else.

"You help them by helping *me*," he said instead.

"Helping you?"

"Come back to the safe house with me. I'll get the sergeant to send over whatever he can from the Kitsilano Killer file. We'll put it together with what you know about the Ricksons, and we'll try to work out what Hanes's message means."

"So you actually *do* think it's a clue like the ones from last time."

"I do. Let me tell you what makes me so sure that he'd stick to his own pattern."

She leaned forward a little, and he was relieved to see her expression brighten with hope as he explained what his connection—a longtime guard at the prison—

had told him about the killer. The other man was reg-
imented in his day-to-day routine. Compulsive, they
called him. The guard even made a joke about Hanes
Standard Time until Lucien shut him down with a glare.
The only time he ever made any kind of waves when
was he was forced to go outside the routine. Fire drills.
New programs or new staff. It actually made him an
ideal inmate. If there could really be such a thing.

Their soup arrived, and they paused their conversation to let Lauren set it down. Lucien picked up the
thread again as soon as she was gone.

"Hanes has only deviated from his regime twice,"
he said. "Once, when he had been battling pneumonia.
And again now, with his escape. That's it."

"But why now?" Raven asked.

"I'm not an expert on psychoses or anything, but
based on my experience of compulsive criminals, my
theory is that something—some change—triggered him
to run. And if I were going to stretch that… I'd say he
probably wants to fix whatever that change was." Lucien paused and set down his spoon as his mind leaped
forward, connecting dots.

"What?" prodded Raven, picking up on the sudden
change.

He shoved back his chair. "C'mon. I've got an idea.
We're going to need to write it down, and I think we
should do it in private."

Chapter 7

Raven followed Lucien back out to the SUV without argument, and she didn't comment on the fact that he paused to tell the uniformed officers to trail them back to the former safe house. She kept silent as they climbed into the vehicle, and said nothing as they started their short journey.

One of Lucien's thumbs tapped the slightest beat on the steering wheel. But even if he hadn't been moving at all, Raven would still have been able to feel his energy. It had breakthrough quality, and she was sure that whatever theory had come to mind, it was a good one. She was relieved. But she didn't let herself get carried away by it. Jim's and Juanita's lives were still on the line, and she didn't want to get her hopes up too high, only to have them swept away.

I'll breathe again when they're found, and when Hanes is back in jail.

The minutes in the car went by quickly, though, and in what felt like not much more than a blink, they were sitting outside the familiar house while the two officers did a security check of the perimeter. As they made their stealthy movements, the familiar guilt at keeping Lucien from his real police work crept in.

Raven let herself steal a glance in his direction. If he resented letting his fellow law enforcers do the job that he was more than equipped to do, then he was covering it up perfectly. Aside from the still-tapping thumb, he showed zero visible sign of agitation. It didn't do much to assuage Raven's self-reproach, and she wasn't quite able to stop herself from wanting to apologize for holding him back. But she barely had a chance to open her mouth before the other two cops signaled the completion of their task, and Lucien's quick reaction stopped her from speaking at all.

He swung open his own door and hopped out, stepped briskly to Raven's side of the SUV and pulled the handle there, as well. He helped her climb out, then spun toward the house. His movements were determined and sure, and they propelled Raven to hurry along beside him. Together, they moved up the walkway and into the house. Once inside, Lucien still didn't slow. He quickly locked the door behind them, kicking his shoes off before the click was even complete, then calling over his shoulder as he moved up the hall.

"Let me show you something," he said.

Raven scrambled to unlace her own shoes, and by the time she caught up to Lucien in the kitchen, he'd already procured a pad of yellow paper and a pen from somewhere. He set them on the table, then yanked out a chair and gestured for her to sit. As she plopped herself down—slightly breathless from the hurry—Lucien joined her and immediately began to scrawl something across the paper. For a second, the scratch of the pen was the only sound. Then Lucien slid the notepad across the table. But he no sooner had it in front of her than his hand slapped down and covered whatever he'd written.

Puzzled, Raven lifted her eyes to his face. She could clearly see that his urgency had taken a backseat to hesitancy.

"What is it?" she asked.

"It's Hanes's pattern," he told her.

He didn't offer any further explanation. But Raven didn't need him to. She knew the murderer's pattern perfectly. She's been *inside* it. And the idea of seeing it laid out on paper was an altogether unpleasant one. It was too clinical. Too detached. No words could properly encompass the fear that filled the yawning days of being held captive.

But if he wrote it down, he has a good reason, she assured herself.

She swallowed. "It's okay. I can handle it."

"You sure?" he replied.

She nodded, and after studying her face for another moment, he released the pad and let her take it. For a second after he lifted his hand, the words swam in front of Raven. But then Lucien's fingers came to her elbow, grounding her as he always had, and the tidy lines of his block-letter printing solidified enough that she could read them.

DAYS 1 & 15: HUSBAND

DAYS 5 & 17: WIFE

DAYS 10 & 19: DAUGHTER

DAYS 15 & 21: SON

Lucien's hand tightened on her arm. "Raven?"

She shook her head. "I'm okay. I just… I need a minute."

She glanced down again. She knew exactly what the numbered days meant. The first was when Hanes's victim was taken. The second was when the evil man killed them. The time in between was how long he felt was sufficient for the police to find them. It was precise. Almost to the hour, she'd heard the lawyers say. And as she'd suspected, seeing it on paper—trying to label the moments as a part of a plan rather than just as something purely heinous—fell short. It didn't come close to knowing intimately how the pieces fit together. It was also impossible not to be thrown straight into the middle of the memories. Raven couldn't help but see just how *she* fit in. She was the daughter, of course. Taken nine days after her father's disappearance, which was five days after her mom went missing, and five days before Hanes got to her brother, too. The fear had already been surreal.

Raven shivered. She'd lived in the cold and the dark for more than an entire week. She didn't lose track of time because Hanes didn't let her. Each morning, his voice had trickled in—disembodied and, more disappointed than pleased—to announce just how long her family had been under his control. Then he'd toss in a half-empty bottle of water and disappear again.

Over the course of those almost nine days, Raven had had no illusions about what was coming. She'd been well aware that the whisper of day fifteen meant her brother had been captured and that her father was undoubtedly dead. On day seventeen, when she knew her mother was gone, too—she'd wept so hard that her lungs burned and her body ached and she doubted that she'd even make it to her own, predetermined date of expiry. But for some reason, she'd still tried to survive. She'd tried to chew through the bonds on her hands, cutting her lips horribly in the process. Attempted to climb up and out. She'd begged and pleaded and bargained. All her futile fight to escape had earned her was hurt. Plenty of pain and suffering. Torn-off fingernails and a broken foot. Countless bruises. Gashes that eventually needed a total of eighty-three stitches. She was starving and half-dehydrated and so delirious than when the ninth day of captivity came, she simply assumed that she was dead already.

But then came Lucien.

His voice—strong and reassuring and *not Hanes*—had cut through the dark and freed her. He'd called her by her name and told her to hang on. A dream taking over from a nightmare.

Raven didn't realize she'd closed her eyes until Lucien spoke, his words sliding into the fog of memories, and pulling her out, just as they had three years earlier.

"We don't have to do this," he told her gently.

She dragged her lids open and stared down at the words. She started to say that they *did* have to. For Jim and Juanita, and for every other person who might come into contact with the man who murdered her family. But as she looked at the timeline again, she saw something she hadn't noticed the first time around. Under the little list, Lucien had added another word.

HOURS?

Raven jerked her attention up to the detective. "You think he's speeding it up."

"With Hanes's preference for order, I think there's a strong possibility that he's adjusted his pattern. Made it syncopated. Here. Let me show you."

He dragged the paper toward himself and made

a couple more marks on the pad. But before he even finished writing, the next piece of Hanes's pattern slammed into Raven head. It was like a physical assault. Her brain reverberated like she'd been struck with something hard, and it nearly took away her breath.

"Their daughter." Her voice was so low that she could barely hear it herself, and Lucien clearly didn't hear it at all, because he'd started talking again.

"So we have to work slightly backward," he was saying. "But since we know his wife couldn't be found after about eleven this morning, we can guess that Jim was taken quite early. Probably seven or so, which fits with when Juanita last saw him, too."

Raven was barely listening. She was too busy thinking about the photograph on Jim's desk. A young, blonde woman with a crooked smile. She was roughly the same age as Raven, and had recently finished medical school somewhere down in the United States, then bought herself a house locally. Jim was so proud of her. What was her name? It seemed imperative to remember.

Samantha? No. That wasn't right. Sandra? No. Not it, either.

Lucien at last noticed that she wasn't paying attention. "Hey. You still with me?"

"You have to call it in, Lucien," she urged, ignoring his question.

"What?"

"Their daughter," she said again, this time loudly. "If Georges Hanes took Jim at seven this morning, he'll be after her by four o'clock. That's less than an hour from now, Lucien."

God. What is *her name? Sarah?*

"Sally!" she gasped abruptly.

"I'm sure the guys at the station have got it under

control," Lucien replied, his voice infused with both confidence and reassurance. "With Hanes's involvement, they would've contacted the family first thing."

"I *was* Sally," Raven told him.

And she knew the statement was enough, because he stopped arguing, grabbed his phone from his pocket and dialed a number without another word.

As the line rang on the other end, Lucien was tense. He thought he shouldn't be. The VPD were thorough. Sergeant Gray would've followed up with the Ricksons' children immediately. He would've ensured that both the daughter and son—assuming there was one of each, as per Hanes's pattern—were under close watch. Except for some reason, knowing all of that didn't ease the tightness in his jaw. By the time his boss's voice mail picked up on the fifth ring, Lucien was holding the phone so hard it stung. He slammed his forefinger to the screen without leaving a message.

Raven spoke up right away, her voice wavering. "No answer?"

Lucien refused to let her see any of his own concern, and he kept his reply on the lighter side. "As much as I'd love to believe the sergeant's at my beck and call, I'm sure he thinks otherwise."

"But you're going to try someone else, right?" Her eyes were pinched in a way that made him sure she was holding in tears.

"I'll give Dispatch a call right away, sweetheart." The endearment slipped out before he could stop it, but if Raven noticed, she didn't say.

She just gave him a quick nod. "Hurry, Lucien. Please."

He turned his attention back to the phone and hit the

second number on speed dial. This time, the call was answered quickly.

"This is Dispatch," said a perky, female voice on the other end.

"Is that Geraldine?" Lucien greeted, relieved to have reached someone he knew well enough that he wouldn't have to offer a big song and dance in exchange for information. "It's Lucien Match here."

"Detective! I heard you were on vacation! You calling in while you're sipping a mai tai somewhere?"

"Hardly."

"Yeah," Geraldine replied ruefully. "I guess I would've been surprised if you'd said yes to that. What can I do for you, Detective?"

"You in the loop about this deal out at the cemetery?" he asked.

"The Hanes thing? Yeah, I know a little bit. Everyone on shift does."

"What I'm trying to figure out is who was assigned to contact the family. Specifically Sally Rickson, the daughter. Any way you can get me that info?"

"Yeah, just a quick sec." The sound of a keyboard clacking carried through the line. "You worked the original case on this one, didn't you?"

"I did," Lucien replied.

"I remember the girl. The one you saved. She was the same age as my daughter. Pretty. Not too tough looking. But she had to be, to come through that ordeal in one piece. What was her name? Rachel?"

"Raven," he corrected automatically, then glanced her direction.

He expected to find her attention on him and the call, but her eyes were pointed at the window, her face pale. Her lower lip was pulled in under the upper one, and she held her hands clasped tightly together in her lap. Lucien had enough experience with the victims of violent crime to recognize the signs of imminent collapse.

If she has to go through this a second time, she won't come out in one piece again.

The thought hit him like a punch.

He didn't know how true it was. He sure as hell didn't want to assume that Raven lacked the strength to overcome more adversity. But a person could only have so much resilience. They could lose only so much before they hit a breaking point.

"Detective?" The dispatcher's voice jerked him back to the phone conversation.

He cleared his throat. "You got something for me, Geraldine?"

"Sure do. Looks like Sergeant Gray was in attendance at Sally Rickson's home."

"I tried Gray on his cell already. Who was he with?"

"Um. Let's see." There was another quick clack. "Detective Singh, and Constables Friesen and Lewis. They've got one patrol car, plus the sergeant's vehicle out. You want me to try their radios?"

"Please."

Lucien waited, strumming his fingers impatiently on his thigh as silence filled the air. He wanted to reach for Raven. To pull her in and offer her reassurance. But the desire to do so had nothing to do with maintaining a professional calm, and he wasn't sure he could pretend that it did.

How did I keep it under wraps those other two months?

Right then, it didn't feel like it would've been possible. Every time he looked at her, the emotion crept in a little stronger. It hadn't even been a day, and already it wanted to overwhelm him. It made his chest ache. He couldn't possibly have been numb to it before, could he?

Without meaning to, he let his gaze slip back to her again. She was watching him now, her oh-so-blue eyes trained on his face. Her expression was as worried as it had been a minute earlier, but there was still hope underneath. She believed in him, and instead of making him feel more pressure to deliver, it filled his rib cage with warmth. The need to drag her into his arms grew again. He wanted her close. Closer than close. Flush against him, her scent filling her nose, her warmth seeping into him. He wanted to taste her lips again, and not feel like he needed to apologize for it, or excuse it. He started to pull the phone away from his ear, but Geraldine cut in once again, forcibly reminding him why he couldn't give in to his urge.

"All right," the dispatcher said. "Sorry about the delay. Had a hard time getting anyone, but I finally got in touch with Constable Lewis, and the news isn't good."

Lucien did his best to keep the blast of nerves to himself, eyeing Rave as he said, "Hit me with it."

"The uniforms picked Ms. Rickson up from a shift at the hospital and escorted her in for questioning. She agreed to waiting things out in a secure location, but requested to grab a few things from home. The uniforms took her to her apartment, where she disappeared from her bedroom."

"From her bedroom?" Lucien repeated, his puzzlement temporarily overriding his deep concern.

"The uniforms were equally confused. And this is where it goes from bad to worse. Lewis said that in retrospect, she thinks someone was *in* Ms. Rickson's room when they arrived. The consensus is that the culprit dragged her into the closet, held her there until her MIA status was noticed, then used the ensuing chaos to take her away from the scene." As Geraldine explained, her voice lost any and all hints of its perkiness. "Clever son-of-you-know-what, isn't he?"

"Clever," Lucien agreed. "And sick."

"No doubt."

"Any news on where the sergeant is at the moment?"

"According to Lewis, he took a team out to canvass Ms. Rickson's neighborhood," the dispatcher stated. "You want Lewis's direct line?"

"Please."

"Got a pen?"

Lucien reached for the notepad and paper, and as he finished scrawling out the number, his eyes landed on Raven once again. It was obvious that she'd heard some—if not all—of what he'd just been told. Every ounce of color was gone from her cheeks. She was swaying a little in the seat. He signed off as quickly as politeness would allow, then reached for her hand.

"It's going to be all right," he promised.

Raven shook her head. "You don't have to say that just to make me feel better."

"Have I ever done that?"

"Yes."

"What? When?"

"Every time we've ever been faced with a dangerous or frightening situation. So. A lot over the two months we lived together." She smiled for the barest second before her mouth drooped again. "She's got to be so scared."

Lucien debated refuting the statement, but there wasn't much point. No one would know better than Raven did just how Sally Rickson was feeling.

"You know that first and foremost, I'm a cop," he said. "And cops don't give out false promises. So every reassuring thing I've ever said to you has been either the truth, or something I believed to be completely true."

Instead of brightening at all, Raven looked even more despondent. She actually pulled her hand away, and dropped her eyes, too.

Surprised, Lucien spoke up right away. "Hey. What did I say wrong?"

"Do you seriously not—no, I guess not." Her blue gaze came up, and she let out a sigh. "You're right. You're an amazing detective. And if you really believe you can save them from Hanes, then I believe you can, too."

Her words had an edge, and he couldn't quite pinpoint the source. It was an edge he didn't *like*. His fingers shot out on their own, and brushed over her chin—as if they were trying to wipe away the unidentified undertone—and for a second, she leaned into the touch. Then she gave her body a small shake and pulled away again.

"You said you were going to ask for some digital files to be sent over?" Now her voice was cool, and Lucien liked that even less. He wanted to demand to know what was going on in her head. She didn't give him a chance.

"We're running out of time," she said. "If we're using your theory about the shortened pattern, then we're at hour nine already."

Lucien wanted to argue, but he couldn't. She was right. It was an extraordinarily small window, and their task was a daunting one. Only four hours until things escalated again. So he set aside his personal needs in favor of his professional obligations, and nodded instead.

"Okay," he said. "I'll fire off a text to Sergeant Gray and ask him to call me as soon as he can. I want to know that status of the Ricksons' son, too. And in the meantime, let me grab the old laptop from the desk in the office, and we'll see what the station's given us."

Relief flooded Raven's face. "Okay."

He fought both a desire to touch her face again, and the bit of resentment that reared up at not being able to do it, then pushed to his feet and slipped out of the room.

Chapter 8

As much as she wanted to, Raven didn't let herself sink into two minutes of sadness while Lucien dug out the laptop. She didn't allow herself to wonder why he'd left the computer there at all, or to think about the fact that it might be another sign of some kind, or to get sucked back into wondering why he'd bought the house in the first place. Instead, she seized on his words—*cop, first and foremost*—and tried to apply them to her own thought process. She might've preferred to find something else at the top of Lucien's priority list, but at the moment, his sentiment was appropriate. Jim and Juanita—and now Sally, too—needed to be put ahead of all else. Above emotions and what-ifs and regrets.

Raven stood up from the table and moved restlessly from the kitchen to the living room, her mind working. *So what's the first thing I would do if I were a cop?* The answer came almost as quickly as the question formed. *Find Jim and Juanita's son.*

But as far as she was aware, the Ricksons didn't *have* a son. Or at least they'd never mentioned one.

Raven paused her pacing, realizing that thought probably should've come up earlier. She'd been too overwhelmed by everything going on to pause and note it.

But they must *have one, or someone else would've said something. The police would definitely have mentioned it.*

A throat clear and Lucien's gruff voice drew Raven's attention away from thoughts.

"That was always one of your favorites," he said with a little nod toward her hands.

She cast a glance down and saw that she'd unconsciously lifted up a small soapstone carving from a little set that rested on a shelf beside the TV. It was a wolf, smooth and vaguely warm under her touch. There were very few personal decorative items in the former safe house, but this was one of them. And Lucien was right; it was a favorite. Not because it stood out from the other seven that sat there—two ravens, two whales, two seals and a second wolf—but because she knew he'd picked it out. He'd told her how he thought it was unfair that the wolf be alone. And even though he'd laughed as he said it, Raven had gotten the feeling that underneath his sheepish humor, he'd meant it, too.

She gave the little ornament a squeeze and brought her gaze up to Lucien again. He was still staring down, and Raven let herself have an indulgent moment of breathtaking appreciation. He was truly the best-looking man she'd ever met. From the top of his six-foot-two frame—capped with his gray-dusted, otherwise-dark hair—to the bottom of his sock-clad feet, there wasn't a bit of him that didn't deserve a second glance. His shoulders were wide and strong, and perfectly filled out the charcoal-gray shirt he wore. His waist was narrow, his hips lean and his legs visibly powerful underneath his athletic pants.

The temperature in the room seemed to spike by a hundred degrees, and a little voice in Raven's head pointed out that she'd clearly been crazy to brush off his comforting touch a few minutes earlier.

"Not my best look, I guess," he said, noting her attention and gesturing to his sports gear. "Didn't have time to change."

"No. You look good. Um. Fine, I mean." Raven's face was already warm from the fact that she'd been caught ogling, and it heated even more at her awkward fumbling of words. "And we match, right?"

Lucien's mouth tipped up a bit as he eyed her own running gear. "That's true." He held out the laptop, then gestured toward the couch. "Should we get started?"

Raven hesitated. Part of her wanted to point out that the professional thing to do would be to set up at the kitchen table. Colleagues didn't cozy up together on a couch while they combed through files. But a stronger part of her wanted the excuse to be a little closer to him, and it was a fight she didn't think she could win.

Taking a small breath, she set down the soapstone wolf and moved to the couch. Trying to at least err on the side of keeping a reasonable space between them, she settled onto one of the corner cushions. But the caution didn't do much good. Once Lucien had plugged the cord into the wall, he dropped his large frame directly to the middle.

It's just practical, Raven told herself. *We can't look at the screen together if we're sitting five feet apart.*

But reasoning it through in her head didn't exactly

transfer over to real life. When Lucien's knee met up with hers so that he could balance the laptop between them, a jolt of electric attraction hit Raven hard enough to make her breath catch in her throat.

Practical.

She tried to think it even more sternly this time, but it was difficult to make the word stick. She was too aware of every little movement. And it got worse again, because Lucien spoke, and his voice was low and somehow managed to rumble through her whole body, setting each and every one of her pores onto high alert.

"Sorry," he said. "This'll take a minute or two. System wants me to update a few things before it'll let me in."

"It's fine." The statement was a half lie.

Their current position was both pleasant and torturous at the same time. Lucien's outer thigh was warm enough that Raven could feel it seeping into her, despite the two layers of pants. His tap on the keyboard as he did what needed to be done made his elbow bump up against her forearm. The little rubs sent a vibration up to her shoulder, which in turn bloomed out to her chest. Each touch only dragged out the torment, and she couldn't help but wonder if the physical pull had always been so strong, or if the long absence had intensified it.

She could recall moments of wanting him, and specific times when their casual intimacy made her warm all over. Lucien, slipping out of the bathroom in a towel because he forgot to grab something from the bedroom. A power outage that equaled an evening spent huddling together under a blanket on the couch, trying to keep warm. Numerous occasions where she'd fallen asleep beside him on that same couch, and once when she'd woken up to find that he'd carried her to her bed and tucked her in there instead.

But it was different back then. Raven just wasn't sure how.

Those days together seemed endless. And even though the drag of time had been scary, it had also let her fall slowly.

Fall slowly?

She acknowledged that slightly sarcastic voice with an invisible nod. It was as far she was willing to go at the moment. Not because she was in denial. She knew exactly how she felt about Detective Lucien Match. How she'd felt about him every second since she met him, and how those feelings only deepened over time, and how they hadn't faded away over their separation. But now the slow fall was over. And she was well acquainted with the pain of how it ended.

Maybe that's it, she thought. *I know there's an end in sight, and I'm subconsciously trying to grab on to as much as I can while I have the time.*

It made just enough sense that Raven believed it might be true.

"Almost there," Lucien murmured. "Got the email up. There's a file of pictures here, and a note from records, saying they'll send the rest shortly."

His announcement alerted her to the fact that she'd unconsciously closed her eyes, and she pulled them open quickly, not wanting to be caught in yet another embarrassing moment. But the second her gaze landed on the screen, she wished she'd kept her lids sealed tight. Because an image opened right at that moment, filling the laptop with something she'd hoped to never see again—the inside of the dark hole where Lucien had found her on the day she should've been executed.

* * *

Even before Lucien realized his mistake, he felt the immediate tenseness in Raven's body. Their legs and arms were touching, and she went from being distractingly soft and pleasant to being as rigid as a two-by-four. A surprised question on his lips, Lucien started to turn. Then the picture on the screen caught his eye, and he didn't have to ask. Automatically, his hand shot out to slam the computer shut, but Raven was quicker. Her slim fingers closed on his wrist, stilling him.

"Don't." She said it just above a whisper, but her tone was surprisingly firm.

Lucien didn't pull his hand back just yet, though, and he cursed himself for not thinking to preview the file before opening it up.

Aloud he said, "Give me a second, and I'll get rid of it."

She took a deep breath, and shook her head, then spoke again, her voice even stronger. "No. I'm okay. I just wasn't expecting it."

Her eyes flicked to the screen, and her fingers tightened on his arm.

"You don't need to look at it," he said quickly. "Let me—"

She cut him off. "Maybe I do, though."

"Raven…"

"No, I mean it. I spend my days helping people learn how to deal with their trauma, but I keep my own behind this… I don't know. A barbed-wire fence in my head, or something." Her hand dropped from his wrist, and she reached up to touch the photo on the screen. "It looks brighter in this shot."

He stole a second-long look at the picture, then brought his attention immediately back to her face. "I think it *is* brighter. It was lit up so the techs could get a good overview of everything."

She was quiet for a moment before replying, "Do you remember how dark it was when you got there?"

"I do," he said.

It'd been so pitch-black that—even just a few feet into the entrance of the hole—he hadn't been able to see his own feet. He'd damn near fallen a half a dozen times on the way. And when he actually reached the top of the nearly sheer drop, he hadn't seen Raven, either. Instead, he'd heard her shallow breaths and small whimpers. His relief that she was alive had been as thick as his concern that she wouldn't stay that way for much longer.

"You called my name," she added.

"Yes. I remember."

"It probably sounds ridiculous, but it was like your voice *was* the light." Her cheeks were tinged pink with embarrassment, but she didn't retract the statement.

Lucien didn't argue, either. Instead, he brought his knuckles up and ran them over the color. Slowly.

He knew what she meant about the light, but as far he was concerned, she was the one who'd parted the darkness. When he'd called her name on that day three years ago, there'd been a brief moment of silence. No breathing, no whimpers. Lucien's relief had evaporated. Then *her* voice carried up. Cracked and so broken that he hadn't quite been able to discern what she'd said. A disbelieving greeting, maybe? But it hadn't mattered anyway. He'd climbed in, feetfirst, sliding his body down the hole and letting himself drop the rest of the way. Four feet more—or thereabouts—but he hadn't known or cared. All he was sure of was that saving her from the fate of the rest of Hanes's victims was the most important thing. He'd landed almost on top of her, and in spite of her situation, she'd reached out to steady him, then asked if *he* was okay in a raw rasp.

"I would've died," Raven said.

The statement made Lucien's heart drop with remembered fear that it might be true. Because right after she'd asked the question, she'd keeled over, straight into his arms.

"We don't know that for sure," he replied, his voice gruff with emotion.

In response, her hand came up to his, her warm palm sending licks of heat through his skin. "Yes, we do. And you know I don't just mean from my injuries."

Lucien swallowed against the thick lump in his throat, then nodded. There wasn't much point in denying it.

After she'd passed out, he'd held her for an hour. Right up until the paramedics arrived. Even after that, he'd carried her out himself. Then stayed by her side, riding along to hospital. Sitting by her bed and holding her hand and measuring her breaths. Fending off the doctors who said he should go home and rest. They'd told him her fainting was borne of exhaustion and lack of food, and assured him that she'd be fine. Lucien had believed them, but he'd still felt a deep need to be there when she regained consciousness. It was a compulsion.

Raven's fingers moved a little more, threading through his. "I'm sorry if I never thanked you properly for saving me. It hurt to talk about it. It *still* hurts, even just to think about it. But I owe you so much."

"No thanks were ever necessary," he assured her gently. "And you don't owe me anything."

It was true. At least as far he was concerned. The only thanks he'd needed were watching her open her eyes. Feeling how they landed on him, and seeing the recognition there.

Until that moment, Lucien didn't believe in love at first sight. He wasn't sure he'd really believed in love at all. Even if his career hadn't brought him face-to-face with the worst moments of humanity, his personal life would've already set him up for failure. His father had been a drinker and serial cheater and a manipulator. A very angry man, who took out everything on Lucien. His birth mother had died when he was born, and his stepmother, who'd been with them since Lucien was a year old, eventually gave up. She left both of them without ever looking back. In a practically textbook reaction, he'd spent his life avoiding serious relationships. He was conscious of it, though, and had accepted it. So when the moment struck—when a woman he didn't know, who hadn't heard his name, or learned any bit of his story, but who somehow threw out an invisible rope and tugged him in—he'd been stunned. She'd eventually learned it all, of course. She'd gotten to know him more than anyone else in the world. But in those seconds, he'd been speechless. Powerless. Unable to do anything but stare at her, just like he was doing at the present moment.

"I don't not owe you anything," she told him. "I owe you *every*thing."

"Literally nothing," he insisted.

She shook her head, the smallest of all smiles turning up her perfect lips. "Weirdest argument ever."

Even if she was right, he couldn't muster up any of his own good cheer. He wanted her to see that saving her life had changed his own for the better, too. For her to understand what he was feeling but couldn't say. He just wished he was better equipped to do it. He reached up and gave his ear a nervous tug. He'd never been great with words. But he'd never felt the lack so acutely, either, and he wished—badly—that he was a smooth talker.

He cleared his throat and lifted both of his hands to cup her face. Words still didn't come. The bad old memories swirled around in his head, mingling with the good ones, and mixing with the present. After a heavily weighted minute, it was Raven who spoke. Just one word, but somehow, she made it sound like an ache.

"Lucien."

It was all he could take. Overcome, he dipped his face down and pressed his mouth to hers. For a moment, she was still. Just receiving the kiss. Her lack of reaction very nearly made Lucien pull away. Then— as if she sensed his intention to separate—her hands came up and landed on the back of his neck, holding him there. And more important, she came alive. Her lips moved with his, tasting and exploring, setting off the metaphorical fireworks that had waited under the surface for what felt like a millennium.

Earlier, Lucien had thought the brief contact between their lips had been a kiss. He'd been wrong. So very mistaken.

You were an idiot to hold back, he said to himself. *A complete fool to waste two months living together, when the whole time, it could've been like this.*

His role as a detective and the consequences of that role? Secondary. His second-guesses about whether or not he could be the man she deserved? Tertiary. No doubts. Raven was the only thing in his sight lines. He needed her more than anything else.

The pace of the kiss—the deepness of it—intensified. Her tongue came out to meet his, and all coherent thought took a backseat. Raven's hands were in his hair now, tugging and twirling. Her body had shifted forward, and her soft curves pressed to his chest. The quick, staccato beat of their hearts rose between them, and it was impossible to tell where his ended and hers started. Their gasps were intertwined; their mouths were one. The words he'd been trying desperately to find had found a different, more thorough outlet.

He didn't want it to end. But when they paused simultaneously to gulp in a breath, Raven leaned away—just a little bit—and Lucien saw that a couple of tears had escaped through her long dark lashes. They were making their way down her face.

Guilt flushed through him. "Raven—"

"Don't," she said quickly, her eyes opening wider. "Please. Don't tell me again that you're sorry."

"You're crying."

"It's not your fault. I'm just overwhelmed by everything."

He ran a hand over his head. As if he could physically scrape away the worsening self-reproach. What had he been thinking? *Almost* kissing her had been bad enough. At least he'd had the presence of mind to stop it before it went farther. This time, though…he'd been swept away by his want. Caught up in the moment, when he should've been paying attention to Raven. What kind of man didn't notice when the woman he was kissing was *crying*?

Her hand landed on his arm, and he realized he'd just done it again—become wrapped up in himself rather than attending to her obvious hurt.

He tried again to apologize. "Raven…"

She stopped him a second time. "I mean it, Lucien. Do *not* tell me you're sorry."

"Raven."

"And stop saying my name and making it sound like that."

He pressed his lips together for a second to stop himself from doing it again, then sought some alternative words. "I didn't mean to—"

"Uh-uh," she cut in. "That's going to be an apology, too." She sighed and wriggled back, lessening the intimacy of their pose. "I know what you're going to say, anyway. We can't do this. We shouldn't do this. There's a professional line, and we should stay on the correct side of it."

He wanted to argue. To tell her where the "professional line" could take itself. Except her words perfectly echoed his own concerns. They aligned with every excuse he'd made when he'd walked away three years ago—the same reasons that he'd played out in his head, every time he got the urge to call Raven.

But they seemed awfully far away and unimportant a minute ago, didn't they?

Lucien opened his mouth—maybe to voice the thought, maybe not—but he didn't get a chance to say anything, because Raven's gaze flicked to the laptop, and she spoke first.

"Looks like something else came through from your contact at the station," she said, and Lucien took that as a sign that she was correct. It was time to get back to the other side of the professional line.

Chapter 9

It took all of Raven's willpower to stay focused on the files open on the screen. It was a daunting task. The feel of Lucien's mouth was too fresh in her mind. And though there was a now a comfortable few inches between them—the laptop rested on the table instead of their knees—it was impossible not to be conscious of his nearness.

And that kiss...

It had been the kiss to ruin her for all other kisses. The one she'd been waiting on for three years. She'd imagined it. Dreamed of it. Played out the ways it could have happened in the past, and the way it would happen if they'd ever met up again.

And it made you cry.

She didn't know where her tears had come from. Not specifically, anyway. She just knew that one second, she was clinging tightly to Lucien, her body alight with pent-up desire, and the next she was fighting a burn in her throat while her eyes betrayed her. And the rawness was what made her sure that whatever prompted the unexpected tears, it wasn't joy at finally getting what she'd always wanted. This was more intense. It felt almost like sorrow. Which really didn't make much sense at all.

She was thankful that Lucien hadn't pushed for more of an explanation. It would've been too humiliating to try to explain that it wasn't just the situation that had overwhelmed her.

She eyed Lucien's handsome profile, trying to puzzle through the conundrum. Why, when the man who unknowingly held her heart kissed her, would she feel such an overwhelming sadness? Why, looking at him now, did it threaten to creep up again? She finally had confirmation that he was just as attracted to her as she was to him, and yet she couldn't manage to drum up some happiness at knowing it.

Drawing in a breath, she forced her eyes back to the laptop, and made herself ask a generic question about the scanned notes on display.

"Is that a police report?" she said.

Lucien nodded without looking her way. "This one is from the Sandora file."

"The Sandoras were the second family targeted by Hanes, right?"

"Yep. It was actually their case that alerted us to the fact that he was handing out clues about his victims' locations. Figured it might help us now to have a quick revisit of the old clues to get us going with the new one." He clicked a couple of times, and a photograph of a yellow note took the place of the file. "This was the one that gave it away."

The existence of the clues was common knowledge,

but the contents of them had never been publicly shared. Raven leaned forward to get a better look. The words were written in tidy block letters, and they would've been unnerving in their oddness, even if she hadn't known they'd been left behind by the man who'd killed her family.

SADDLE UP, they read. *THE WILD RIDE IS COLD AND OLD, BUT CLOSE TO HOME.*

Raven fought a shiver. She didn't want Lucien to think she couldn't handle the details.

"How did the Sandoras help you figure it out?" she asked.

"You remember there was a manhunt underway already?" he replied.

She nodded. "Yes. Because the VPD had Hanes's identity from the beginning, right?"

"Yep. But not because the task force was clever enough to figure it out. Hanes left his ID at the first abduction scene."

The revelation stunned Raven. "What?"

He leaned back on the couch, and she pretended not to notice that his knee was brushing hers once more.

"Part of his game," Lucien said. "It was a detail we never released to the press. In fact, you're one of about two dozen people who're now aware of the fact. So if anyone asks, you're an official consultant on the case."

Raven frowned. "Okay. But I don't understand. He *wanted* you to know who he was?"

"Only so we could use the clues he'd left. His address was invalid, and nothing about his ID helped us with actually pinning him down. He was—is—too smart for that. But knowing his name did give us access to bits and pieces of his life, all of which connected him to the victims in random ways."

Raven's attention swung back to the computer, her brain searching for the meaning behind the clue on the yellow note. Something about the words jogged a memory she didn't even know she had.

"David Sandora..." she said. "He was found by some kids at an abandoned stable, wasn't he?"

"That's right," Lucien agreed. "The stable had been swallowed by a sinkhole a decade earlier, and no effort had even been made to recover it."

"So this clue...it had something to do with what? Horses?"

"Yep. Turned out that Hanes was a regular at the track. An employee there called our tip line to tell us she recognized his face, and it was actually the clerk who took the call that had the light-bulb moment. The clerk knew where David had been found, and she also remembered reading somewhere that he'd once worked as a horse trainer. She put it all together, brought it to the task force and suddenly everyone realized the notes were more than insignificant crazy talk."

Raven stared down at the screen for another moment, remembering her own clue—the only one she'd been familiar with until the current moment. She started to mention it, but before she could, her eye was drawn to something else. There was another file open behind the photograph of the note, and a small section of words was visible behind the picture. She blinked, and her breath caught a little as an idea formed.

"Does that say that Hanes worked as a custodian at the hospital?" she asked.

"Could be. Guy couldn't—or maybe wouldn't—hold down steady employment, so he went through a lot of jobs," Lucien told her. "Why? Does that mean something to you?"

"Do you mind if I…" She trailed off without finishing, then reached across his lap without waiting for an answer to her half-asked question, and she clicked on the other file.

The top of the digital paper was labeled with the words *Georges Hanes: Career History*, and it had to have at least thirty titles listed below the header. But there was only one that interested Raven at that moment. She sought it out again.

"Vancouver Heart Hospital," she read aloud. "Building service worker. Morgue." She met Lucien's eyes. "Before he retired into the caretaker position at the cemetery Jim Rickson was a pathologist."

"At Vancouver Heart?"

"I'm about 90 percent sure of it. And the clue kind of fits, too, right?" She tried not to let hope bubble up, and tried even harder not to let any of it show as she added, "If he really *wasn't* talking about me, I mean."

"I was already convinced that he wasn't. This just solidifies that," Lucien said, his fingers strumming thoughtfully on his thigh. "A life for a life. And death is the morgue's business. Good police work, Detective Elliot."

Her face warmed. "Funny."

He gave her knee a quick squeeze, then pushed to his feet and dragged his phone from his pocket. "I'm gonna give the boss a call and make some coffee. You want tea?"

"Always," she said.

She watched him step from the living room to the kitchen, then turned back to the computer and flicked through the other photographed clues, only half listening as Lucien spoke with his boss.

"Sergeant," he was saying. "Nice of you to take my

call this time around." Pause. "Yeah, you heard me right." Another pause. "Nope. But you'll wanna listen to this."

His words faded way in the background, though, as her own clue popped onto the screen. In fact, the whole world kind of slipped away as Raven stared down at words.

DIG AROUND. ALWAYS DARK AND FULL OF MYSTERY, MY SPARKLE IS A SURPRISE.

She knew, obviously, what the message referred to. Hanes had driven her out to a long-shut-down mine, and that was where Lucien had found her. But she hadn't ever looked at the note itself. Doing so now gave her a deep chill. It was impossible not to picture Hanes writing it down, a small, smug smile on his face.

She'd been told that he confessed in court that he wrote out the obscure hints beforehand, then planted them somewhere. A fail-safe, in case the investigators were successful in their search for one victim, the clue would be there to lead them to the next. She hadn't seen the one left in the hole with her—the one that the task force wasn't able to decode in time to save her brother. It'd been far too dark. And her attention was elsewhere, of course. But that didn't stop her from wondering if her mom had seen the note about her. If the serial killer had left it somewhere visible in her case.

Oh, Mom, she thought. *I kind of hope you saw it, and I hope you were sure someone would be smart enough to figure it out.*

Her heart ached sharply in her chest as it always did when she allowed herself to consider the family she'd lost. She hated Hanes for taking them from her. She wanted to stop him from ever having the power to hurt anyone like that again. The need was a burn, almost as painful as the acute loss.

She brought up her gaze just as Lucien was setting his phone down on the counter.

"All right," he said, speaking as he moved toward her. "The sergeant is sending someone to check the morgue. I think it'll—" He paused, clearly catching belated sight of her face. "Hey. What is it?"

"Tell me how you found me."

Lucien looked understandably surprised. Over the two months they'd spent together, he'd tried exactly three times to tell her a little about it. And all three times, Raven had shut him down. In fact, over the last few hours, she'd talked more about Hanes and her own tribulations than she had in the past three years. But now she felt like she needed to know everything she could, so she could arm herself.

"Please," she said, and Lucien sat down beside her and started to talk.

Lucien spoke on autopilot, recounting the events that had led up to the moment he found her at the bottom of the hole in the mine. He told her that while he hadn't been a part of the task force assigned to tracking Hanes—another case had him busy already—he *had* attended an all-hands-style meeting. The Kitsilano Killer had had the entire city on edge. The sergeant was growing more and more agitated, and the pressure was reaching a critical level. It'd been late in the evening on day eighteen of Hanes's pattern. Each member of the Elliot family had already been taken. The two senior members had been found dead, and the final hours were creeping toward Raven's demise, too.

Some of it, he was sure she'd heard before. A fair

amount of details were gone over at the trial, and she'd been present for nearly the whole thing, only excusing herself a few times when things got to be too much. She'd even been prepared to testify. Thankfully, Hanes's own words were enough to put him away, and Raven was never called to the stand.

Lucien explained it all, anyway. Carefully, but without leaving anything out. What he was more concerned with, though, was keeping an eye on Raven's reaction to the information he was sharing.

When he'd been acting as her personal bodyguard, she'd made it abundantly clear that she didn't want to discuss the specifics of the original Hanes case. She'd almost fallen apart once when he'd brought it up. He didn't blame her. He didn't push her. It wasn't a part of his assigned task. His job was to keep her alive and unharmed, and if she preferred to steer their interactions away from her family's murder, then so be it. It was actually probably the reason they'd gotten to know each other on such a personal level. They were able to talk about their life paths and their dreams. Their favorite movies and their pastimes. Very little had been off-limits. With the exception, of course, of the Kitsilano Killer. Now, though, Raven's eyes were fixed on him, and she showed no sign of shying away. So he pushed on.

"I left that emergency meeting pretty much the way I came in…" he said to her. "Without much of a clue where the search was going, or knowing if it was going anywhere at all. The task force had already been split in two. One group was focusing finding Hanes himself, and the other…"

"Was looking for me and my brother," Raven filled in.

"Yes. And at the end of each day, they'd get together

and try to see if any puzzle pieces overlapped. It was the final thing everyone did before they went home. *If* they went home. But on *that* day, no one wanted to do it. They knew they only had hours left to save you, and fitting the pieces together seemed too final." Lucien paused, silently recalling the details of that particular day.

There'd been a palpably thick sense of dread hanging over the entire station. The two rooms they'd dedicated to the case as war rooms were full to the brim. Cops. Forensic techs. Clerks. Puzzle solvers who'd come in from God knew where. No resource had been spared. There was coffee flowing, and a pile of sandwiches sat in the middle of a couple of tables in each of the rooms. A local shop had donated the food, but no one seemed to have the stomach to indulge in eating any of it.

"Every person there was in for the long haul," he said. "I think some of them had literally not gone home in days. I was doing my best to close off my other case so I could pitch in more, too. I'd worked through the night, and had driven out of town to follow a lead. I was in my car in an alley outside this lowlife's house, waiting for him to come out so I could ask him a few questions. The sun was just coming up, and a guy walked up with a roll of posters in his hands. He started sticking one up on the wall, and I was kinda half watching him do it. And then the poster itself caught my attention. It was an advertisement for some event at the mining museum."

"Once of those coincidences you're so fond of talking about," Raven replied.

He nodded. "I remember sitting there, thinking it was too obvious. Who wouldn't have thought of a mine, the moment something sparkly was mentioned? And who knows? Maybe they *had*."

"But you didn't wait to find out."

"Well. I did aim to loosely follow some kind of protocol at first. I made the call directly to the sergeant, but damn if I could get a hold of him. Or anyone important. I sat there for a half hour, thinking someone *had* to be about to call me back. No one did. And my witness never came out of the building in that time, either."

"And you broke all the rest of the rules to come and get me." Raven's expression grew soft, her gaze focused on him in a way that made him want to reach out to stroke her cheek.

He closed his hands into fists to keep from giving in to the impulse, and replied, "It was quicker—and possibly a lot stupider—for me to just place a call for immediate backup, then hightail it outta there. Completely lost any chance of solving that other case in the process, by the way."

"Do you regret it, then?"

Her tone was light, and he knew she was kidding. That didn't stop a hint of fierceness from entering his response.

"Regret it?" he said. "It was the best damn decision I've made my entire career."

Her expression faltered, just for a second. It was long enough for Lucien to realize he needed more than the *hint* of fierceness. Forgetting his resolve not to reach for her, he unfurled his fingers and dropped them to her hand.

"I lied just a second ago," he admitted.

Her forehead creased. "About what?"

"I told you that I called in my hunch because of protocol. That wasn't true. The call was an afterthought. I was already pulling onto the highway when I realized that I might not get to you in time, and I wanted to make sure someone knew where I'd gone."

"Oh. Well. That barely even qualifies as a lie."

He drew in a breath. "It doesn't sound like that big of a deal, I know. But my lack of playing within the rules was an issue. The sergeant told me once that if there were a dictionary for cop stereotypes, he was sure my picture would be under *hothead*."

Raven's frown deepened. "You?"

He suppressed a chuckle at her obvious disbelief. "Yes, me."

"But you're so *calm* all the time. I don't think I've ever seen you get more than a little annoyed."

"Acting impulsively was a bit of an issue for me for, oh, I don't know? The first fifteen years of my career."

Her dubious expression didn't change. "I honestly just can't picture it."

Now he did laugh. "I abandoned my own case—and the witness I was supposed to interview—so I could chase down a lead that wasn't even a lead. I didn't stop and look for a connection between Hanes and the mine and you. I just did it. If that's not the very definition of impulsive, I don't know what *is*."

"But your instincts were right. There *was* a connection. Hanes worked in that jewelry store. I was in the local paper for finding and returning that engagement ring that'd been missing for fifty years. And besides that…if you *hadn't* followed your gut, then I would've died."

"Sergeant Gray told me that was the only reason I still had a job. Like I said. Best damn decision I ever made."

"For you career."

"What?"

"You said it was the best decision you've ever made for your career."

A small, dim light bulb tried come to life in the back of his head, but he couldn't quite put his finger on what it was trying to illuminate. There was just a flicker, and then it was gone.

"It made all the difference," he said. "I was a good detective before I met you. Excellent track record, actually. Except for the part where I let myself act without thinking, got write-ups for coloring outside the lines and felt the need to go toe to toe with my boss every time we disagreed. I used to be completely single-minded—just honing in on the endgame and nothing else, running over whoever got in the way. I stopped being like that the moment I met you."

She shook her head a little. "I don't understand, Lucien. I made you a better cop by taking away your focus? That's kind of a contradiction, isn't it?"

Once again, he struggled to find the right words. He wanted to say something meaningful. Something powerful. In the end, he settled for straightforward.

"Knowing you helped give me a bigger view of the world," he said. "So it didn't just make me a better cop… It made me a better person."

Raven's cheeks went a touchable shade of pink, and Lucien couldn't resist. He dropped his fingers from her hands and lifted them to her face. The way she leaned into the caress—her eyes closing a little while her lips parted—sent a new wave of want through Lucien. He inched forward, anticipation licking through his veins. Self-control was an illusion. No matter how much he told himself he shouldn't let anything more happen, the undercurrent was too strong. He bent his neck a little more.

"Lucien." Her breathy voice just barely carried above the noisy rush of blood through his body.

He made himself pause, his lips close enough that his reply was just a murmured vibration. "Yes?"

"Your phone."

"What about it?"

"It's ringing?"

"No it's not."

"Yes. It is."

Lucien pulled back and glanced toward the table. The electronic device was, in fact, ringing. Loudly, actually. And even from where he was, he could see his boss's name flashing on the screen.

Dammit.

The man had timing.

For a second, Lucien considered ignoring it. As quick as the thought came, though, it was gone. Lives were in the balance. Including Raven's. Not answering wasn't an option, no matter how much he wanted it to be.

Chapter 10

Raven would've liked a moment to enjoy the fact that Lucien had just come as close to a romantic confession as she'd ever hoped for. Or maybe not quite as close as she'd always *hoped* for. But possibly as close as she would get. Except she didn't *get* a moment. Because almost as soon as Lucien picked up the phone, Raven knew it was bad news. His mouth—which she'd been just a hairbreadth away from a few heartbeats earlier—set into a line as he greeted his boss, then listened for a second. He gave her knee a little squeeze, then stood up and moved restlessly through the room, talking as he moved. And she didn't even have to really listen to the conversation to figure it out, and the one snippet she did hear clearly confirmed it anyway.

"No," said Lucien. "I agree. The hospital was a good conclusion. Too bad it wasn't the right one. We'll just have to look for another connection between Jim Rickson and Hanes."

It made her heart drop. They were going to have to start again. Look for something else in the clue. The idea was overwhelming.

She tried to remind herself that the task force was diligently working on it, too. Sergeant Gray and the other VPD officers wouldn't rest until Georges Hanes was behind bars again. They'd dedicate serious time to trying to figure out exactly what the message meant. But knowing it was still little consolation while the Rickson family suffered the consequences of the killer's escape.

Raven's eyes sought the computer again. There had to be something there. She reached out and started to pull it in so she could take another look, but stopped as another name on the list of Hanes's employers drew her attention.

Dan's Pork and Poultry.

She frowned, unsure why that particular listing seemed to stand out. She couldn't think of a way that the clue related to farming. Or to Jim. He wasn't exactly the agricultural type. In fact, the closest he came to raising pigs or chickens was his prize-winning barbecue sauce. Three years in a row, he'd come in first in some kind of contest. And Raven only knew about that because of the plaques he had hanging over his desk. Right that second, she could actually picture the gold-embossed wood really easily for some reason. But it had nothing to do with the riddle.

She shook her head, trying to clear it of irrelevant details, and reached for the computer again. But she stopped a second time and almost gasped as a new idea hit her.

"Lucien!" She looked up as she said it, and saw that he was just about to stick his phone into his pocket.

"You're going to want to keep that out so you can call Sergeant Gray back."

His hand stilled. "Why? What'd you find?"

"Dan's Pork and Poultry."

"Er. What?"

"Jim won a couple of prizes for the sauce he makes for pork ribs. Dan's Pork and Poultry in on Hanes's list of employers. And the message was written in pig's blood. So…it wasn't the *words* that he wanted us to see?"

Lucien's eyes widened with understanding. "You're suggesting that the medium itself is the message."

Raven tried not to let herself show too much excitement. "It makes more sense than what he actually wrote, doesn't it? What if the words are just a misdirect?"

"It'd definitely fit better with Hanes's need to assert his cleverness." He pulled the phone out, hit a button, then waited only a moment before speaking quickly into it. "Hey, Sergeant. Yeah, it's me again. I've got another possible lead."

As he gave a quick rundown of her theory—God, how she hoped she was right this time—Raven turned back to the computer. She pulled up the search engine, thought for a second, then typed in a few keywords.

Pork, shutdown, abandoned, pig.

The laptop took its sweet time processing—long enough for Lucien to finish his conversation and seat himself beside her again—but when it finished, Raven was startled to see that an immediate possibility came up. Right at the top of the page was a newspaper article detailing the recent closure of a pork-processing facility. The thumbnail photo showed a tall barbed-wire-topped, chain-link fence surrounding some kind of building.

"Can that really be it?" Raven asked. "Can finding it really be that easy?"

"Might as well have a quick look." Lucien leaned past her to click on the news story, then read the first bit aloud. "'In the wake of a quality-control scandal, Orion Meats temporarily closed its doors today. The company will be on hiatus while the allegations are investigated by health authorities. Until then, the warehouse is closed to public and staff alike.'" He paused there, lifting his eyes to meet hers. "Sounds like a place Hanes would choose. I'll call it in."

Raven waited again as he stood up and placed yet another call. Hope was already springing up again. The more she stared at the picture of the shut-down warehouse, the more she felt it. It would fit Hanes's MO just right. Somewhere slightly foreboding. Off the beaten path. Unlikely to be carefully patrolled. And quite possibly the easiest place to obtain a container of blood that was going to be used as paint. Which meant he'd probably been planning for a while.

Raven swallowed, and focused on scanning the rest of the article as she tried to fend off the wave a nausea that threatened.

There weren't many more details. A bit about the internal complaint, a bit about the number of employees who would be out of work. A statement from the owner. And an address. The last thing gave Raven pause. It was close to their current location. Really close.

Her gaze flicked to the clock. Her best estimate was that they were somewhere close to hour thirteen. That meant that if they were right about Hanes's sped-up timeline, there were only two hours left until Jim wouldn't have a second more in the world. And they were literally twenty minutes away.

She bit her lip and glanced up toward Lucien. He was back to pacing, his voice low—not quite audible—but slightly intense nonetheless. She knew without asking what he'd say if she even *hinted* at what was going on in her mind. Then—like he knew she was vaguely plotting something—he glanced her way. Before she could drop her gaze to hide her thoughts, he averted his own eyes. It made her frown. What was *he* thinking, that he had to look away? It only took a second more to find out.

He tapped the phone off and turned a grim look her way. "Two pieces of bad news."

"The first is that the task force hasn't been able to track down the Rickson's son. Literally no sign of his existence so far. Sergeant's digging deeper. Thinks maybe he was estranged from the family."

"That might make sense. Jim and Juanita talked about Sally all the time. But they never mentioned a son even once."

"They'll keep looking. Maybe we'll even get lucky and wherever he is, he's too far for Hanes to get, too." Lucien sighed, ran a frustrated hand over his hair, then gave his head a small shake. "That's not the more pressing thing right now, anyway. In that five minutes between calls, the sergeant got the news that a semitruck flipped its load on Highway One. Which wouldn't matter too much to us, except it's right by the exit that's nearest to the processing plant. Boss says it's already backing up like crazy. Side routes will be nuts going that way, too."

Sweat dampened Raven's upper lip as she stated the obvious, "So it's going to delay getting someone to Jim."

"Yeah. I'm afraid so." His eyes dropped to his phone, and she knew he was checking the time.

"Two hours left," she said quickly, the sweat spreading to include the back of her neck.

"Two and a quarter," he corrected.

She didn't argue that fifteen minutes made no difference. She knew from experience that it *did*. But it wasn't her point at the moment, either.

"How long?" she asked.

No explanation for what she meant was necessary.

"Under normal circumstances, it'd be forty minutes."

We could be there in half that, she thought.

Aloud, she said, "And how long now?"

"Sergeant is guessing an hour at best."

At best.

It didn't sound hopeful at all.

"Can't they just… I don't know…force their way through?" she asked. "Isn't that the point of emergency services?"

"It is," Lucien agreed. "Apparently, it's going to be so rough getting in that they're sending a medevac chopper instead of trying to come in on the ground. But the crew will get there are fast as they can. I promise."

She closed her eyes, trying to ward of the sudden sting of tears. "What if it's not quick enough?"

She felt the air shift just a bit, and she knew he was coming her way. In a second, he was going to sit down and try to comfort her. And she was sure that if he did, she'd abandon the plan that was coming together in her head. She needed to head him off.

She opened her eyes, pushed to her feet, and—pretending not to notice Lucien's surprised expression— she stepped around the coffee table and moved toward the kitchen. There, she grabbed a glass and busied herself with filling it with water from the sink on the freestanding island. But as she took a sip, she let her eyes roam the room in what she hoped was an unobvious way. She almost immediately found what she sought. A set of keys on a black ring, decorated with a gunmetal-gray letter *L*. It hung where it always had when they'd lived there before—on a hook beside the light switch.

Raven lowered her glass, thinking maybe she would send out a feeler or two before jumping too quickly.

"Does the sergeant have backup plan?" she asked, hoping she sounded more casual than she felt.

"He's putting out a call to see if anyone's already on that side of the accident," he told her.

"You mean *this* side," she said. "With us."

"Yeah. Technically, I guess. Wish I hadn't sent Constable Davies and the others away. But there's not much *we* can do about it."

The slight emphasis Lucien put on the word "we" made her certain that if he couldn't see through her, then he'd at least already considered and rejected the idea of going on their own. She set the glass down. But she didn't even get in a small step toward the keys before she saw that Lucien was watching her a little more intently. She grabbed the glass again. Took another sip. More slowly, this time. Then she set the glass down. Only the moment before she let it go, she gave it a little shove. And down it went. Not just spilling the water, but also rolling across the island and making its way toward the ground.

Raven heard Lucien react. She saw him hurry from his spot a few feet away. But both his startled exclamation and his rush to save the glass from shattering were just background for her getaway.

Lucien realized what was happening about a tenth of a second too late. And his mistake only compounded.

When he clued in to what Raven was doing, he jerked away from his intended target. His fingers brushed the glass, which then hit the tile. Dozens of shards sprayed out, and he had little choice but to lift his arm to cover his eyes.

The amount of time it took for all of that to happen was also—not so coincidentally—exactly how long it took Raven to dart across the kitchen and grab his keys from the hook. Lucien dropped his arm just as she was slipping out of the room.

Cursing the fact that he hadn't considered that she might make a run for it, he tried to give chase. Once again, her very effective distraction impeded his progress. His foot hit a patch of the spilled water, sending his body into an unintentional lunge position.

Dammit.

He fought to right himself, and slipped again, sending his knee almost to the floor.

He cursed aloud this time. "Dammit!"

Gritting his teeth, he grabbed a hold of the counter and pulled himself up. A little slower and a little more cautious. When he was up and stable, he stepped wide around the mess, then loped through the house toward the front door, his mind tossing self-directed criticism at him as he moved.

He'd *known* Raven had realized they were closer than anyone else. He'd seen it in her face. Heard it in her voice. What he *hadn't* known or seen, though, was that she'd make an impulsive move like this one. He'd assumed she would ask. Suggest. Argue and cajole. Not just bolt and steal his keys and presumably his vehicle.

His hand landed on the doorknob. His twist yielded nothing. He tried again before realizing that Raven had bought herself another few seconds by locking the dead bolt. With a growl, he reached up and snapped it back to the open position, then dropped his hand back to the handle. For a second, worry crept in under the frustration.

What if I get out there, and she's already gone? He shoved the question aside with a silent, snarly answer. *She won't be. And if I have to throw myself in front of the car to stop her, I will, so help me—*

The thought cut off abruptly as he flung open the front door and found his SUV parked right at the stoop. The vehicle was running. Raven sat at the wheel, her face equally guilt ridden and determined.

Lucien reached for the door, but as he did, the lock clicked shut. Then the window rolled down just an inch.

"I want you to get in," Raven said, her voice matching her expression.

"Funny way of showing it," Lucien replied.

"I *want* you to get in," she repeated. "But only if you're not going to turn into a rabid bear and try to wrestle the keys away from me."

"A rabid bear?"

"You know what I mean. We've already wasted time that we could've spent driving to the pork place. I don't want to waste any more fighting about whether or not we should go. *I'm* going. I'd prefer it if you'd come."

In spite of the situation, Lucien's mouth tried to turn up. He ordered it—firmly—not to.

"I don't recall you being quite so stubborn the last time we met," he said.

She tipped up her chin. "And I don't recall you tossing around insults. Are you getting in, or not?"

"Unlock the door, and I will."

"Solemnly swear that you won't try to sabotage me."

"I solemnly swear that I won't sabotage you."

Her eyes narrowed suspiciously. "That was too easy. What's the caveat?"

He sighed. "I don't solemnly swear that I won't spend the entire drive trying to talk you out of doing this. Or trying to convince you to stay in the car when we get there."

For a second, she didn't move or speak, and he thought she might actually just drive away. Then her shoulders relaxed, and the locks clicked open again.

Relieved, Lucien yanked on the handle, climbed in and closed the door again before she could change her mind.

"By the way…" he said as Raven put the SUV into Drive. "That wasn't an insult."

"What?"

"Stubbornness is actually a trait I admire."

She didn't answer, but the blush in her cheeks was enough of a response all on its own. Once again, Lucien's mouth betrayed him with a small smile. The circumstances were terrible on every front. Yet he couldn't stop himself from liking the fiery side of her. He'd seen glimpses of it during their months together. He would never in a million years refer to her as meek. This, though, was something other than just a gritty will to live. It was more. Or a drive to *do* more. A heroism that made Lucien's chest expand. It made him *happy* to know that she had it in her. He liked it.

Not gonna dare tell her that, though.

He didn't need to encourage the recklessness, and he sure as hell didn't want her to put herself in danger. So he remained silent as Raven guided the car up the driveway, then out onto the road. But he did steal a glance of her profile, and the moment he did, regret crept in. For a second, he couldn't place it. He studied her face for a few more moments, trying to figure it out.

Would she really have left without him? He honestly couldn't say. She didn't have a death wish, and she had a healthy fear of Georges Hanes.

And yet...

Her delicate jawline was set—not quite stiff enough to be called rigid—but definitely determined. Even from the side, he could see that her eyes were utterly focused. The only hint of nerves was the way she briefly sucked her lower lip between her teeth. As quickly as she did it, though, she released it. Then she blew out a small breath as if to steady herself, and her jaw went still again. The regret pricked at Lucien again, and this time he was able to place it.

You should have been there, said a voice in his head. *You should've witnessed her growth. Supported it. Not left her alone to keep dealing with everything on her own.*

He turned his gaze to the side window and watched the scenery go by, growing more agricultural by the second. He couldn't deny that he agreed with the voice's statements. Every part of him was screaming that he'd wasted three years. She'd grown without him. Become stronger. He didn't resent that. Not really. He wasn't self-centered enough to think that her healing process would've been better if he'd been around. He just regretted every moment of not seeing it happen.

If there was anything to resent, it was his own idiocy at leaving.

So tell her that, urged the voice.

He swiveled his head back in her direction, his throat raw. His eyes raked over her, drinking in her features.

The soft, dark hair. The creamy, makeup-free skin. The lips he now knew were softer than silk.

The gravity of their current situation took a backseat to need to tell her how he felt.

"Raven."

Her name came out so rough and low that it didn't carry above the light rumble of the engine. He swallowed and tried again, but she spoke first.

"I think we're almost there," she said, lifting a hand from the wheel to gesture out the front windshield.

Lucien automatically turned his attention in the direction she'd indicated, and he immediately spotted a large, concrete sign.

Orion Meats, it read.

Underneath the plain black lettering was the silhouette of a cartoon pig and a large arrow. It was a sharp reminder that there were more pressing things at play than the ache in his heart.

"You know I really am going to ask you to wait in the car, right?" he asked as Raven turned off the paved road onto a packed gravel one.

"And you know I'm going to refuse," she replied without looking his way.

"We have no idea what we're walking into."

"If Jim is in there, then we know that Hanes isn't. You said yourself he's obsessive and won't deviate from his pattern."

"He's *already* deviated," Lucien pointed out.

"In a way that would make you think he's there, waiting to attack?" she countered. "Why would he put out the puzzle pieces and bait us with this game of his if he was just going to kill us the second we figure out the first clue?"

He gritted his teeth. As much as he didn't like it, she

was right. His instincts agreed with her assessment of the situation. Hanes would be pleased if they solved his riddle and found Jim.

And if he wanted to kill Raven, he would've done it by now.

The thought was dark, but also true. Hanes had had both the opportunity and the means, and Lucien had meant it earlier when he told her that he believed the serial killer didn't want to harm her. Whatever his end-game was, it wasn't to see Raven dead. Lucien's own surety of that fact was the only thing that stopped him from pulling out the spare cuffs he kept in his glove box and snapping them to her wrist.

Admittedly, as the SUV slowed, then came to a stop, the temptation to do it was still high. His hands practically itched to secure her, and he had to force himself to look away from where she gripped the wheel in order to stop himself from following through on the urge. He focused on the big building in front of them instead.

It was exactly as it had looked in the online picture. Barbed wire, chain-link fence. Yellow caution tape twisted across the entrance, and the concrete building loomed up behind it.

"It's ominous-looking, isn't it?" Raven's question had an audibly nervous quaver.

"You can still opt for waiting in the car," he reminded her.

In response, she lifted an eyebrow, then clicked open her seat belt and swung the door wide. She jumped out and started up the drive toward the concrete structure, and his only choice was to follow her. He popped open his glove box, cast a half-wistful glance at his cuffs, then reached around them to grab his holster and weapon before hopping out, too.

Chapter 11

Raven's heart was beating so hard it hurt.

She wasn't sure what scared her more—the thought of being wrong and not finding Jim at all, or the thought of finding him too late. She was glad when Lucien caught up to her, and she didn't protest too much when he overtook her to place himself as a shield between her and the big building. But even his presence couldn't quite buffer the fear. Her legs wanted to slow. Her body wanted to turn back. And her mouth wanted to tell Lucien that he was right—she'd be better off letting him do the police work while she waited in the SUV. Like the good civilian she ought to be. She made herself stay the course anyway.

The gray building only got bigger as they got closer, and by the time they reached the metal gates, the processing plant seemed huge. There was an unpleasant, lingering odor in the air, too. Every time the breeze picked up, it drew the scent with it. Raven didn't consider herself to be particularly squeamish, and she knew well where the meat she ate came from. But at the moment, she wondered if she'd be able to stomach a piece of bacon ever again.

"I won't judge you if you want to back out," said Lucien softly, his voice alerting her to the fact that she'd paused in her walk in spite of her resolve to keep going.

Raven breathed out and looked up at him. There was nothing acrimonious in his statement, and his face was open. She knew he really *wouldn't* judge her if she asked to lock herself in the car. He'd probably prefer it. But she didn't detect any pressure in his voice, either. He wouldn't gloat if he got his way. She started to concede. But her mouth no more than opened before the sound of shattering glass cut her off. And Lucien went from being just a man to being a cop.

"Get behind me," he ordered, his hand already at his waist, reaching for a weapon she didn't even know he'd retrieved.

With shaking limbs, she did as she was told, then whispered, "Should I go back to the car?"

"Too late. Don't know who can see us from where." He paused. "Unless you're willing to give up looking for Jim and leave altogether."

"No. No way."

"Then put your hand on my waistband, and move with me."

His grim tone scared her even more. She tucked herself closer against his back and slipped fingers to the spot he suggested. Together, they took a few steps forward. The air was almost silent now, with no more glass breaking, no follow-up voice calling out, the only sound their own muted footsteps and the far-off trill of a bird. But the quiet was as nerve-racking as the noise.

Raven had to work to keep from gripping Lucien too tightly. She didn't want to impede his movement or make him think he needed to pay more attention to her than he did to the task at hand. Willing herself to appear calm even if she couldn't *be* calm, she followed behind. Under the caution tape. Through the surprisingly unsqueaky gate and up the cracked path. He led her past the front door to the side of the building, then kept going.

Lucien didn't look around as they walked, but Raven could feel that his body was on clear alert anyway. He stayed that way until they hit a small set of descending stairs. There, he guided her down to the bottom and at last paused in front of the door. His gaze went up first—checking to see that they were out of sight, she thought—then came to her next.

"I want to give you my gun," he said, his voice low.

Raven blinked. "What? Why?"

"I want you to stay in this spot while I go inside, and I want you armed."

"I'm not staying here! You literally just told me I couldn't go back to the car."

"Up there, you're exposed."

"Down here, I'm trapped."

Lucien's mouth was set in a stubborn line, visible even in the darkened doorway. "Trapped with a weapon. If someone gets this close, you can shoot them point-blank."

Raven's throat tried to close at the suggestion, and she had to clear it in order to answer. "If I try to shoot someone, I'll probably hit my own foot instead."

He surprised her then, by reaching out and placing his free hand on one of her arms, both his expression and his tone intense. "I need you to stay safe, Raven. Nothing matters more to me than knowing you're okay."

Her throat tightened again, this time for a different reason. "How do you think *I* feel, Lucien? You want to give me your gun and walk into God knows what completely unarmed while I stand out here alone having absolutely no clue if *you're* safe or not?"

For a second, he said nothing. An unnameable tension roiled between them. The air was so thick with emotion that Raven could practically feel it. She half expected Lucien to drag her in and kiss her for all he was worth. And she mostly wished he would. So long as it didn't equal a goodbye. But after a few more moments, he just muttered something incomprehensible and dropped his hand to his side.

"Have you got a bobby pin hidden in that hair of yours?" he asked, sounding annoyed and resigned at the same time.

"A bobby pin?" Raven echoed. "No. Why?"

"Because if we're going in, I'd rather not risk walking back out in the open." He jerked his thumb toward the door behind him. "Need to find a way through there."

"Oh. Why don't you just try it first?"

"What?"

"Like this."

She leaned past him to grab the door handle. She gave it a twist, then nearly lost her grip in surprise when it actually turned and clicked. As the door started to swing open, Lucien's arm snaked around her body and his hand landed on hers, stopping it.

"Guess they're even less keen on security than I would've thought," he said, his voice beside her ear and even lower than before. "Hang on. Let me do it."

She yielded to the suggestion, shifting a little so that he could ease the door the rest of the way open. A dim hallway stretched out in front them, silent and even more foreboding than the building as a whole. It made Raven's pulse quicken nervously. She had an urge to ask if Lucien was sure he wanted to go this way—being exposed abruptly seemed more favorable. But she was afraid that saying anything would echo down that long hall, so when he gave her the smallest nudge, she took a few steps in. Lucien moved more quickly, obviously feeling a confidence she couldn't muster up herself.

"You good?" he murmured from somewhere near the top of her head.

She forced a nod, but couldn't quite make herself utter an affirmative aloud. It would've been a lie. She hated the way she couldn't see her feet when she looked down, and how she had no idea if she was going to stumble into a wall or thump down a flight of stairs or crash into some unseen person just ahead.

Why hadn't she grabbed her cell phone before running out of the house? Even putting aside the need to call for help, its flashlight app would've been enough light to illuminate their way. She started to ask Lucien if he had his, then remembered she'd seen it sitting in the center console before she ran off for the second time. She was sure that if he'd taken it with him now, he'd be using it. There was no choice but to keep going the way they were.

But the dark pressed down on Raven. It reminded her far too much of her own harrowing, near-death experience three years prior. The bad memories hovered on the edge of her mind, much closer to the surface than she liked. It was a physical pain. One she had no interest in enduring all over again. Her flight instinct was rearing its head, and she didn't know how long she could resist it.

Then, like he'd read her thoughts, Lucien's warm,

strong hand shot out to take hers, and his touch grounded her. Just as he had been three years ago, and as he'd continued to be for the two months that followed, he provided her with the means to overcome the darkness.

Using one of the techniques she taught her clients, she focused on the immediate, concrete sensation of their intertwined fingers. She noted the pinpoints of heat, and how their hands fit together perfectly. She inventoried the rough patches of his palm, and let herself enjoy the vaguely scratchy feeling against her own soft skin. Each detail let her breathe easier, distracting her from the trap her own mind tried to set. And in just a few moments, they reached the end of the hall that had previously seemed never ending. Another door waited there, its outline extremely faint in the blackness.

But this time, when Lucien leaned close and again asked if she was okay, Raven was able to nod and mean it. She even squeezed his hand and took the first step.

Lucien would've preferred to be in front of Raven. Just the thought of her walking into the potentially dangerous unknown was enough to set his teeth on edge. He could tell, though, that she needed this moment to flex her emotional strength. She was fighting hard against her fear—which was evident in just how tightly she clung to his hand—and he wanted her be able to face the terrible memories and move past them. He'd be a support beam where needed, but he knew she really had to do it on her own. He didn't have to be a grief counselor himself to understand that. So he didn't fight to get past her as her fingers gave the door handle a tug; he settled for gripping his weapon with his own free hand. Preparing for the worst. Bracing for anything but.

Thankfully, as the door inched open, the only attack came from a miniscule amount of light and a gust of rot-tinged air. The scent was just shy of gag inducing, and Lucien suspected that any plans the processing plant had put in place for reopening, they were a long way off now. Maybe abandoned altogether. Whatever the case, by the time the door was fully widened to reveal a landing and two flights of stairs, the pungent aroma was dominating the space. It made him want to be anywhere but there even more than he already had before.

Raven let out a little cough, then pulled her hand out of his to cover her mouth. "Oh, God. It almost makes the abandoned mine seem like a spa."

Lucien chuckled, then immediately regretted it, because the smell permeated his mouth as well as his nose, and a gag threatened harder.

"C'mon," he said quickly, trying to draw in as few breaths as possible as he spoke. "Let's head down."

Raven's attention flicked from the ascending staircase to the descending one. "You're sure that's the right way?"

"Hanes likes dark, deep holes. And even if he didn't, I have a feeling that smell is coming from upstairs, and I'd like to avoid getting closer if possible."

"Good point."

They moved toward the steps, then started down. The bad smell didn't disappear completely, but each stair lessened its strength somewhat, and by the time they hit the bottom, the air was more stale and damp than it was putrid. The dark was thicker again, though, and Lucien automatically reached for Raven's hand. She moved a bit closer, her gaze swinging back and forth.

"Which way now?" she asked.

Lucien swiveled his head in either direction, just as

she'd done. He frowned. They stood on a concrete plat-form, which was exactly like the one on the floor above. Only instead of any doors, there was simply a blank wall in front of them and corridor on either side of them.

"It's not helping the horror-movie feel, is it?" Raven said, her worried tone at odds with her attempt at humor.

Lucien tightened his grip on her hand. "Hanes knows how to pick them."

Her responding exhale was audible. "Yes, he does. So I guess whichever way is the most horrible will be the right way, and we just need to—" She cut herself off abruptly, and her head swung to the left. "Did you hear that?"

He tipped his ear in the direction of her gaze and strained to listen. After a second, he shook his head.

"I don't hear anything but a little bit of a breeze," he admitted.

"But there shouldn't *be* any wind, should there?" she replied. "This basement is mostly underground. I mean, there *could* be windows. But why would one be open right now?"

Kicking himself for not making the connection him-self, he nodded. "Good deduction again. I swear you're a better detective than I am."

Her mouth tipped up. "Not even close, Lucien."

He stared down at her curved lips, overcome with a desire to kiss them. It felt like the natural thing to do, but he fought the urge, and gave her hand a squeeze instead.

"Let's go left, then," he said. "But carefully, with you behind me again, okay?"

"You can't always be my armor, Lucien."

"Maybe not. But I can damn well try to do it as long as possible." His hand dropped hers, then came up to touch her cheek. "I know you don't need me to get by, day-to-day, Raven. You've been fine without me these last three years. But I'm here right now, and you're not going to get rid of me."

Her expression was hard to read in the dark, but he saw her eyes find his mouth—like maybe she was thinking the same thing that he had a moment earlier— and he willed her to make the move that he hadn't.

But she just let out a tiny breath, dragged her gaze back up, then said, "All right. Lead the way."

Covering his disappointment, he turned to face the hall on the left. She positioned herself as he'd suggested, her hand on his waistband and her body close enough that he could feel its warmth. As their slow, careful walk up the hall progressed, regret clouded Lucien's mind, and their pace gave it time to fester.

He hated the back-and-forth between what he wanted—which, simply put, was Raven and nothing else—and what he knew was right. Which was something he *couldn't* put simply. Raven deserved the very best. He was thirty-eight—nearly thirty-nine, if he was being honest—and if he hadn't yet found a way to manage a relationship, how could he give *her* that perfection? She was just barely thirty. Plenty of time to fall in love with someone else. To take it slow and make mistakes and figure out what *she* wanted. Even if it shattered him in the process.

But if it's so right to keep fighting it, then why does it feel so wrong?

The question nearly made him stumble. It was a stupidly obvious one. Something he'd only managed to avoid asking himself because of the space between them. Now that they were together again, it seemed like the thing he should've started with.

So stop *fighting it.*

Once again, his feet threatened to trip over themselves. It *was* a solution, though, wasn't it? Let go of his self-doubt and embrace the fact that three years had done nothing to quell his desire. Put it all out there, and let Raven make the decision. If she didn't choose him, at least he'd have given it a shot.

No time like the present.

He could've argued against the thought. Pointed out the obvious details. Like the fact that they were in the basement of a meat-processing plant in the midst of searching out the latest victim of a serial killer. But an old flicker of impulsivity drove him to ignore those facts. He started to spin, a declaration on his lips. He only got as far as a half turn—just enough to send Raven bumping into his back—before the rattle of something loose under his feet made him stop and pivot back. He was glad that he did. Under his feet, the ground crunched in a way that it definitely shouldn't have.

Surprised, Lucien looked down. He was even more surprised to note that visibility had improved. He could see that the tiles were a sandy color, and also that they were cracked. A glance a little farther up told him that it got worse. Pieces of flooring were broken and spread out, the wreckage extending all the way from where they stood to a corner about fifteen feet ahead. And at that corner, the concrete under the tiles was exposed. As Lucien frowned at the destruction, a bit of crushed ceramic lifted up, blew forward in a small cloud, then settled again.

"Raven," he said, careful to keep his voice to a murmur, "I think we've found the source of that wind."

Her hands—which had moved from his waist to his

shirt when she bumped into him—tightened on the fabric, and her reply was just barely audible. "Okay."

He wanted to offer to let her wait where she was, but he knew she'd say no. He'd try to convince her. She'd argue. Then win. So he forewent the hushed fight, and instead nodded toward the shattered floor ahead.

"We're going to move even more slowly," he said, his words still a whisper. "I don't want to be surprised by whatever it is that's waiting around that corner. And when we get there, I want to have a quick, careful look before we turn. Work for you?"

"Slow, careful, no surprises," she replied just as softly. "Yes. Definitely works for me."

But once they'd inched forward over the broken tile, made their way to the corner, and Lucien leaned forward to take his surreptitious look, he realized that *no surprises* wasn't on the menu at all.

Chapter 12

When Lucien didn't lean back right away, Raven took an automatic step closer.

"Wait," he ordered.

His tone wasn't particularly urgent, but he did lift an arm to block her way. She halted because she didn't have any choice. That didn't stop curiosity from propelling her to bend over his elbow. What she saw made her gasp. And she understood why Lucien hadn't pulled back. Just ahead—bathed in dim light from a cracked, very small, very dark-tinted window above—was a gaping hole that spanned the majority of floor. She knew, also, why he'd blocked her from moving forward. Another few incautious steps, and one or both of them might've fallen straight in.

But what's it doing there? she wondered.

She quickly scanned the space, searching for an explanation. The light filtering in through the cracked window illuminated a few things. The first was simply that the space around the corner was just an open room. Not huge. Maybe eight feet by eight feet. It had no doors, and no other exit. The second was a pile of dirt—almost to the ceiling, and spreading out the length of the back wall—on the opposite side of the hole. The third thing was shovel, propped up in a corner. Its presence made Raven's hands want to curl into nervous fists. The fourth and final thing that she saw in her quick visual sweep was an oddity. A rock. Almost baseball shaped. Sitting on the ground right in between the wall with the window and the hole itself. For a second, she just stared at it, puzzled. Then it hit her.

The shattering glass we heard before... Jim.

She didn't realize she'd said it aloud until Lucien answered her.

"You're right," he said, his tone dour. "He's gotta be down there." He edged into the room—careful to keep a ways back from the hole—and called out, "Mr. Rickson? Can you hear me?"

There was no answer.

"Mr. Rickson?" Lucien repeated, his voice a little more urgent. "My name is Detective Match, and I'm here to help."

Raven waited tensely for a response, her eyes roving over the space again, and her mind working.

Hanes had dug the hole. Somehow, someway. Probably not starting with the shovel, but undoubtedly finishing with it. Then he'd dropped the caretaker into the pit. But Jim hadn't given up. Maybe he'd taken a random chance. Or maybe he'd heard their approach. Either way, Raven was certain that the older man had tossed the stone up toward the window in a last-ditch effort to draw attention to his whereabouts.

So why isn't he saying anything now?

"Jim!" Lucien said it sharply, paused for a moment, then turned back to Raven. "I need to go in."

She knew without being told that he didn't just mean the room. She swallowed. "How?"

He swung back to the dimly-lit space and tucked his weapon away as he scanned the area. "There's gotta be something in here I can use. A rope? Wish we had just a bit more light, so I could—"

She didn't wait for him to finish. She knew if she disclosed the idea that had popped into her head, he'd protest. So she didn't bother. Sweeping past him and ignoring his half startled, half concerned curse, she made her way to lip of the hole where the rock sat waiting.

Up close, the space between the wall and the hole was smaller than she expected. Two feet wide, at best. And the hole itself was a strange draw. Her eyes wanted to hang there. To sink into the blackness, even though it made her heart *thump-thump-thump* three times faster than it ought to be going.

One wrong move…

She knew it was only seconds that ticked by as her thoughts tumbled in, but the world felt slow just the same.

Had Jim experienced the same raw terror that she had? Was it lessened because of the shorter period of time? She tried to remember if the first hours had been the best, because she still had hope, or they were the worst because of the immediacy of it all. She honestly couldn't say. It all blurred together in a mess of hopelessness, fear, resignation and desperate optimism.

And does it really matter right now?

She could hear Lucien calling her name. Warning her to back up. To let *him* do *whatever* she was trying to do.

He was moving toward her now, too—his feet shuffled on the broken ground—but with far more caution than she'd taken. He muttered something about getting both of them killed, and Raven realized with a start that he was right. If both of them tried to occupy the narrow space, at least one of them would wind up in the pit with Jim. And not in the way Lucien was planning.

She forced her gaze away from the hole. Moving quickly and surely, she bent down and grabbed the rock from the ground. She fixed her gaze on the crack in the tinted window, drew back her arm and threw as hard as she could. The glass exploded outward with a surprising force. The light in the room quadrupled, making Raven blink as she tried to adjust her vision to accommodate for the sudden onslaught. Breathing out, she lifted her gaze to Lucien.

"Better?" she asked.

His expression—which she could now see perfectly—was unimpressed to say the least, and his reply was flat. "Your idea was good. Your execution was more than flawed."

"It worked out okay." She tried to make it sound light, but she could tell that Lucien was genuinely frustrated and worried, and guilt tickled at her. *How would I have felt, if he'd jumped toward the hole with no warning?*

She took a step in his direction, an apology on her lips. But her sorry was swept away as her foot caught on a piece of broken tile. Her arms flailed, her heart dropped and the world swam as the two-foot gap between her and hole became two inches. She wanted to scream, but her throat was both raw and closed at the same time, and no sound came out. She just barely managed to gain control of herself in time to scramble back from the edge of the pit. Without even thinking about it, she threw herself straight in Lucien's chest and buried her face in his shirt. His hands came up immediately—one to hold her close, the other to run soothingly over the back of her head.

"I'm sorry," he murmured into her hair.

Her mouth worked in silent surprise for a second before managed a muffled response. "You're…what?"

He pulled back, his familiar brown gaze fixing intently on her face. "I'm sorry. I said I needed more light, and you came up with a plan to get it. You didn't *tell* me the plan, because you knew I'd fight you on it. I don't want you to keep doing rash things because you don't trust me to listen to you and be reasonable about it." He touched her cheek with his thumb. "Forgive me quickly so that I can get to Jim."

Heat crept up Raven's face, and not from the caress. In the panic, she'd momentarily forgotten their purpose in being there—*her* purpose in her mad dash to the rock.

"Forgiven," she said, not bothering to waste time arguing about having nothing to forgive.

He stared down at her for another heartbeat, then leaned forward. Raven braced herself for the warm, firm feel of lips. She tingled with the anticipation of it. But in the end, he just gave his head a small shake, stroked her cheekbone once more, then stepped away.

Even though he could feel Raven's eyes following him as he took a look around, Lucien made himself focus on searching out a solution for getting to Jim Rickson. He didn't curse himself for not seizing the moment and kissing her. Maybe it was counterintuitive or contradictory, but in the split second when she'd teetered on the edge of the manmade hole, a flash of something unexpected had slammed into him. A sense of future. Instead of fearing that they couldn't have one and being infused with a slap of carpe diem, he was overcome with the realization that he wanted the long haul. Which was the exact reason he needed to get to Hanes and put the man back where he belonged. Preferably as quickly as possible.

After a moment of searching, his eyes landed on a piece of coiled rope, and—shoving aside the uneasy sensation that Hanes had left it there deliberately— he stepped toward it, snagged it up then scanned for a place to anchor it. Almost too quickly, he found the perfect spot—the bottom of an exposed beam in the wall beside the dirt pile. There was no chance the concrete hadn't been carved out there on purpose, and as much he hated to do exactly what Hanes clearly wanted him to do, he didn't see another option. The only positive about the smug preplanning was that Lucien was sure there would be no sabotage. Gritting his teeth because he was unable to stop himself from picturing Hanes's stupid smile, he swung the rope around the beam and tied a secure knot, then gave the nylon a hard tug to ensure it would hold. Next, he wound the free end around his waist before finally making his way back to the edge of the hole. There, he paused. He had a funny feeling that the length of rope was going to take him *exactly* to the bottom of the pit. It might've bothered him more if Raven's voice hadn't carried through the air and lifted him above the disquiet.

"Be careful, Lucien," she said. "Please."

"I will," he replied.

He offered her a small smile to show her he meant it, then grabbed a tight hold of the rope and started his rappel into the hole. His descent was slow, but in spite of the unhurried pace, the dark came quickly. The walls of the hole seemed to narrow, too. At first, Lucien was sure it was an illusion. A paranoid claustrophobia. The farther he got, though, the more he realized the pit was funnel-shaped and slightly curved. As though the digger had grown tired or lazy—or both—as he got nearer to his endgame.

Or maybe Hanes just wanted you to feel like you were sinking into a pit of hell.

He ignored the dark suggestion and kept going.

When the rope started to run out—maybe about fifteen down—he reduced his speed even more in anticipation of hitting the ground. Sure enough, seconds later, the bottoms of his shoes found purchase on the uneven dirt.

He exhaled, then tipped his head up and called, "I made it down."

Raven's reply came right away. "Do you see Jim?"

"I don't see anything," he admitted. "But I'm going to go on feel. Hang on."

He kept a firm hold on his tether and moved with care, mindful that wherever the other man was, he was undoubtedly injured.

"Jim?" he said. "Mr. Rickson, are you here?"

For a long-seeming moment, Lucien heard nothing in response.

The space is only so big. A few steps should take me crashing into him. Probably lucky I didn't land on him to start with.

The thought spiked his worry. *Shouldn't* he have immediately encountered the other man?

"Jim?" he repeated, spinning in a blind circle.

Even though it was already as close to absolute blackness as it could be, he closed his eyes as bent to reach out and find the other man. The moment his lids sank shut, though, he realized her *could* hear something. Breathing. Shallow. Weak. But undeniably there. Relief flooded in.

Keeping his eyes shut, he concentrated on following the sound.

To the left.

Two steps.

He took them, then paused again.

A little bit more.

He moved again. Stopped again.

Right here.

He opened his eyes and crouched down. And found nothing.

"Jim?"

He dropped from his squat directly onto his knees, then pushed his palms forward in the darkness. At first, he met only air. After a moment, though, his fingers hit a wall. Frustrated, he started to drop his hands. His quick movement landed his knuckles on a hard surface, too smooth to be a part of the hole itself.

He reached out again, aiming for the same spot. He didn't hit it on the first try. Instead, his fingers found the wall again. This time, he didn't pull away. Instead, he dragged his hand down over the dirt, seeking whatever he'd touched a moment earlier. As he perused the surface, he realized something. The wall continued to dip inward, creating a hollowed-out space. He continued to follow the slope, and at last his fingers again found the unnaturally smooth surface. It had a familiar feel, and it only took a second to place it—the toe of a work boot. Cautiously, he pushed his hand up a little. It landed on a denim cuff, and the touch earned him a raspy groan.

Thank God.

He flattened his palm and gave the jeans a light pat. "I don't know if you can hear me, Jim, but my name is Lucien Match. I'm a detective with the VPD, and I'm a friend of Raven Elliot, as well. We're here to get you out."

A word carried through the dark. "Raven?"

Lucien breathed out, his relief compounding. "Yes. She's up at the top of this hole, and she's going to be very glad to know you're alive."

"My wife…"

He was glad the other man couldn't see his face. He wasn't sure he would've been able to disguise the sharp stab of emotion that hit him in the gut.

"Let's get you out of here first, okay?" he replied, his voice rougher than he would've liked. "Then we'll talk about everything else."

Jim didn't respond, and it only took a second to realize that his breathing had already regained the slow, shallow quality it'd had a couple of minutes earlier.

Unconscious again, Lucien thought.

He wished he had enough light to give the man a thorough once-over. As it was, he had no idea how extensive the injuries were. Whether anything was broken, or how hard it was going to be to move him. Broken bones were a strong possibility. A concussion was likely.

"But how severe?" Lucien muttered to himself, running a worried hand over his head as he tried to decide what to do next.

Then Raven's voice carried down through the shaft, reminding him that he hadn't yet confirmed the fact that he'd located Jim. "Lucien?"

"Still here," he called back. "Jim's here, too, and he's in and out of consciousness, but he's alive."

She said something that sounded like, "Thank God," then raised her voice and added, "I hear sirens. They're getting closer. Should I try to go out and let them know we're here?"

"No." As soon as the word was out of his mouth, he realized he'd said it too sharply, and before he could retract and adjust, Raven spoke again.

"Do you think Hanes is out there...watching?" she asked.

He adjusted his position on the floor and peered up, half hoping he'd find her face looking down at him. The angle was wrong, though, for seeing anything other than a gray blur.

"It's hard to say what Hanes is up to this time around, but even if he's *not* out there, you don't need to worry about giving a heads-up about our location. They'll find us," he told her.

"You're not just saying that to try to keep me safe?"

He couldn't stifle a chuckle. "Not this time. Don't get me wrong. I'd definitely exaggerate to keep you here. But this time, I mean it."

He couldn't hear her sigh, but he sensed it as she said, "I guess I'll have to believe you."

Lucien laughed again. "I guess you will."

"But he did hang around sometimes, didn't he? I remember it from the trial."

"He *claimed* to stick around the scenes in case we were able to solve any of his puzzles in time. But who knows if it's true. He definitely managed to keep busy in between his grabs. His plans were elaborate. Carefully planned, too. In fact...with the shortened time frame, I don't know how he's keeping up with any of it."

"If it helps, I don't think he dug this hole," Raven replied. "At least not the whole thing."

He adjusted again, this time so he could rest his shoulders against the curved wall as he answered. "No?"

"No. I took a bit of a look around. There's some kind of notice up on the wall. Utilities repair. And there're some stakes and caution tape stuffed in behind that pile of dirt, too. I think Hanes just took advantage of what was already here."

"Well. At least I feel a little less like we're fighting against someone with super powers. Been a question a few times."

"Trust me. He's very definitely human. But the worst *kind* of human."

"Agreed."

There was a pause, and when Raven spoke again, the tremble in her voice was audible, even with the space between them. "Did you see any sign of him at the mine when you found me?"

"No. But I wasn't looking for him."

"Right. The whole single-minded thing you had going."

"Worked in my favor that time."

"Yes," she said, her tone noticeably warmer. "Mine, too."

Lucien closed his eyes. In spite of the fact that Jim Rickson was beside him, hanging on to life by who knew how big a thread, and in spite of the fact that he could now hear the sirens, too—in spite of everything really—the conversation felt intimate.

"I don't know if I ever told you how relieved I was to find you," he said. "We all were. Them, because it ended that feeling that they were chasing someone who really couldn't be caught. Me, because it was *you.*"

For several long seconds, Raven didn't reply. Lucien half wondered if he hadn't spoken his admission aloud.

He cleared his throat and started to repeat it, but she finally answered, just as the sirens came to a muted crescendo, then cut off.

"Why did you leave, Lucien?"

The question was a searing knife in his heart. Hot and cold at the same time. And words failed him, of course. He scraped a frustrated hand over his chin and tugged at his ear, his mind forming the sentences that his mouth wouldn't.

I wasn't good enough for you, Raven. I'm probably still not. But I've been feeling a little selfish since the second I first saw you today. So forgive me for that, too, okay, and give us a chance?

Why couldn't he just come out and say it? Why couldn't he just tell her how he felt? How he'd always felt? He opened his mouth, hoping something close would make its way into the world. Instead, it was a groan. Not from him, but from the man lying beside him.

He turned his attention down to Jim, whose eyes were open, but far too glassy. "Help's almost here, Mr. Rickson." As if on cue, authoritative voices overhead announced the arrival of an emergency crew. "See? That's them now."

"Juanita…" said the other man.

It pained him to realize the even with the lack of lucidity, Jim Rickson could express more with one word than Lucien could muster up at all.

Chapter 13

There was a part of Raven that wanted to holler at the emergency responders to wait. To please just stand outside the door for five more minutes before they came in and did their thing. She made herself stow the desire to do it, and instead called out so that they'd be found more easily. But even after the three men—two firefighters and an off-duty cop, it turned out—had stepped in, gathered her quick version of events, then started discussing a retrieval plan, Raven couldn't shake the feeling that she'd finally been about to get an answer for the question that she couldn't let go.

Three years, she thought, moving out of the way as the three men settled on a course of action and got to work.

It'd been a permanent part of her heart for that long. Since the moment Hanes was sentenced, and Lucien turned down those courtroom steps and walked away.

A scene remembered far better than she liked. It'd been like the ending to a movie. Only a sad one. Because if the scriptwriter had had any kind of conscience or decency, she or he would've made sure Lucien turned around, ran back and scooped her into his arms. Which never happened.

For the first while, she'd assumed he'd call. She'd given him space, because she'd thought maybe he needed it. Time to process the ending of the nightmare that was the Kitsilano Killer. Paperwork. But days went by. Then a week. And *she* wanted to call *him*. But doubt had crept in. She'd told herself that maybe there was a good reason he wasn't calling. That she should wait. There'd been a follow-up—several, actually—with a family-liaison officer. Her subtle probes hadn't yielded a thing. Neither had her too-casual walks by the station, nor the one time she'd dared to sit in her car outside Lucien's apartment. It was that evening that had really been her wake-up call. She remembered it almost as well as she remembered what Lucien's shoulders looked like as he disappeared from sight.

She closed her eyes for a few seconds, recalling the humiliating moment.

It'd been evening and almost dark. The sky was overcast, but the rain hadn't started yet. The tall structure that Lucien called home had been cold and lifeless, and Raven had thought it hadn't suited him at all. She was wondering if the inside was different—what personal touches he might've added—when the sharp tap on her window had interrupted her imaginings. She'd looked up to find a uniformed officer standing outside. The woman had informed Raven in a crisp tone that a neighbor had called in a "concern." And Raven had taken off as fast as she could, vowing not to reduce herself to that level ever again. Yet no matter how much time passed, she'd never quite been able to let it go.

A throat clear made her drag her eyes open, and she saw that Lucien was out of the hole now, his mouth slightly curved up, but eyes pinched just enough to give away his worry.

"Holding up okay?" he asked. "Didn't want to wake you if you needed some beauty rest."

She let out a shaky laugh. "If only it were that easy. I'm not asleep, and I'm holding up okay." It wasn't a lie; physically, she was completely sound. "What about Jim?"

He nodded toward the hole. In the few minutes that Raven had been lost in her own thoughts, the small emergency crew had rigged up a retrieval system that consisted of a stretcher and a lot more rope. They were just lowering it into the ground now.

"Only room enough in there for two people," Lucien added. "They had to get me up and out before one of them could get down to assess him."

"But you think he's going to be okay?" she asked.

Some undefinable emotion passed so quickly over his face that Raven almost thought she'd imagined it. But when he spoke, his voice had a hint of roughness to it, and she knew it wasn't just in her head.

"I think he'll be fine," he stated. "Holt—the fire-fighter who went down first and took my place— already relayed up that Jim was lucky. Suspected concussion and dehydration. The hospital will confirm that it's nothing worse, but Holt was pretty confident. Said he was a nurse before getting on with the fire department."

Raven breathed out. "That's good news."

"Yeah. Not bad, all things considered." He paused,

shifted from one foot to the other, then sighed. "There's something else."

She automatically tensed. "What?"

"Another message."

"But we were expecting that, weren't we?"

"We were." He shifted again.

She narrowed her eyes. "But you don't want to tell me, because you think I'll run off again."

"I *know* you will, if you think you can save Juanita. I'm just trying to think of the best way to slow you down while still keeping my promise to listen to you."

A laugh burst out of Raven's lips before she could stop it. She saw the off-duty cop swing a curious look her direction, and she covered her mouth to try to contain herself. The laughter still made its way out, but at least it was muffled.

"I'm serious," Lucien said.

"I know you are," she replied.

"And it's *funny*?" He sounded so genuinely puzzled that she had to stifle another laugh.

"It's—" she cut herself off with a blush.

"It's what?"

"Nothing."

"No, seriously. You can't laugh at a man, then not tell him what makes it so funny. We have sensitive egos."

Her face warmed even more, and she tossed a quick look at the rescue crew before dropping her voice and saying, "It's funny because it's cute."

Lucien's mouth twitched. "Not a word I've heard used in conjunction with my name."

"Trust me. It applies."

"All right. Fine. I'll be cute, you be stubborn, and we'll both take it as compliment?"

"Ha-ha. Very funny."

Raven's lightened mood lasted for about ten more seconds, and then an increased commotion near the pit drew her attention and sobered her again. The two men at the top of the hole were straining with the makeshift pulley system, and the man below—Holt—was yelling up instructions. Even though she knew they were doing everything carefully, it still made her worry. And it reminded her that no matter what momentary amusements there were, the situation was as grave as ever.

She swallowed and turned back to Lucien. "What did the message say?"

"'Pretty yellow flowers, all in a row. I'd go back, if they'd let me,'" he told her. "I asked Holt to send me a picture of the message, and he said he would. But my phone's still in the car, so why don't we get out of here so we can take a better look?"

"What about Jim?"

"We'll check in on him once they get him out. They've already put in a call for an air ambulance. Right now, we're more in the way than anything else, and it'll be even worse when the chopper and EMTs get here."

Raven took a breath. She wanted to protest. But as much as she felt compelled to stay and help Jim, there wasn't a lot she and Lucien could do as far as medical care was concerned. They would really be doing more for him if they focused on the next steps. On where Hanes was directing them now, with the new clue.

On Juanita.

"Okay," she said. "Should we let them know we're going?"

"Yeah. Give me one second, okay?"

He paused after her said it, and something in his stance gave her the feeling that he was about to lean over and give her a kiss. As if it were a daily thing. A habit. But as quickly as it came, the sensation was gone. He turned and stepped toward the men on the other side of the room, already speaking to them as he moved.

Raven stared after him. It wasn't the first time she'd tensed with anticipation of a brief meeting of their lips. And she knew it wasn't just because of their earlier moment of intimacy, either. It was something she'd experienced with Lucien a hundred times. One of those things that contributed to her belief that there was more to their relationship than professional obligation.

Can I really go through that again?

The thought sent a stab so sharp through her chest that she almost couldn't catch her breath. It worsened when Lucien spun her way and smiled.

Can I? she thought again. *Can I have my heart broken all over again?*

"You ready?" he said, completely oblivious to the turmoil in her head as he closed the gap between them.

She nodded, because she didn't really trust herself not to say anything related the pain in her rib cage. "Ready as I'll ever be."

"Good," Lucien replied. "Let's get back to the house and work on that clue."

Right. Focus on that, she ordered silently. *What did it say? Pretty yellow flowers, all in a row. I'd go back, if they let me.*

She frowned. It was typically vague, just how Hanes liked things. But what did it mean? Something to do with gardening? She thought of the flowers that Hanes had left on her family's gravesites, then moved to her house. Was it related? She let the questions and possible answers roll through her head for the entirety of the short walk back to the SUV. And it wasn't until they were already buckled in that Raven remembered something important. It wasn't the message itself that mattered. It was what the note had been written in that was key. She opened her mouth to ask, but Lucien answered before she could say it aloud.

"Chalk," he said as he turned the engine over, then put the SUV into Reverse. "Hanes wrote it in chalk."

They both stayed quiet for the duration of the ride, and while Lucien wouldn't have called it a companionable silence, it wasn't an uncomfortable one, either. He was sure that Raven's mind was doing the same thing his was—searching for some connection between Hanes and Juanita and a chalk-related past. He didn't have much personal information about Juanita, but he'd already decided to go for the most obvious choice.

A school.

Even if chalk was used less and less, and the blackboards had been traded in for whiteboards and dry-erase markers—or even digital Smart Boards, in some cases—Hanes was the right age to remember the strokes of pale color and the calcium dust in the air. Seeing it on the wall had thrown Lucien back about thirty years, too.

So it's a place to start, anyway, he thought.

And as they pulled into the driveway, Raven voiced a question that matched up with his unspoken conclusion.

"Where did Hanes go to school?" she wanted to know.

"Officially? At least ten or eleven of them, from what I remember." Lucien cut the engine, did an automatic visual sweep of the area, found no sign of disturbance, then reached for the door.

"Because he was kicked out?" Raven asked.

He paused with his fingers on the handle. "Not of the schools. The foster homes."

"Right. His parents died in a fire when he was a baby."

"Yes. Or so he claimed."

Raven's forehead creased. "What do you mean?"

"Hang on," he replied. "Let's go inside first."

He pushed the door open and hopped to the ground. By the time he reached her side of the SUV, she'd climbed out, too and was waiting for him. Side by side, they walked up the path to the house, and he explained what he knew. Or to be more accurate, what he *didn't* know.

"About 90 percent of what Hanes shared with the VPD about his life was suspected to be a lie," he told her. "A lot of it was unverifiable. His identification was valid. Ish. Or somewhat legally obtained, anyway. That's how we were able to get such extensive employment records. Good, tax-paying citizen that he was." He paused to unlock the door, then started up again as he'd dragged his feet out of his shoes. "The stuff before he started working is spottier. There *are* records of a Georges Fredrique Hanes in the system. But *our* Hanes's middle name is most definitely David. And the fire—wherever it happened—was never tracked down."

"But none of that was brought up at trial," Raven said, following him to the living room.

"No. It wouldn't have been helpful to either party. What Hanes might've gained in sympathy, he would've lost in credibility. We would've seemed like we were struggling to pin him down."

"But you still think we should start with his schools?"

"Definitely. It seems logical, if not likely."

She sighed. "But it's Hanes. So logical doesn't necessarily equate with likely."

"True enough." He settled onto the couch, pulled

the earlier-abandoned laptop closer, then gestured to the spot beside him. "Let's look at the schools anyway. It's still our best lead."

It pained him to see the way Raven eyed the ample space hesitantly, then bit her lip before joining him. It made him want to toss aside the laptop and pull her into his arms. There'd never been a hint of awkwardness between them before. He was sure it'd been caused by the kisses and the touches and the half-spoken declarations. He could feel the questions and uncertainty in the air, and he was afraid it would become a rift if it went on much longer. Without meaning to, he started to lift his hand from the keyboard to reach for her. He only moved half an inch, though, before the computer chimed a notification.

This is exactly why you need to get this case closed, he thought. *No stopping and starting. No interruptions.*

He forced his hands to stay on the computer, and tried to be grateful that it was more cooperative in booting up now than it had been before.

He cleared his throat, clicked to the file folder, then keyed in a search for the list of schools. It popped up right away, and Lucien clicked again. The list appeared. Staring at age eight, it was shorter than Hanes's record of employment, but still longer than any child ought to have.

"Any of these look familiar to you?" he asked, tipping the computer toward Raven.

She scanned the files, then shook her head, her face despondent. "They're all here, in BC."

"Yes?"

"Juanita grew up in rural Saskatchewan. Her family owned a farm there. And she didn't move here until she was twenty."

"So I guess that'll rule out a childhood school connection. Unless it was kindergarten for Hanes."

Raven nodded, her face drooping even more, her attention flicking back to the screen.

"Fifteen elementary schools," she said softly. "Six high schools."

"Nine of the twenty-one are verified," he replied.

"It's…"

"What?"

"I don't feel *sorry* for him." Her voice was thick. "I don't. At all. The man's a monster."

"But psychologically, you see what might have led him down this path?" Lucien filled in.

"I don't *want* to see it. I don't *want* to think there's a reason." Now her voice wasn't thick; it was one gasp shy of a sob.

Lucien had no choice. He pushed the computer away, turned then pulled her into an embrace. She didn't resist. She buried her face in his chest, her shoulders shaking. He pressed the side of his face to the top of her head and ran his fingers over the small of her back in a slow circle.

"Listen to me," he said. "You don't *have* to understand. You don't have to be sympathetic and you don't have to accept that lives can play out this way. That's not our role here. There are plenty of people who get a rough start—a tragic start—and they rise above it. We're not Hanes's advocates or counselors or his *any*thing. There are people for that. And that's okay. It doesn't make us less human."

She lifted her head and met his gaze, her eyes shining with tears that quickly made their way out to join the streaks already on her cheeks. "I hate him."

Lucien's hand slid up her spine, then came to rest on the back of her neck. "So do I."

"I can't *stop* hating him."

"You don't need to."

"But I know it's unhealthy."

"This isn't a forgive-and-forget situation."

"But—" Her voice broke, and she tried again. "But something has to give. Somewhere."

He pressed his forehead to hers and moved his fingers around to cup her face. His thumb stroked gently back and forth over cheekbone. He ached to ease her obvious pain. He ached for *her*.

"Raven…"

Her mouth was so close.

Too close. Your eye is on a different prize.

He inhaled, pulled back and dropped his hand. "I won't let Hanes get away. I promise. I'll make sure he's locked up in the deepest, darkest hole that the prison system has, and I'll personally throw away the key."

Her gaze flicked to his mouth for the briefest second before she leaned back, too. "I thought cops didn't make promises."

"I'm not making the promise as Detective Match."

"You're not?"

"No. I'm making it as *Lucien* Match."

"Is there a difference?"

He frowned a little, wondering if the question was more weighted than it ought to have been. He shook off the worry. Their already-short timespan wasn't growing any longer.

"Detective Match answers to the VPD," he told her. "And Lucien—*I*—would rather answer to you."

Raven studied him for a long second, her now-dry eyes boring into him like she was trying to read his thoughts. Maybe trying to find out if there was any jest to his words. He didn't look away.

Say yes, he willed silently. *We get through this. We put Hanes back where he belongs. And then we move on, together.*

"A deep, dark hole?" she said, echoing his sentiment from a minute earlier.

"The deepest and the darkest," he replied firmly.

At last, her expression softened, and she nodded. "Okay, Lucien 'the man' Match. I'll take that offer."

"Hold me to it. You're the boss now." He touched her cheek once more, then turned back to the laptop, even more eager than before to get the job done.

Chapter 14

Raven wondered if Lucien knew what his words had done to her heart. If he had any idea how it felt to hear him separate himself from the job. He might not even have meant it the way she wanted him to—and maybe he wasn't even aware that he'd said it—but there was a steady thrum of hope running through her anyways. It made her blood warm and her brain buzz, and when Lucien murmured something about wondering where else chalk might be found, an idea burst from her mouth.

"Gymnasts!" she said.

He turned a puzzled look her way. "Uh. Gymnasts?"

"They put chalk on their hands."

"Yeah, I know. But…"

"What?"

"I'm having a hard time picturing Hanes in a leotard at any stage in his life."

She didn't let his amused smirk or the wry comment

deter her. "Okay. Fine. Pool halls. They put it on the cues, right? So that—" The look in his face stopped her. "What? What is it?"

"Lou's Pool Hall."

"Okay."

"Hanes worked at this place. I remember because he stayed there longer than most of the other ones. Stuck with me. Lou's Pool Hall. He did equipment maintenance," he explained. "Can you think of anything that would connect that to Juanita?"

"No," she admitted. "Not off the top of my head, anyway."

Lucien sat back, his frustration showing in the set of his jaw. "This would be a lot easier if we had full access to her life like we do with Hanes."

An idea popped into Raven's mind. "Maybe we do. Pass me the laptop."

Without asking why, Lucien handed it over. Raven quickly loaded the search engine, then pulled up her social media accounts and logged in. From there, she searched her friends list for Juanita. A few seconds later, she had the older woman's page up. She played around for another few seconds before she found what she was looking for—a "Getting to Know Your Friends" questionnaire that Juanita had filled in. She turned the computer toward Lucien.

"This came up in my feed a couple of weeks ago," she told him. "I remembered it because about ten of my friends did the same quiz, and it kept coming up over and over. I didn't look at it carefully at the time, but…"

Lucien's eyes moved over the page. "This is good, Raven. *Really* good."

"It is?"

"Look." He swung the laptop back her way, then

tapped the screen about three quarters of the way down. "Right there."

"How did you meet your significant other?" read the question.

And underneath that, Juanita had typed an answer.

"I was at a pool hall with my girlfriends. Jim made a bet with his friend that he could get my number. He challenged me to a game, and he made me promise that if I lost, I'd give him my number. I let him win."

"It's just the kind of detail Hanes likes," said Lucien. "Significant, but not that easy to figure out."

Raven nodded. "And far more subtle than the school idea."

"I'm going to let the sergeant know. Do you want to poke around on the local news sites and see if you can find a location that fits?"

"Sure."

While Lucien stood up, pulled his phone from his pocket and stepped to the kitchen, she grabbed the laptop and typed in the search using the same parameters she'd done for the pork-processing facility. Her efforts weren't as quick or fruitful as they had been with Jim's location.

Shut-down pool halls aren't big news, I guess, she thought, scrolling through the results.

There were a half dozen websites with addresses. Coupons for a few places. One small article on a fist-fight outside one of the halls, only noted because one of the parties involved was a celebrity chef of some kind. Nothing that stuck out at all.

Raven sighed and tried to think of a word or two to add to make the search more effective. But as her fingers hovered over the keyboard, she heard Lucien sign off from his phone call, and she looked up at him instead of typing in anything else. She could tell from his stormy-eyed expression that his conversation with his boss hadn't gone well.

Her stomach dropped. "What's wrong? Is it Jim?"

"Jim's fine," Lucien said quickly. "Stable. Awake and lucid, too. But there's a bit of an issue. He told Sergeant Gray that he and Juanita don't *have* a son."

"So Hanes deviated from his usual plan?"

"I don't know. I honestly can't see it happening."

"A mistake, maybe? Could he have *thought* there was a son?"

He exhaled noisily. "I can almost see that even less. He's so damn meticulous."

"But there must be some explanation."

"Yeah. I just wish I had any idea what it might be." He paused and shook his head. "Bit of good news, though. The second I said the words *pool cue*, the sergeant jumped on it right away. Told me that the owner of an out-of-the-way pool-table manufacturer got busted last year for a gun charge. Boss kept an eye on the place, so when a pipe burst and flooded it a couple of months ago, he was made aware. The whole warehouse had to be gutted, and financial issues meant it never got put back together. In particular, the floor gave out and left a gaping hole down into the ground. Sound about right?"

Raven wished she couldn't picture it as well as she could, but there was no denying that the description ticked all of Hanes's boxes. "So should we—"

"No."

"You didn't let me finish."

"Didn't have to." He tossed his cell onto the coffee table and sank back down onto the couch. "You were going to ask if we should go there. Maybe not even ask. Maybe suggest in a kinda bossy way."

"Ha-ha."

"Uh-huh. You know it's true. And before you remind me that I just promised that you *are* the boss, I should let you know that my *other* boss refused to give me the name of the pool hall solely because of our so-called shenanigans. And yeah…he actually used that word."

Raven couldn't help but laugh. "Did you remind him that we saved Jim's life?"

"Twice. I also reminded him that we have the internet and could simply look it up. Then he reminded me that I like my paychecks."

"Not an unfair point."

"Nope. He also said that if none of that deterred me, then to just be aware that the place in question is on *his* side of the highway, and that everything is still ridiculously backed up."

"Covered all of his bases, didn't he?"

"Man didn't get made sergeant because he wasn't shrewd and thorough." Lucien threw an arm onto the back of the couch. "But I don't like feeling like I'm just sitting here with my hands under my—" The buzz of his phone cut him off, and he lifted an eyebrow as it danced over the table. "If that's the sergeant, telling me he's already got Juanita, I think I'll be almost as annoyed as I will be relieved."

Raven made a face and tried not to be too hopeful that the unlikely suggestion might become reality. "Answer it."

"Yes, ma'am." He grabbed his phone and glanced down. "Unknown number." He shrugged, then pushed his thumb to the screen anyway. "This is Match."

Raven could hear the reply on the other end—a man's voice, a little hesitant and nearly overridden by cell-phone crackle. "Is this the detective? The one in charge of Sally's case?"

"Who am I speaking with?" Lucien replied.

"This is Henry Gallant. I'm Sally's boyfriend."

Lucien met Raven's eyes, and she shook her head. She didn't know Sally well enough to say whether or not she had someone significant in her life.

But...

"Wouldn't your boss have mentioned it if he knew about a boyfriend?" she whispered.

Lucien nodded, and as he spoke into the phone again, his voice took on a smooth, placating tone—one Raven was sure he reserved for questioning during police business.

"No worries, Mr. Gallant. I'm just going to put you on speaker so my colleague can hear you." He gave the screen a quick tap, then held the phone out. "Okay. Just so we're on the same page and there's no misunderstanding...you said you're Sally Rickson's boyfriend?"

On the line, a car horn honked, and Henry Gallant dropped a curse, then immediately apologized. "Sorry, Detective. Trying to make my way out of Vancouver International, and the traffic's nuts."

"You just got in?"

"Yes. I live in Toronto."

Both of Lucien's eyebrows went up. "Do you mind if I ask how you got this number?"

The rush of a car engine surged, then died out. "There was a message on my phone when I landed. The guy said he was with VPD and he found me in Sally's call log, and was looking to talk to me about a few things. Kind of vague, with a number to call. So I tried to call *her* first, but I couldn't get her, so I called the VPD number. Voice mail, so I tried Dispatch. A friendly woman named Geraldine said Detective Match was the one to talk to." There was a momentary break in his speech. "Is something wrong, Detective? Is Sally okay?"

Raven could hear the worry slip into the man's voice, and her suspicion of him eased into sympathy. But Lucien clearly wasn't quite ready to let his distrust go.

"Forgive me, Mr. Gallant," he said. "I just wasn't aware that Ms. Rickson *had* a boyfriend."

Henry noisily cleared his throat. "I don't think anyone was."

"That's going to need a bit of an explanation," Lucien stated.

"Look," replied the other man over the roar of more traffic. "It's a little awkward. Sally and I met at a singles event last year. I was visiting from Toronto and went out on a whim. I had no intention of meeting someone. I just…uh. You know."

Raven's face warmed a little, and Lucien swiped a hand over his mouth, obviously trying to cover his amusement.

"Yeah," he said in a perfectly blasé tone. "I know."

Henry cleared his throat again. "Anyway, I met Sally at the singles event. We connected. But I'm nine years younger than she is, and I think it makes her uncomfortable, so we haven't exactly been advertising it." He paused. "But really, Detective. Can you tell me what's going on?"

Lucien's fingers strummed on his knee, and Raven was sure he was trying to decide just how much to disclose.

"In all honesty, Mr. Gallant," he said after a moment, "it's probably best to have an in-person discussion. But I know how I'd feel if I were in your shoes, so I'll tell you what I can without going into too much detail. Can you hang on for a second?"

"Sure."

Lucien gave the phone a couple of quick taps, then lifted it to his ear and stood up, pacing the room as he talked like he always did. His explanation made no mention of Hanes and no mention of Jim and Juanita. His speech was efficient and comforting at the same time—the perfect, practiced blend.

Lucien the man, and Lucien the detective.

Unconsciously, Raven closed her eyes, thinking about it. Hadn't she just been feeling elated about the fact that he'd separated the two? Hearing him now, it seemed impossible to believe that it could ever really happen. The two parts of him were fused.

And is it even fair to expect it?

It was why, even when she questioned how come he'd left three years ago, she hadn't worked hard to pursue him. She kept coming back to that.

And if you keep coming back to it, doesn't that mean it has some merit?

In sudden, desperate need of a moment to herself, Raven pushed to her feet, mumbled an excuse that she was almost positive Lucien didn't hear, then rushed out of the room.

When Lucien clicked off the phone and turned back to Raven, he was surprised to find her spot empty. His initial reaction was an unreasonable moment of panic, and her name burst from his lips before he could reason with himself.

"Raven!"

He immediately rolled his eyes at his own outburst.

Relax, he ordered silently. *She probably went to the bathroom, and she won't appreciate being hollered at.*

He fired off a quick heads-up text to Sergeant Gray, dropped his phone back onto the table then settled onto the couch. His foot tapped and his knee twitched. He was undeniably antsy. He'd eased Henry Gallant's concerns as best he knew how, then directed the other man to head to the station. He had faith that someone there would do the rest. He was certain, also, that the task forced was working thoroughly on the pool-table tip. On top of all of that, he was relieved that Raven was kept safely out of the thick of it. He had no interest in dragging her back into it. Or himself, for that matter. But he couldn't quite curb his desire to be doing something more.

He eyed the doorway that led to the hall where Raven had undoubtedly headed.

"I just want it to be over," he murmured under his breath.

Because as long as Hanes is on the loose, we won't ever be able to move on.

Lucien scraped at his chin, then leaned his head back and closed his eyes, trying to breathe away the uncomfortable sense of powerlessness that nagged at him.

He had to acknowledge that the last three years were on *his* shoulders. He had to own the fact that he was the one who'd left. He'd always told himself it was nobler. Better for Raven. But Hanes's escape made him increasingly sure it'd been a mistake. The man was like a dark shadow, hanging over the possibility of a future.

He opened his eyes and sought the doorway again. Raven still hadn't reappeared, and his concern twitched back to the front of his mind, overruling his melancholy. He stole a glance at the little clock on the corner of the laptop's screen. He felt like he'd been brooding for an hour, but it'd really been more like five minutes.

Long bathroom break.

"You're being paranoid." Even as he said the words aloud to himself, he stood up and took a step toward the hall. "Raven?"

He paused and listened for a response. He didn't get one.

"Raven!" he repeated, a little louder this time.

This time, he *expected* to get an answer. Even if it was just a shout to give her another minute. He got nothing, and his paranoia was starting to feel justified.

He strode through the doorway and up the hall at a near run. The bathroom door was wide open, and he rushed by without bothering to look in. He didn't even have to think about which way would offer the easiest escape route—the never-used master suite at the end of the hall had a private balcony. His feet took him past Raven's old room, then past his own. With an unusual lack of caution, he flung open the door to the master suite.

"Raven!"

He swung his gaze back and forth. His eyes found the closed sliding glass doors first, and he stepped toward them and gave them a sharp pull.

Locked.

His worry ramped up even more.

"What in God's name is—" He stopped muttering abruptly as a light squeak carried in from behind.

He faced the hall, and for a second, he spied nothing. Then the squeak sounded again, and he saw a flash of movement. It only took him a puzzled second to figure out that one of the doors was gently swinging back and forth.

Raven's door.

Wishing like crazy that he'd thought to grab his gun, he moved quietly out of the master suite. He pushed himself against the wall and slid along, thankful that his sock-clad feet made no noise on the hardwood. At the edge of the door frame, he paused and considered his options. Call out her name again, as he'd done without reserve so far? Sneak a careful glance into the room? Or go for broke, aim for surprise and just burst his way in? He was really leaning toward the last option. If Raven hadn't responded to her name yet, she was unlikely to do it now. A sneaky glance only worked if someone wasn't waiting for it.

And if someone is *waiting for it...*

The thought that she might be being held against her will made Lucien clench both his jaw and his fists. It also made a surprise attack more than preferable.

Preparing to pounce, he bent his knees. He only got that far, though, before the door let out a noisier squeak, swung all the way inward then thumped dully against the wall. Lucien tensed in anticipation of an assault. Instead, his defensive position was met with the sound of wind. For a second, he didn't react. His hands stayed up; his body stayed poised.

Make a decision, he ordered silently.

Exhaling a silent breath, he counted to five, then inched forward. The door flapped again. He took another step. Then another. And when he got a full view of the room, he wasn't sure whether he wanted to laugh, cry or just plain curse his own overactive cop brain.

Raven was there. On the bed. And she was out cold. *Really*, really out cold, by the look of things. She was sprawled over the mattress one arm above her head and one leg hanging off the bed in the most uncomfortable-looking sleeping position Lucien had ever seen. The window was partway open, and cold air was blowing forcefully through it.

Kidnapping...O. Naptime...1.

Shaking his head, he took a moment to study Raven's sleeping form. She probably hadn't meant to doze off. He'd bet his left leg that she'd just wanted a moment alone, had sat down, then given in to exhaustion. He didn't blame her, either. The day felt like a month, and it wasn't even over yet.

He stared at her for another few seconds, debating whether or not he ought to wake her. She'd probably be less than thrilled to sleep through anything important, and she might even be mad that she'd wasted what could've been productive moments. But the fact that she'd fallen asleep, contortionist style—then continued to sleep through his yells—told him she needed what small amount of rest she could get.

"Take what you can get, sweetheart," he murmured.

He started to leave, but another blast of wind cut into the room, and he decided to take an extra moment to close the window. Careful to keep quiet, he moved across the room, reached over her sleeping form and slid the glass pane shut. Another glance at Raven prompted a need to make her more comfortable, too. Very gently, he lifted up her awkwardly skewed leg, then shifted her so that her whole body was properly on the bed. He tugged the throw blanket up, tucked it over her shoulders, then stepped back with the intention of exiting. As he turned, though, Raven let out a sleepy noise— part sigh, part murmur—then rolled over and spoke in an equally sleepy voice.

"Lucien."

He brought his attention her way, an apology for waking her on his lips. He went still, though, when he realized she hadn't woken and spotted him. Her eyes were closed, her lips just barely parted. She'd said his name her sleep. The realization made his heart expand to the point that he had to press his palm to his chest to ease the ache, and he felt a need to touch her.

Does she have any idea what she does to me? he wondered.

Her lids fluttered slightly, and as much as he tried to stop himself from doing it, he couldn't help but give in. His hand dropped down to brush away a loose strand of hair. The barest contact made his throat scratchy with raw emotion.

"Every day…" he murmured. "I've thought about you every day. Even when I wanted to think about anything else."

Her lids fluttered again, and he knew he had to leave the room. Because if he didn't, his need for her would only compound. He'd wake her. Take her into his arms. Kiss her so hard that there'd be no doubt as to how he felt. He'd beg her to forgive him for being an idiot for the last three years.

And then… A rush of want hit him so hard that he nearly groaned. *Get a hold of yourself, Match.*

He did his best to shake off the rush of feeling and desire, then—without daring to hazard another look in Raven's direction—he spun toward the door. He didn't make it a single step, though, before she said his name again. And this time, he was sure she was awake.

Chapter 15

For several groggy seconds after she called out to him, Raven thought she was dreaming again. Lucien stood just a few feet from her bed, and that was an embarrassingly frequent theme in her dreams. She waited for him to turn. To move toward her and sweep her into his lap and kiss her breathless. He didn't move, though. And it was the stillness of his body that made her sure she was awake. In her dreams, he was never still.

But she was definitely in bed, the haze of unexpected sleep hanging over her. She stared at Lucien's back, and started to say his name again. Before she could speak, though, he pivoted to face her, and his pained expression washed away the last bit of grogginess.

"What's wrong?" she said automatically, pushing up to a sitting position. "Is it the Ricksons? Did something happen?"

He shook his head, his features clearing. "No. None of that."

"What is it?"

He took a step toward her, eyed the bed, then stopped again. "I didn't mean to wake you up."

"It's fine. *I* didn't mean to fall asleep."

"I figured."

He shifted from one foot to the other, and his eyes drifted to the bed again. The look was quick, but something about it made Raven warmer.

She cleared her throat. "Did you hear from the sergeant?"

"Not yet."

"And everything else is okay?"

"Yeah. Everything's good."

She studied him for a second, noting the way his fingers drifted to his ear, and the way he held his shoulders a little too stiffly. She could tell he was covering something up; she just had no clue what it was. Or why.

"Lucien, if something's wrong, you might as well just tell me now and get it over with."

"Nothing's wrong."

An unexpected surge of irritation pricked at her. "If you don't want to tell me what it is, that's fine. But I'm not an idiot. I could see that you were upset the second I woke up."

He flinched, almost like he'd been struck, and Raven realized it was probably the first time she'd ever lost her temper in front of him. She wasn't quick to anger in general, and with his hard line to her heart, Lucien was the last person she'd ever have thought to direct any annoyance toward. Feeling bad, she tried to reel it in. But her conscience and her mouth had other ideas.

"Do we lie to each other now?" she asked. "Because

what I remember from three years ago is that you were the one person I had left to trust."

"Raven." The single word wasn't enough to slow down the torrent of her own.

She shook her head. "My parents and my brother are gone. My friends from before try not to pity me, but I can feel it anyway. And new people treat me differently when they find out who I am. There's a taint around the edges of my life, and I don't care how melodramatic that sounds. Three years ago, you made me feel normal and hopeful, and I won't let you turn around and treat me the same way as everyone else."

He stepped forward, reached for her, but she stood quickly and moved out of touching distance.

"I deserve more than that," she said.

"I can't…" Lucien trailed off.

She had no idea what he was thinking, no idea what he was trying to say. But the frustration was too high, her emotions too close to the surface.

"I need a minute, Lucien. A *few* minutes. That's why I came in here in the first place."

She stepped to the door, but his voice—surprisingly anguished—stopped her before she could make it all the way the out.

"Stay. Please."

She spun back, and was startled to see that the broad-shouldered man had sunk down onto the bed. His face was aimed at his lap, one hand on the back his neck, the other tightened on the blue-flecked quilt. He looked more broken than Raven would've thought possible. Her anger dissipated. It took most of her willpower to keep from rushing back to him.

"You *do* deserve more," he said. "And that's the problem."

She was genuinely surprised. Whatever she'd been expecting, it wasn't a declaration that she was right.

"I don't understand," she replied, inching closer in spite of her resolve to stand her ground.

He replied without looking up. "Only two things have ever mattered to me like this. My job. And you."

His job.

Why did it always have to come back to that?

"I don't want to stop you from doing your job," she told him automatically.

His eyes came up to meet hers. They were very close to red-rimmed, and their familiar coffee-colored hue was pained. But there was a hint of puzzlement there, too.

"Why would you be stopping me from doing my job?" he wanted to know.

Her face warmed. "By asking you to give me more."

His puzzled expression deepened, his forehead crinkling into a frown. "You think that being treated the way you deserve to be treated hinges on my work?"

"I keep you from doing it."

"How?"

"By turning you from a detective into a bodyguard."

"I'd *rather* protect you than solve murders, Raven." He said it slowly, like he was trying to figure out why that idea might bother her.

She let an exasperated noise out. "It's basically a demotion."

"Bodyguards everywhere might disagree."

"Not my point, and you know it. You spent years working to get where you are. Five minutes with me, and I'm asking you to make that second best?"

"Are you?"

"What?"

"*Are* you asking me to make my work second best?"

She felt the flush in her cheeks spread down her throat. "I wouldn't do that. Why do you think I—"

"Why do I think you what?" he prodded.

Raven swallowed. How had the conversation turned from her being mad at him, to him trying to make her admit that she wanted selfish things from him?

She tried—a little desperately—to turn it around again by asking the one question she knew he didn't want to answer. "Why did you leave, three years ago?"

But this time, he didn't balk or try to change the subject. "Because of everything you just said. Because I'm not good enough for you."

"What?"

"I'm not—"

"No. I *heard* you. I just can't believe that's what you said."

"But it's the truth. You deserve perfection. I can't give you that."

"I don't want perfection, Lucien. I want you." As the admission burst out, her skin went from hot to scorching, and she wanted to bury her face in her hands.

And Lucien's mouth was quirking up. "Is that supposed to be a compliment?"

She dropped her eyes so she wouldn't have to see his amusement at her expense, and muttered, "Don't make this worse than it already is."

He stood up and stepped in front of her so quickly that she almost stumbled back. But both of his hands landed on her forearms, holding her securely in place.

"Raven." His voice was thick. "Look at me. Please."

Reluctantly, she brought her gaze up. And even though she knew how close he was, staring up at him still took her breath away. His face was tipped down, his expression intense. She couldn't help but drink in every detail of him.

She could see the lighter flecks of caramel and the darker flecks of cocoa in his irises.

She could see the beginning of his salt-and-pepper stubble, and the little ridges of his lips.

She could smell his light, masculine scent.

She could feel the heat of his chest.

There was the ever-present crease just between his brows, and there were tiny laugh lines at the corners of his eyes, new since they'd met last.

She loved it all. She wanted to touch it all. And for the first time in her life, she truly understood what it meant to yearn for something.

"Raven," he said again, his fingers coming up to her chin. "There could never be something bad about you wanting me, so I sure as hell can't make it worse."

It took her a second to figure out that he was replying to her embarrassed grumble from a few moments earlier. With him standing so kissably close, it was hard to think straight.

She tried to force out a steadying breath, but all that came was a breathy little gasp, so she gave up and shook her head.

"If it's not bad," she said, "then why do you keep looking at me like it is?"

"It scares me," he admitted, his voice dropping lower.

His mouth skimmed from her eyes to her mouth and then back again in way that made Raven shiver. Her pulse beat against her veins unsteadily, and she inched forward.

"Why?" she whispered.

The hand on her chin slipped to the back of her neck

and his fingers tangled into her hair. "What if I let you down?"

"You won't."

"You don't know that, Raven. But you *do* know my family history. What my dad did to my stepmom…what she did to us…"

"You're not them."

Their bodies were flush against each other now, and Raven could feel that in spite of his protests and self-doubt, he wanted her as much as she wanted him. His free hand had made its way to her waist, and he was holding on like he was never going to let go. And yet he still argued.

"If I hurt you, I'd never forgive myself," he said.

She lifted her arms and put them on his shoulders. "I'm willing to take the risk."

His expression was torn, a battle clearly raging inside. Raven wriggled even closer. A little groan escaped his lips.

"This job, Raven."

"I don't want to talk about the job, Lucien."

"But if I—"

"Lucien."

"Yes?"

"Please."

"Please what?"

"Shut up and kiss me."

He gave her a final look—a hungry, all-consuming one, temperature-spiking one—then dipped his mouth down and devoured her.

Lucien refused to regret a single second of it.

Not the little rip he made in her shirt as he tore it off.

Not the bruise he was going to have from stumbling into the bed frame as she propelled him toward the bed.

Not the moment of awkwardness where she confessed to taking birth control for medical reasons, nor the moment of embarrassment—and relief—where both of them confessed to not even have been on a date over the years of separation.

And definitely not the way she looked and felt when he met her eyes, slid between her thighs and eased into her.

Not even the time it took away from working on the case.

It was all perfection; obligation and worry be damned. How *could* he regret it? Raven was still wrapped around him, her petite frame tucked against his large one like it was meant to be there. Like it'd been there a thousand times before. Just how he'd imagined it would be.

At some point, she'd managed to slip into his T-shirt, and he was already anticipating taking it back, bathed in her light, soapy scent. Maybe he'd hold off on washing it. Hang on to it like a lovesick teenager. He smiled at the analogy, but then immediately thought about how it didn't even come close to describing the way he felt. Yes, he loved the current moment. All of the passion-filled moments that had led to it, too. But he didn't want to freeze time. He just wanted more of it. For Raven to do this a hundred times. For her to put on a hundred different shirts, a hundred, postsex times so that he'd never *need* to not wash one.

He traced a lazy hand over her back, relishing the way she snuggled a little closer. Her breaths—and his own—had finally evened out, the exertion fading.

But not the excitement, said a voice in his head.

He acknowledged it with a mental nod. Her nearness was already stirring his desire all over again. He smiled again, and flattened his palm against the dip just above her hip.

Three years, you've been waiting, Match. Not a pleasant wait. You tolerated it, though. But now that you've been together once, you're going to become insatiable?

According to his body, the answer was a clear yes.

He slid his hand lower. Slowly. Down to the edge of the T-shirt, which ended high on her thigh. He paused there so he could stroke her velvety skin.

Raven squirmed, let out a little sigh, and her fingers flexed against his chest. "If you keep doing that, I won't be held accountable for my resulting behavior."

He chuckled and kissed the top of her head. "If you're trying to deter me, you're doing it all wrong."

She leaned away, but if it was an attempt to put a little space between them, it backfired. The movement drove his palm down even more—straight into her rear end—and she groaned.

"Lucien!"

"It was an accident."

"Yeah, right," she grumbled.

He laughed again. "But I *am* still waiting on the *resulting behavior.*"

"Very funny." She started to say something else, but he bent and cut her off with a kiss, just because he could.

"Are you going to say *that* was an accident, too?" she asked breathlessly when he finally pulled away.

"Hmm. Does it mean I'll get away with it?"

"No."

"Damn." He leaned back and dragged his fingers up

to a more respectable spot on her back, then closed his eyes and drew in another Raven-scented breath before murmuring, "I could get used to this."

There was a silent moment before she answered, and when she spoke, it was in a serious tone. "I'm *already* used to it. Is that weird?"

He didn't have to think about is reply at all. "No."

She was quiet for a second again, then sighed. "But we have to get up, don't we?"

"Probably a good idea. I left my phone out in the living room."

"Well. That explains why Sergeant Gray didn't interrupt us."

He laughed, kissed the top of her head then sat up to search for his discarded pants. His boss and the case—and Hanes, thank God—hadn't even been on the periphery of his mind during their time in bed. In fact, it'd all felt very far away. Like a lifetime had passed since he'd hurried through the house in search of her. But now that he was reminded of it, the urgency of the situation was hurtling toward him again.

He yanked his pants over his thighs, then sat back down, his brain switching back to cop mode. An idea was trying to take solidity. His fingers tapped his thigh as he watched Raven move to the closet to thumb through the clothes she'd left behind three years earlier, and that he'd never had the heart—or the desire—to get rid of. She grabbed a pair of jeans, then turned toward him, holding them out.

"Hope these still—" She stopped, her eyes hanging on his face. "What?"

His fingers stopped moving, and he answered slowly. "What if there *is* a brother?"

"In the Rickson family?"

"Yes."

"Jim out and out told your boss that there wasn't."

"I know. But he also didn't know about Sally's boyfriend."

She stepped into the jeans and zipped them up, frowning at him. "It's not exactly the same thing. I mean. Jim would know if—oh."

Lucien nodded. "He might *not* know. It's not outside the realm of possibility that he could've fathered a child somewhere else."

She snagged her bra from the footboard of the bed, then stepped to the dresser and opened a drawer, pulling out one of her own cotton tops. "But how would Hanes find out?"

"Not sure yet." His gaze lingered on her as she started to pull off his T-shirt.

"Close your eyes," she ordered, pausing midyank.

"Seriously?"

"Yes."

"You realize how thoroughly naked I just saw you."

"But you weren't *staring* at me."

He couldn't stop his sudden smirk. "I was most definitely staring."

She shot him a glare—one that looked like a cover-up for amusement—then tore his shirt off and tossed it right at is head. By the time he'd fumbled it off his face, Raven was already back in her bra. Lucien couldn't say it made the view any less interesting. The black fabric—designed for running, he was sure—hugged her breasts perfectly, and the hint of cleavage was just enough to add a bit of temptation.

"So damn beautiful," he murmured.

Pink crept up her cheeks, but she eyed his naked

chest for a moment, and said, "Ditto," before pulling her shirt on.

Grinning a little, he watched her for another second, then dragged his own shirt over his head, stood, and held out his hand. "C'mon. Let's go see if the sergeant has any news for us."

Palms clasped and fingers intertwined, they made their way out of the bedroom and back to the living room. As they stepped in and moved toward the laptop, the screensaver—a digital clock moving in a slow circle—caught Lucien's eye. When he saw the time, he stopped so short. So much so that Raven jerked forward, her hand slipping free and her shin bumping the coffee table.

"Hey!" she said, turning to face him. "What happened?"

He turned a wry look her way. "Just realizing not as much time went by as I thought."

"Isn't that a good thing? Time is something we don't have to waste."

"To waste?" he echoed. "Okay. There's the proof that I should drag you back to bedroom and dedicate another hour or two to ensuring that three years was worth the wait."

"What do you—" Her mouth stopped working for a second, and her eyes went wide. "Are you implying that wasn't long enough to be *worth* it?"

"Are you saying it *was*?" he teased.

She wrinkled her nose. "I can't tell if you're insulting me or just fishing for a compliment."

He took a step, grabbed her hand again and gently pushed lips to her palm. "Neither." He dropped her fingers and pulled her closer. "I just want to treat you how you deserve to be treated." He dusted a kiss across her lips, and relished the little catch in her breath. "Satisfy you in ways that—" On the table, his phone jumped to life, startling him, and he shook his head and finished his sentence differently than he'd planned. "In ways that only my boss can perfectly interrupt, apparently."

Raven laughed as he released her, but before he could turn fully away, one of her hands shot out to clasp his forearm. "Hey, Lucien? Just in case I don't get to tell you before Sergeant Gray interrupts again…it was worth it, and I happen to be *very* satisfied."

As he snapped up the phone and prepared to issue a greeting, he had to remind himself to keep his grin from entering his voice.

Very satisfied.

Hearing it made his heart expand. It also made him realize something. In spite of all the perfection, he did have one regret. He hadn't yet told her he loved her.

Chapter 16

With the silent, self-directed promise to get the declaration out, Lucien was sure it was going to be hard
to stop himself from trying to hurry through the conversation with his boss, no matter what the other man
had to tell him. As soon as he'd offered his greeting,
though, the awkward throat clear on the other end told
him it wasn't going to be so simple, because it wasn't
his boss at all.

"Uh. Detective Match?" said a vaguely familiar voice.

It only took him a second to place it. Sally's alleged
boyfriend.

"Mr. Gallant? Is that you?" Lucien said.

"Yeah. It's me."

"Everything all right? Did you make it to the station all right?"

"I did. Gave a statement, and they told me to stay
close in case they had any more questions, or in case I

thought of anything. I'm at Sally's place now. They said it was all clear, but they put a car outside, just in case."

Henry sounded worried, and Lucien offered an automatic reassurance. "That sounds about right, Mr. Gallant. They clear the scene and do their thing quicker than most people think. That being said…is there something *I* can do for you?"

"I *did* just remember something, and it might be nothing, but… I guess it could be important, too. I tried to call the number they gave me, but I got voice mail. I didn't wanna wait, just in case."

"Understandable."

Raven gave Lucien a nudge, then pointed emphatically at the phone. He nodded his understanding and tapped the screen, then set the phone back on the table and sat on the couch. Raven joined him.

"Okay, Mr. Gallant," he said. "I've got you on speaker again. Go ahead and hit me with the details."

"A couple of weeks ago, Sally did one of those mail-order DNA tests."

Lucien tensed and exchanged a look with Raven. He was already sure of what Sally's boyfriend was about tell him.

"And?" he prodded. "What were the results?"

There was a pause. "I dunno."

"You don't know what?"

"The results. That's why I thought it might matter."

Lucien gritted his teeth and tried not to let his frustration seep into his reply. "I'm not following, Mr. Gallant. If you aren't aware of the results, how could they be significant?"

"Oh." A sigh carried through. "Sorry, Detective. I think I'm overtired, and quite frankly, I'm worried as all hell about Sally. Starting to feel like I can't keep things straight." He sighed again. "Anyway, the guy at the station was asking me if Sally has any brothers or sisters, and I said no. Because she doesn't. She told me her mom *couldn't* have any more children."

"Okay."

"Then she got that DNA test done, and I was on the phone with her when she got the results via email. She was excited at first, but then she got a little weird. I asked her what was wrong, and she changed the subject. So I just thought…" There was a shrug in the trail-off of his words. "It *could* matter, right? I've seen TV shows where stuff like that happens."

Now it wasn't irritation that tried to filter through. It was excitement.

"It absolutely could matter," Lucien told Henry.

"Yeah?"

"Definitely."

Henry's relief was palpable, even though the phone. "That's good. Great. Is there anything else I can do?"

"Maybe just check one quick thing for me," Lucien replied.

"Yeah. Name it."

"I'm assuming forensics would've grabbed it, but before I start making calls…is Sally's computer there?"

Henry's immediate reply surprised him. "Your forensics guys don't have it. They *can't* have it. Someone stole it this morning. She sent me a text and said she thought she'd left it in her car overnight, and when she went out to check, it was gone."

Lucien's finger strummed against his knee. "Did you tell the folks at the station?"

"Twice."

"Okay. I really appreciate all of this. I promise to do what I can."

"Thank you." There was a pause, and then Henry said, "Detective Match?"

"Yes?"

"I really want her to be okay. I *need* her to be okay, if I'm being honest," the other man admitted. "I'm scared. And I'm not even sure she knows how much she matters to me."

Lucien forced himself not to steal a look at Raven. He knew precisely how Henry Gallant felt, and he had a feeling that if he glanced her way, it would be written all over his face.

"Talk to you soon, Mr. Gallant," he said, then clicked off the phone, his mind and his heart engaging in a quick battle.

He wanted to tell her right then and there. He didn't want another moment to slip by without her knowing precisely what was in his heart. Contradictorily, though, he didn't want the first time he said it to be overshadowed by the circumstances. Or for her to think—even for a single second—that he was *only* declaring it because of the life-and-death pressure. In the end, he was saved from having to make a hard-and-fast decision by the fact that Raven pointed to his phone.

"You're buzzing again," she told him.

He glanced down and realized she was right. A text message from Sergeant Gray had come through, but Lucien been oblivious to the vibration in his hand. With a rueful shrug, he swiped his thumb over the screen, and read through the unusually long message.

"Bad news?" she asked right away, her tone neutral, but her expression tense.

"Some bad news and some *great* news."

"Please, *please* start with the great."

"They found Juanita Rickson. Alive. She was at the pool-table-manufacturing place, just like we suspected."

Relief flooded into Raven's face. "Oh, thank God."

"Sergeant said she's doing okay. No life-threatening injuries, but they've got her sedated."

"Has she had a chance to see Jim?"

"If not, hopefully they'll find a way to connect them soon. Fingers crossed for side-by-side beds," he said with a small smile.

"Best of a bad situation, I guess," she replied. "Did Hanes leave a clue for Sally?"

"Yep. Sergeant's going to send me a picture shortly. He said in the meantime, I'd probably want to know that it was written in ash. The burn kind, not the tree."

"Ash," Raven murmured, closing her eyes for a second, then opening them and frowning. "What was the bad news?"

Lucien felt his mouth set into a line. "Press."

"Press?" she repeated. "Someone leaked the story?"

"Yeah. The Hanes bit was already out there because of the APB. But the sergeant said someone hinted that he may have started killing again, and now it's bogging things down because a group of reporters is trying to get the scoop. Someone tailed the officers who went after Juanita. Now Gray's been asked by the mayor to give an official statement."

"That's not good news for Sally."

"Agreed."

"I feel like we need to do something." Her frustration was clear in her voice, and Lucien reached over to give her knee a reassuring squeeze.

"We *are* doing something. Jim and Juanita were found because of your ideas," he reminded her.

Her face only sank more. "How do you keep going with it all, Lucien?"

"All what, sweetheart?"

"The work. Trying to solve cases like this. You finish one, and another comes along, and you solve it, but then there's another. And every time there's a risk that you *won't* solve it. It's just so overwhelming."

"It *can* be overwhelming. Intimidating and depressing, too."

She made a face. "Not really helping."

"Look…" He moved his hand up to thread his fingers through hers. "There are cases that don't get solved, bad guys who go free and things that never leave you. Sometimes, you get five in row, and four never get wrapped up. But you have to keep going, because that single case did. And on the next five, that other single one might not get solved if you give up. It's the same with your job, isn't it? You don't walk away from your client if they don't have a breakthrough on the first session."

"No. Definitely not."

"Even when it's hard, the rewards outweigh the frustration."

He kissed the back of her hand, then let her go as his phone signaled another incoming message. It was the promised photo from Sergeant Gray. A quick click zoomed in on the soot-colored words, which were scrawled over a slab of broken concrete.

SHORTEST TO TALLEST, SIDE BY SIDE. TAKING ONE IS THE ONLY CHOICE.

When he held it out for Raven to see, she exhaled a shaky breath and leaned against him. "I know we're focusing on what the message is written *with*…but I can help but wonder what the words mean, too. Do you think Hanes would really write just random thought?"

"Not in the slightest," Lucien admitted. "But we have to work with what we know will bring us results."

"I guess so." She sat back up. "So what does the ash mean? Something to do with the fire that supposedly killed Hanes's parents?"

"It's the best place to start. Do you know much about Sally?"

"No. Just what her parents have told me. And it's definitely not enough to figure out what her life has to do with ash."

"Okay. Different solution them. Talking to Juanita's not feasible at the moment, and even if Jim's still lucid, he probably doesn't need the added stress, so if we can find a way around that…" He trailed off as an idea popped to mind. "I can't believe I'm going to suggest this—I think we should take a drive over to Sally's place and take a look around for anything that might relate to ash or fire."

"Really?"

"Yeah. It's not an active crime scene, and Sally's boyfriend is there. He might have info for us, too. But don't get too excited," he said. "I'm probably going to get my butt handed to me when the sergeant finds out. I'll be living on the streets."

She jumped to her feet and held out her hand, and then—with an utterly serious look on her face—replied, "Don't worry. I make enough money to support both of us."

Raven kept her mouth shut for most of the ride over to Sally's place.

Her blurt-out—which more or less equaled an offer to live together—was bad enough, considering that they hadn't even started to discuss the consequences of sleeping together.

Are there consequences? She clamped her teeth together and refused to give in to the need to ask, replying to the question silently on her own. *Of course there are consequences.* But another silent moment prompted a follow-up question. *But what are they? And why didn't we talk about it?*

She could hazard a guess as to her own reasons. Lying next to him had just felt too normal to prompt a "what now" conversation. It didn't feel like a momentous change. Never mind that in her head, it should've altered everything. It had, the hundred times she'd imagined it. But in reality, it was like her whole life sighed contentedly. *Finally.* And that was that.

But now, she wondered if it was too much of an assumption to think it was the same for him. And she couldn't say anything. She was afraid if she did, she'd give away the three-word sentence that kept playing through her mind.

Her mouth went a little dry at the thought.

She loved him. It wasn't ever a question. She'd loved him for the two months they'd lived together. She'd loved him for the three years they'd spent apart. But feeling it and saying it were two different things.

She stole the smallest glance of Lucien's profile. As always, he was heartbreakingly handsome. His exterior matched his interior, too. Just the right mix of hard and soft, strong and kind. Yes, she loved him. So much that it was almost painful. But even if sleeping together hadn't changed anything, admitting it aloud would undoubtedly set a new course. One where—in spite of his assurance that he *liked* being her bodyguard—he might be forced to make a choice.

I love you.

In a way, it was an ultimatum. Because there was no going back. Either someone said it back, or they didn't. If they did, it meant something big. A commitment. And if they *didn't* say it back…

Raven swallowed. Her heart couldn't take the thought, so she focused her gaze out the window and tried to concentrate on something other than her feelings for Lucien.

At least keeping silent has the added bonus of not drawing attention to the fact that I really shouldn't be here at all, she reasoned.

It was true. She couldn't quite shake the worry Lucien was going to change his mind about their course of action. He'd already violated more than a few rules, and she was afraid that he was going to come to his senses at any moment. That he'd remember that aside from her personal investment in the Hanes case, she had no reason to be involved. He could call her a "consultant" all he wanted, but when it came down to it, she was just a civilian.

A civilian who's in love with the cop who's working her case.

"Shut up." She accidentally muttered it aloud, then blushed as Lucien immediately turned her way.

"What was that?" he asked.

"Nothing," she lied quickly. "I think we're almost there." She pointed to the four-way stop just ahead. "If that's Diver Avenue, then we need to go left."

Sure enough, as they reached the red sign, she could see that she was right. Lucien flicked on the turn signal, eased into the intersection then tapped the gas as they rounded the corner. But he slowed again almost right away.

"That's strange," he murmured.

Raven's heart tapped a nervous beat. "What?"

"Henry said there was a patrol car stationed outside. I don't see one."

Raven scanned the street. There were a number of cars parked up and down the side, and a few in driveways, too. But none of them was topped with blue and red, and none looked like an unmarked vehicle, either. The nervous tap in her chest became a thrum.

"That's the house there," she said, pointing again. "Juanita told me about the fountain in the front."

It was distinct. All metal, shaped like a bird in flight, a perpetual cascade of water spewing up around it.

"And definitely no cop car sitting in front of it," Lucien replied.

He slowed even more, then came to an idling stop a few houses back from their target. His fingers strummed the steering wheel for a few seconds before he pulled ahead and cut the engine.

"This is the part where you try to make me stay in the car, isn't it?" Raven asked.

He shook his head, just once. "No."

For a moment, she was hopeful. "Oh. Good."

But as soon as she'd spoken, she caught the grim look on his face.

"There's no 'trying' in this case. You're staying in the car."

"What happened to me being the boss?"

He shook his head. "There're far too many unknowns here."

"Are the unknowns lessened when I'm stuck in the car?" she countered.

He didn't budge. "The SUV is equipped with bullet-resistant glass. *I'm* equipped with bullet-resistant training. You, on the other hand, are going to be equipped with a phone set to dial for help."

She crossed her arms over her chest. "Shouldn't that part come first?"

"What?"

"Calling for help. For backup. You promised not to ignore my good ideas, remember?"

"I—" He cut himself off, grumbled something she couldn't hear, then yanked his phone from his pocket and clicked a speed-dial number while narrowing his eyes in Raven's general direction.

On the other end, a woman's voice became audible. "This is Dispatch."

"Geraldine," Lucien greeted, his tone at odds with his scowl. "It's always a pleasure when I get you on the line."

"Likewise, Detective," came the reply. "Making headway in the Hanes case?"

"Actually, yes. Which is why I need your help."

"Whatever I can do."

"First off, can you tell me if a couple of uniforms were stationed at an address on Diver Avenue?"

"Sure can."

Raven uncrossed her arms and leaned closer to Lucien as he reeled off the house number. She was eager to hear the response, and didn't want to miss it. But she was also unsure if she wanted an affirmative or a negative. Had the police been there and left? Or had they never come at all? The former made her worried. The latter filled her with deep unease.

"Detective?" said Geraldine after another few seconds.

"Yep. I'm still here," Lucien replied.

"Is this the same address that Sergeant Gray attended earlier?"

"That's the one," Lucien confirmed. "Should be a car here now, too."

"I'm sorry," said the other woman, "but I don't see anything listed for that address at this point in the day. At last check, forensics finished up and sealed the house."

Lucien dropped a low curse, then met Raven's eyes, and when he spoke into the phone again, he sounded like he didn't want to be asking the question that came out of his mouth. "Geraldine…did you give my number to Sally Rickson's boyfriend?"

"Sally Rickson? She's the homeowner?"

"Correct."

A sick feeling was building in Raven's gut.

"I'm sorry," Geraldine repeated. "I didn't give your number to anyone today, Detective. Is something wrong?"

"I need you to send a unit to the Diver Avenue address." He paused. "Make it two units, actually."

The dispatcher's voice immediately took on a more professional tone. "Yes, sir. I'll advise that you're requesting backup immediately."

"Thank you." He clicked off the phone, then tossed it hard into the console.

He brought his eyes to hers, and the twisting in Raven's stomach became a tornado. She suddenly didn't want him to speak. She didn't want to hear the words that were undoubtedly coming. But she couldn't think of a way to stop him, and her breath cut away as he made the announcement she was anticipating.

"It was Hanes," he stated, somehow managing to

sound both toneless and coldly furious at the same time. "He set us up."

Raven tried to form a reply, but the words wouldn't come.

Hanes.

It couldn't have been him on the phone, could it? Surely, one of them would've recognized his voice. The nuance of his speech. The perpetually smug undertone. Something. Anything. But would they have, over the crackling line? The man would definitely have known just what to say to get them to come. To conform to his plans.

A wave of dizziness tried to take her, and she clutched at Lucien's arm, using his solidity to anchor herself.

"He must've hired someone," he muttered, voicing her own thoughts aloud. "We would've known it was him."

She attempted again to answer, but this time, she was interrupted by a scream, emanating from somewhere near Sally Rickson's house. The sound froze Raven, and she felt Lucien stiffen beside her, too. She followed his gaze to the inch-wide crack of the passenger-side window, and she knew what he had to be thinking. The scream had been shrill enough to carry in, and that was saying something. It'd also been full of terror. Possibly pain. And Raven was 99.9 percent certain that it belonged to a woman.

Sally.

"Lucien," she whispered, breaking momentary stillness. "We need to go in there."

"Not we," he corrected quietly.

She pulled away and shook her head. "I can't stay here."

"You can. And you will."

"Lucien."

"No. I'm sorry, Raven. Either I go now, or we both sit here and wait for backup."

"That's…" She trailed off and swallowed, trying to keep her face from betraying the inner battle she was fighting.

You promised him that you wouldn't stop him from doing his job. You told yourself you wouldn't let it happen. And yet here you are, at the first sign of trouble…

She exhaled. "How long?"

"Give me ten minutes," he said without asking what she meant. "It shouldn't take me more than that to figure out what's going on, and backup should be here by then anyway."

"Please be careful."

"I will." He leaned over to give her a quick, firm kiss, then closed the window completely and added, "Bulletproof glass, sweetheart."

Then he was gone, and Raven was pretty damn sure he'd left with her heart in his pocket.

Chapter 17

Lucien fought to keep his attention on moving forward rather than looking back. The scream had stoked his ingrained need to act. To use his skills and training. But even as he made his stealthy trek from the SUV to the house—quick but not haphazard enough to draw unwanted attention—a voice in his head asked him if it was the right choice.

You could still turn around, it said. *Waiting for backup isn't the worst idea in the world.*

He gave the voice a mental shove as he hunkered down next to a car parked beside the driveway. Waiting might *not* be the worst idea in the world, but it could definitely be the difference between life and death.

What about Raven? argued the voice. *What about her life and death?*

That, he couldn't really fight against. He didn't like leaving her alone and potentially defenseless. Her life was more important to him than all others. But he knew that she wouldn't forgive herself if they could've saved a life and didn't. He would've liked to have left his weapon with her, but abandoning it would've then left *him* futilely unarmed, too. Raven would never have agreed to it. Might've literally held him down until he agreed to take the gun with him. It was almost—but not quite—enough to make him smile as he slid his back along the row of bushes on the edge of the yard.

Ten minutes, he told himself. *That's not so bad.*

He refused to give in to thoughts of all the things that could go wrong, even in that short time frame. He couldn't entertain a single one, or his plan to stay focused might fall out from under him.

Lucien reached the end of the row of bushes, and he eyed the front door. It was closed. From where he stood, he could see a single strip of police tape over the top of it, apparently unbroken. That didn't mean much, though. There were windows and back doors, and Hanes was smart enough not to leave overt evidence of his presence.

Except in the form of a scream.

The reminder made Lucien move faster. With a quick, visual sweep of everything in range—and not letting his gaze hang on the SUV for a second too long—he made a run. Bushes to the unusual fountain on the grass. Fountain to the archway in front of the back gate. There, he paused again and did another quick glance around. There was no sign of movement, aside from the flick of a curtain across the street. He ignored the flick and kept going. The neighbor would undoubtedly call 911, but it wasn't like that was something that concerned him.

Bending his knees to keep his head below the window on the side of Sally's house, he made his way through the gate to the backyard. At the edge of the exterior wall, he pressed his back to the wall, sneaked a fast look around the corner, found it clear then made the turn. It was quiet, the air still.

Lucien's gaze sought the two rear entryways. The first was a set of sliding glass doors that led into the house from a sunken concrete patio. The room on the other of the side of the glass was utterly dark. He moved his eyes to the second option—up a short flight of wooden steps and across a deck. It was dark up there, too, but not utter blackness like down below. He could clearly see a wind chime as well as a set of outdoor speakers, hanging from two posts near the country-kitchen door.

Very quickly, he weighed the options and tried to account for Hanes's general cleverness. Would he be using the darkness downstairs to stay hidden? Or would he be trying to lure Lucien into coming through the upstairs door? Either was plausible, and Hanes probably knew it.

Just make the decision, Lucien ordered silently.

He pushed off the wall, turned and took a step. He stopped, though, before he could actually go either up or down. A window above, just at the top of a vine-covered trellis, had caught his eye. It was cracked open, a bit of sheer drape moving softly behind the screen.

Bingo.

He holstered his weapon and moved toward the wall before he could reason a way out of making the dangerous play. Gripping the wood and ignoring the wobble his weight created, he climbed up, hand over hand. In moments, he reached the second-story window. Careful not to look down, he freed his fingers from the trellis, grabbed the cold, metal-edged glass and gave it a push. For a second, it didn't budge. A curse built up in his throat. Before it could actually make its way out, though, the window gave way. There was a small squeak, and the whole thing opened.

Lucien traded in his curse for a grateful prayer of thanks instead. He forced the screen off, then dragged his large frame into the room. He landed with a dull thump on a wide desk, where he continued to lie, hand on his weapon, breaths coming in shallowly, and eyes trained on the closed door. He listened for any indication that someone had heard his entry. The house remained quiet.

Okay. Time for the next move.

Taking extra care to maintain his own silence, he swung his body around and placed his feet on the floor. Everything stayed silent. Lucien didn't know if that was a good sign or a bad sign. His experience had taught him not to speculate. He kept moving. Slinking stealthily across the floor, hyperaware of the smallest creak. His reached the door, found the knob and gave it a slow turn. If someone was watching from the other side, they'd see it no matter how careful he was, but there was no sense in being incautious. When the handle had reached its full rotation, he gave it a slight push. Hard enough to open it, not hard enough for an unnecessary slam. As it swung, he stepped back. Out of gun range, out of surprise attack range. Neither came his way.

He drew a breath and stepped out of the room. The hallway was near dark, the only light coming from the space he'd just stepped out of. Something pricked at him. *Unease.* He paused and swung his gaze up and down. In addition to the one he'd exited, there were three more doors, each closed.

Two bedrooms and a bathroom, he decided absently.

There was no sign of disturbance coming from behind any of them. The unease grew. Lucien reminded himself that there was a whole other floor—plus the basement—to factor into his search. Time was still of the essence, too. He focused on the stairs, moving quickly and silently toward them, then heading down, pausing at every third step to listen. He was met with the same silence each time. And it continued to bother him. By the time he hit the bottom, his teeth were gritted with nerves, his shoulders were stiff with worry and his mind was probing for an explanation.

Because it's too quiet, he thought.

There should've been some sign of life. Either from the screamer, or the person who'd caused it. Or at least a hint of disturbance. An overturned pot. A dropped item. Instead, the house was eerily, emptily quiet.

Lucien very nearly turned around to go back out the way he'd come in. At last, though, something caught his eye. Just the barest flicker of light, emanating from somewhere on the main floor. It gave him a bit of renewed purpose, and he continued with his exploration of the home, following the glow to a partially open door.

Easy, he cautioned himself silently.

He placed a hand on the slightly cool wood and pushed. The door opened the rest of the way to reveal a small, windowless room. The entire space was dominated by a wraparound desk, and the flickering glow was coming from the computer that sat atop it.

Lucien's mouth went inexplicably dry.

There was nothing on the screen except a rectangular box with the familiar Pause, Play, Rewind and Fast-forward icons showing. It was as though someone had stopped a song midway through, then walked away.

Lucien took a very, very cautious step closer. He eyed

the mouse, sitting innocuously on its pad. Did he press it, or not? Did he wait for backup now? A forensics team to swab the space for fingerprints? Or was he just being paranoid, and letting his cop instincts have a free ride?

He took another step. Then paused. Sitting in front of the keyboard was a piece of paper. It was printed with a series of boxes, each box containing a name and line going to yet another box. Only a heartbeat passed before Lucien realized what it all represented.

A family tree. The DNA test results.

Forgetting his thoughts on fingerprinting the area, he reached for the paper. Even in the dim light, he could still make out the names. Eager anticipation hit, and he scanned the paper in search of Jim and Juanita and Sally. Before he could find them, though, the computer screen flickered, drawing his attention away from the page. He looked up just in time to see a remotely controlled arrow move to the Play button, then click. Immediately, a muted scream filled the air. His mind connected the dots at lightning speed.

The scream was another ploy. A fake. Probably filtered from the computer to those outside speakers he'd noted earlier.

But in spite of the quickness of his realization, it was still too late. He didn't even get a chance to lift his gun before a searing pain hit his temple, and the world snapped into blackness.

The second scream came at the eleven-minute mark—a full sixty seconds past Lucien's promised return time. Raven knew, because she was staring at the clock on Lucien's phone when it carried through the air. And it sent a burst of fear into her heart. Her hand came to the door handle automatically, and it took all of her willpower to keep from simply shoving it open and running toward the house.

Stop. Wait. Think. The silent commands only worked because they came in sounding awfully close to Lucien's voice.

She breathed in, then out, and tried to come up with some reasonable course of action. A *quick* and reasonable course of action.

Her eyes left the house and scanned the street. Where was the backup? The howl of police sirens and the flashing lights?

Her gaze darted back to the house. Why was the scream another solitary one? Where was the reaction?

It doesn't make sense.

She was sure of the thought. She just wasn't sure *why.*

Her hand tightened on the phone.

The phone.

She inhaled and exhaled again, typed in Lucien's four-digit password without bothering to be thankful that she knew it, then hit Redial. It rang once, and a masculine voice filled the line.

"This is Dispatch," he said.

She worked to keep a steady voice as she replied, but couldn't quite manage to keep the words from tumbling out on top of one another. "Oh. Hi. This is Raven Elliot. I'm at a…er…scene with Detective Lucien Match. He was waiting for backup. He talked to Geraldine? But no one has come, and I think something is wrong. He's in the house."

In spite of the babble, the dispatcher responded patiently. "Ms. Elliot, you said?"

"Yes."

"You're on Diver Avenue?"

"Yes."

"Okay. I show that a request was put in, then ninety seconds later was rescinded."

Raven's heart tried to stop. "Rescinded? Who rescinded it?"

"Detective Match," said the man on the other end.

Her brain tried to work out a way for it to be true. Maybe he'd found nothing inside. Maybe he'd used a landline to make the call. Maybe the scream—maybe *both* of them—were unrelated to anything about Hanes at all. But it only took a second to know that they were just things she wished might be true.

"He didn't rescind the request," she told the dispatcher, her voice calmer than her heart or mind. "Detective Match exited the vehicle twelve minutes ago. He headed to Sally Rickson's residence, and he hasn't come back. I'm a-hundred-percent sure he didn't place a call in that time."

She closed her eyes, waiting for an argument. For the dispatcher to point out that she couldn't possibly be that certain of something she couldn't see.

Instead, she got a carefully spoken reply. "And you're calling from Detective Match's phone now?"

"I am," she said.

"And it's been in your possession for all of the twelve minutes in question?"

"It has."

There was the briefest pause, and Raven abruptly knew what it meant. They hadn't considered the cancellation of the request to be problematic because somehow, it had come from Lucien's cell phone. Hanes might not have changed his game, but he'd sure as hell upped it.

"Ms. Elliot." The dispatcher's voice barely carried over the rush of blood, coursing through her head. "I'll send somebody right away. Stay on the line with me while I—"

She hung up before he could finish. She knew he'd argue with her, and she knew she wouldn't listen anyway. So there was no point in wasting time she didn't have. Ignoring the almost-immediate ring of the phone again, she focused on what had to be done.

First...

"I need a weapon," she murmured.

She was sure that Lucien didn't have a gun or anything like that—if there *was* anything that could be called "like that"—stashed away in the SUV, or he would've mentioned it.

Something else.

Riding the line between urgent and frantic, she started her search with the glove box. A quick pop and she found nothing but vehicle insurance, a set of handcuffs and a first-aid kit. She eyed the cuffs for the briefest second before deciding they'd be useless unless she'd already subdued someone. She slammed the glove box shut and moved on to the center console. There was nothing inside but a dented aluminum can. Trying not to lose hope, she twisted around and climbed to the back, folded down one of the rear seats and at last found something that might prove fruitful. A bright orange emergency bag. Her confidence buoyed, and visions of action-movie-style, weaponized flare guns filled her mind.

"C'mon, c'mon," she said aloud to the empty vehicle. "Give me something I can work with."

But the hurried unzip and dump of equipment yielded little. Another first-aid kit. A silver emergency blanket. Three flare tubes that were small enough to fit in her palm, and no flare gun. There were some tools that might've sufficed if she wanted to get close enough to an attacker to use them. But she had no intention of engaging in hand-to-hand combat. Fighting tears, Raven started to shove everything back into the bag. But she stopped as her hand landed on an item she hadn't spied the first time. It was a cylinder. An inch around, and four inches long. And as she lifted it up and read the label, relief washed over her.

Bear spray.

Something she could use at last.

Gripping the bottle, Raven opened the door to as narrow a space as would allow her to fit through it, then slipped out. The temperature seemed to have dropped a few degrees since leaving the house, and she fought a shiver as a gust of cold wind penetrated her clothes.

It's not a sign, she told herself firmly. *It's just the weather.*

But her feet still tried to slow a little. She didn't let them. She'd watched Lucien make his way up to the house, so she decided it was best to follow his path. But she did it at a run.

Car to bushes to fountain to arbor over the back gate.

Raven paused to catch her breath. It was hard. And not because the quick run had stolen much of her oxygen, but because this spot was where she'd lost sight of Lucien. Where she'd sat—helpless and alone in the SUV—as he'd disappeared from view. She'd been chanting *ten minutes* in her head like a personal mantra. And yet he hadn't come back.

And you're standing here, wasting time thinking about it.

Shaking off the thick worry, she grabbed the gate and eased it open. She stopped again, just on the other side, eyeing up the entrances to the house. What would

Lucien have decided? She was sure he would've put his training and experience to good use. But what could *she* use? She didn't have over fifteen years as a cop under her belt. She'd never questioned a killer or sought a confession or put together the pieces of a crime. Not until now, anyway. But she *had* been inside Hanes's game before. And she knew both how clever he was, and how clever he *thought* he was. And Lucien would've known that, too.

She stared up at the house for another few seconds. Two doors. Both still. Both dark.

Both obvious.

She took a small step back and looked for something subtler. And she found it right away. A set of curtains, flapping in a window overhead. The glass pane had been pushed open, and there was no screen. Raven knew right away that Lucien had to have made the climb up. So she took a breath, tucked the bear spray into her waistband, and followed suit. Up, up she went, surprised by her own agility. But she didn't take time to be pleased. She quickly slipped through the frame, slid over the desk just under the window then eased to the carpet. Retrieving the bear spray, she made a beeline for the door. Her heart tripped with nervous anticipation, one part fear, and another part hope. But the latter was dashed by the next series of events.

Her fingers found the knob. They gave it a turn, then a push. But the door wouldn't budge more than a quarter inch.

"No," she whispered. "This isn't happening."

She pushed again. It still didn't move.

"Come *on*."

It wasn't locked. But it was holding firm. She leaned closer, trying to gauge what was holding it in place.

Duct tape.

The sticky, metallic substance was just visible along the frame.

She gave it a poke. Then went still as a rumble carried to her ears. It only took a second to realize that it was the sound the garage door opening.

Abandoning her examination of the tape, Raven raced back to the window. From her position, she couldn't see the detached garage. But she knew it was there. And as she contemplated how many bones would break if she simply jumped out, she heard the crunch of tires, the light squeak of brakes, then a second rumble.

Desperate, she turned back toward the door. She ran straight at it, shoulder first. Once. Twice. And on the third time, it wasn't the silver tape that gave way—it was the frame. With a crack, it flew out. Raven landed on the floor in the hall. But she knew it was too late. No matter how fast she got up, not matter how quickly she ran down the stairs, it wouldn't be soon enough. Lucien was gone. Hanes had him, and even when the sirens at last filled the air, Raven had no idea how she was going save him.

Chapter 18

Lucien woke up groggy. His head ached worse than he'd ever felt it ache before. For a few seconds, disorientation reined. Why did he feel like he'd been chewed up and spit back out again? He moved to lift a hand to his throbbing skull. Except his arm wouldn't budge. And that's when it all came rushing back. The climb into the house. The family tree. The fake scream and the realization that Hanes had outsmarted them. Then the abrupt blackness. But one thought rose above all.

Raven.

He resisted an urge to futilely holler her name. Where was she now? He hoped to God she was okay. In fact, he wouldn't even entertain the idea that she might not be. Backup had to have arrived at Sally Rickson's house by now. There wouldn't have been enough time for Hanes to grab Raven, too. Not while also securing and transporting Lucien himself.

Speaking of time and transportation...

How long had he been out, and where the hell was he? If he wanted to get back to Raven—which he did, more than anything—he needed to figure out where Hanes had brought him.

Fighting the fogginess of his mind, he took a slow, deliberate inventory of both himself and his surroundings. Aside from the thick ache in his head, the rest of his body appeared relatively unharmed. His shoulders hurt a bit, which he suspected was owing to the way his arms had been drawn back and secured behind him.

No. Not just behind you, he corrected silently. *Behind you and around something.*

He flexed his fingers a little, trying to get a feel for it. The object in question was cold and metal and a couple of feet wide. He gave it another poke and decided that he was about 90 percent sure that it was some kind of pipe. Not residential, though. Its breadth was too great for that. Commercial, maybe? Or industrial? Wherever he was, it wasn't in the basement of someone's home. Though that being decided...he *did* think he might be at least partially underground. There was almost no light, and the air had a certain smell. Earthy. Dank. On top of that, his clothes—particularly the underside of his pants—felt damp. Soaked through, almost.

Soaked through.

Lucien blinked as he realized his pants didn't just *feel* wet. They *were* wet. Very wet.

He cast a glance down and spied the reason. Even in the dark, he could see the shimmer of water, catching what little light there was and reflecting it back to him. He was sitting in a puddle, maybe an inch deep.

He lifted his eyes and took a wider look around. Walls surrounded him. Or at least they did on the three sides he could see, and he thought it was a safe assumption that a fourth stood behind him. But there was something off about them. They appeared to be painted, but they didn't look like finished drywall at all. He could swear they almost seemed to be made of a concrete. As he tipped his attention up even farther, he saw that the oddity didn't end with the walls. Or at least not with what they were made of. There was also the fact that they led to blank space. No ceiling.

Lucien craned his neck. Way above was a roof of *some* kind, but he couldn't quite make out what it looked like. He dragged his gaze over the walls again, this time downward. When his eyes hit the floor, his puzzlement doubled. It appeared to have a steep slope, and he was mostly definitely at the bottom.

A room inside a room?

The suggestion didn't quite fit, but he really felt like he *ought* to have a clue as to what his whereabouts meant. Yet the answer remained just out of reach. The pain in his head was trying to expand, too, and that was bogging him down even more. Trying to fight the fog, he closed his eyes for a second. Slowly and silently, he started to count down from thirty. He only got as far as twenty-one before a new awareness crept in. The darkness held a sound. A *trickle*. So steady that it actually bordered on a stream. It was deeply disconcerting, and Lucien didn't know how he hadn't noted it first. Maybe because he'd dismissed it as wind, or maybe because the thump of his headache had blocked it out completely. Now, though, it seemed all-important.

He opened his eyes and searched for its source. His efforts drew a blank. Shifting a little in place, he tried to get a better view. Instead of spying anything more, he just sloshed in the puddle beneath him. He adjusted again and realized something. It didn't matter so much *where* the dripping was coming from. What really mattered was that it was coming in at all. More significant than that was the fact that it was staying. The puddle was growing. The inch-deep water already felt more like two—though maybe his mind was exaggerating it, at least a little—and getting free abruptly superseded the need to understand his surroundings.

Lucien closed his eyes again, this time to search out a solution. A twist of his wrists told him his bonds were of the zip-tie variety, and also that Hanes had used more than one. Not ideal, but slightly less secure than a set of cuffs. He filed away the detail and moved on to the next. His arms were able to move up and down the pipe a little, and that gave him some time-buying hope. If the water rose too high, he could probably force his way into a standing position. At the thought, a vision of himself, standing helplessly in chin-high water filled his mind.

Not going to let it get that far, he growled silently.

He rand his thumbs over the pipe, seeking a physical weakness. The metal didn't appear to be soft or flimsy in any way, and it was hard not to let disappointment flood in. There *had* to be a way out. Hanes was crafty and meticulous, but he was also human, and humans made errors. They got overconfident. Let things slide or forgot small details. Especially people like Hanes, who thought they existed outside the law and who believed they were above all others. As if to bring the idea from metaphor to reality, a scrape overhead announced that Lucien was no longer alone.

He angled his face up and called out softly, "Hello, Georges."

"Lucien. Nice to see you again."

"Interesting statement, considering that I can't see you at all."

A moment passed, then there was a shuffle, and a pale, white face appeared in the open space at the top of the strange walls. Lucien's teeth clamped together as loathing filled him. It was the first time he'd seen Hanes since the end of the trial, and he was once again reminded how much he despised the man. With his plain features and unassuming stance, there was nothing about the Kitsilano Killer than screamed evil. He was the mild-mannered bag boy at the local grocery store. The guy who handed back your change at the pet-food supply place, or the one who smiled at the gas station and asked if you needed a fill. Yet under that was the soullessness of a cold-blooded murderer. Lucien hated the contradiction, even though he'd been around similar ones enough times to be familiar with it. Books and cover. Looks and deceptions.

"Nothing to say to me, Detective?" Hanes called down.

Lucien unlocked his jaw and forced an even tone. "Nothing *nice* to say, Georges. How about we leave it at that?"

"So, then… I take it you haven't figured it out, yet."

"You know I'm not interested in your games."

"This one should interest you, though."

"I'm afraid not."

There was a pause. "So it's your girlfriend who did all the clever legwork."

Lucien's teeth fought to gnash together again. "Leave her out of this."

"Oh, I am," the other man reassured him. "Raven Elliot is quite irrelevant at this stage."

A stab of straight-up fear hit Lucien's gut. "What the hell does that mean?"

Hanes chuckled. "Not *that*, Detective. She's alive, and as far as I know, physically sound. Though she's probably worried about you. I meant what I said quite literally. She's irrelevant. She has no bearing on the 'game,' as you called it. In fact, she was a previous winner, and I have no intention of overturning that."

Even though he knew full well that the man couldn't be trusted, Lucien couldn't quite stop a breath of relief from escaping his lungs. After all, Hanes had no reason to placate him.

"So what is it you want, then, Georges?" he called up.

"I think I'll wait just a little while longer, and hope that you figure it out on your own. I'll give you some more time alone, Detective."

As soon as he'd said it, the tap of feet on the ground echoed through the strange space. Then the air went silent, except for the sound of the trickling water and Lucien's own noisy thoughts.

Time was being wasted, and Raven was being left out. Or at least that was how it felt to her. The police had taken her statement. They'd been attentive to her physical well-being. And then they'd proceeded to speak in hushed tones while they followed up on the leads that *she* had given them. Even Sergeant Gray—who she was sure knew just how much leeway Lucien had given her during the investigation—wasn't providing her with any useful details. The scenario was disheartening and frustrating, and she'd finally asked for a few minutes alone.

The sergeant had complied. In fact, he'd very nicely—almost enthusiastically—suggested that she take a breather in Sally Rickson's bedroom. The room was away from the noise on the first floor, which was currently being used as a base for the search for Lucien.

"*Conveniently* far away from the action, too," Raven muttered as she sank down on the edge of Sally's bed and eyed the door, which was closed but undoubtedly guarded on the other side.

She sighed. She knew it wasn't fair to be angry with the task force, which was being made to go on yet another tangent because of Lucien's missing status. Every person in the living room below was invested in finding him, just as they were hard at work trying to decipher the meaning of the ash from Hanes's third clue. And they'd been effective and efficient with some things so far. Raven had to admit that. They'd figured out that Hanes had cloned Lucien's phone to cancel the call for backup. They'd tracked down the *real* Henry Gallant, and found out that he did live in Toronto, that he had been on a few dates with Sally and also that he was completely clueless as to what was going on. They hadn't yet figured out if Hanes himself had made the calls or if he'd hired someone to do it, but she was sure they would soon. It was all progress. They had the best intentions and the best resources. Not mention that it was literally their job.

Except none of them has been in Sally's shoes, Raven thought. *None of them is in love with Lucien. And none of them is sure their heart will be ripped out if they don't beat Hanes at his game.*

Her throat constricted. She was half-certain her heart was already on its way to being ripped out.

Burdened by the need to be moving, she stood up and paced the room. Her eyes roved over the space in search of some clue that the officers might've missed. They'd gone through it in the same way they'd explored the rest of the house. Quickly. Thoroughly. And fruitlessly.

But there had to be something, didn't there? Hanes liked his clues to be challenging, but there was always a solution. The trick was figuring it out before it was too late.

She slowed both her steps and her gaze. At a carefully measured pace, she scanned the room again.

There was the desk under the window, which was more-or-less empty even before the VPD team got to it. Only a dog-eared address book and a container of pens—knocked over, then picked up again—sat on top. Neither thing screamed of being a clue.

Raven's attention swung from the desk to the small bookshelf. It was tidily arranged. Alphabetized by author name. It was all fiction, and no titles about fire or ash to speak of.

She spun toward the closet, which hung open, evidence of the search on display. Open shoeboxes. A dress, knocked to the floor. Hangers askew. Nothing that stood out any more than the rest.

Raven moved on. The dresser was much the same as the rest. It'd been opened. Rifled through with as much delicacy as anything *could* be rifled through. A pair of flannel pajama bottoms hung out of the bottom drawer, where extra care hadn't been taken in closing it.

Absently, Raven stepped toward the pj's, preparing to tuck them back in. But as she bent down, something under the bed caught her eye. Her heart did a hopeful leap in her chest. She abandoned the flannel before even touching it, moved across the room and dropped to her stomach. The space under the bed was very narrow, the frame only a couple of inches from the floor. And the object that had somehow drawn her attention was quite small, very close in color to the carpet. It was obviously hidden deliberately. She could see how it could've been overlooked. In fact, the only reason *she'd* seen it was sheer luck.

Or maybe fate, she conceded silently as she slid a hand under the bed, reached for the item and realized what it was—a nearly flat, three-inch-by-three-inch box. The perfect place to stow a secret.

Knowing she should probably be calling out to the officer on the other side of the bedroom door, Raven cast a single, guilty look in that direction, then opened the box anyway. She almost laughed at what she found inside. Ticket stubs for a few circuses. A matchbook with a fiery logo on the front. And a flyer for a class on throwing flame sticks.

"Astound your friends," it read. "Delight and enchant with Magic Fire!"

If Raven hadn't known Hanes enough to know better…she probably would've assumed it was a setup. But she was sure he wouldn't have manipulated his own bread crumbs in that way. And even if she hadn't been quite certain if it just based on Hanes's history, there was just something about the placement of the box and its harmless items that made it easy to picture Sally stowing them. The woman was, by her parents' accounts, driven and scientific. Circuses and fire sticks were way outside that. A little kid's dream. Embarrassing as an adult, but no less real.

Raven stole another look at the closed door.

"Just one more thing," she murmured. "Then I'll share it, I promise."

She pulled Lucien's phone from her pocket—glad she'd snagged it back from the pile of evidence-related things downstairs—and opened up the search engine.

Quickly, she typed in the words *Magic Fire*. She was immediately rewarded with a going-out-of-business announcement, which she clicked. Four months earlier, Magic Fire had gone into foreclosure and shut its doors for good. But just six weeks ago, some of the leftover supplies had lit up and destroyed the place. All that was left was a concrete shell. Perfect for Hanes's macabre hobby. Sally was there. No doubt about it.

Raven squeezed the items in her hand for a second. Part of her wanted to tuck them back into the box, stuff the whole thing into her bra, then go back out the way she'd come in—through the window. But she knew she had to give it to Sergeant Gray and his men. Even if she wanted to run straight to the burnt warehouse on her own, Sally deserved the benefit of having the police come for her. And if Lucien was going to be on the other end of the next clue, then he also deserved to have the experts on his trail.

But is *he going to be there?* she wondered.

It would mean a serious break in Hanes's pattern. The pattern Lucien himself swore wouldn't change.

Raven's heart fluttered with worry. If Hanes *had* deviated in this, he might deviate in other things. And unpredictability was a bad thing, where serial killers were concerned. But the alternative was worse. Because *no* shift in the usual would mean Lucien could be very hard to find.

Refusing to accept the possibility, she shoved the matches, advertisement and ticket stubs back into their box, then stood up and made her way to the door. As she'd suspected, there was a fresh-faced, uniformed officer standing just outside.

He acknowledged her with a nod. "Everything okay, Ms. Elliot?"

She bit back an urge to remind him that *nothing* was okay, and instead said, "Yes. But I think I found something. I'd like to give it to Sergeant Gray."

"I can do that for you," offered the young cop.

Raven stared at him, seeing the way things would go. She'd hand him the box. In turn, he'd hand it over. The task forced would do just as she had done and hit up the internet for answers. They'd assemble a team. Retrieve Sally. Which would be a good thing. But after that, they'd move on, and Raven would most definitely *not* be a part of the equation. She'd be lucky if they even shared the next clue with her. And could she really blame them? She wasn't a member of the VPD. She was just a former victim, turned current pain in the butt.

"Ms. Elliot?" the officer prodded gently, his hand out and his eyes on the little box.

She stopped just shy of yanking the box away and clutching it to her chest. "I'd like to give it to him myself."

"Ms. Elliot, you really don't need to—"

"Please."

He sighed, then shrugged. "Sure. Follow me."

And she did. She put her eyes square between his shoulders. She matched his pace up the hall, then again down the stairs. She stood to his side and let him apologize to Sergeant Gray for the "minor interruption." She even pretended not to notice when he waited a couple of feet away for her to say her piece to the boss. But as soon as she was done handing over the information and the box of evidence that proved her theory, she was also done with being under the young cop's scrutiny. And thankfully, her revelation brought a flurry of activity that made it easy to do what she'd decided to do.

She knew her plan was reckless. Possibly crazy. But

she needed to do it anyway. So she slipped out of the living room and into the kitchen. There, she grabbed Lucien's keys from the counter. She'd set them in the ceramic bowl herself, so finding them wasn't an issue. And her actions didn't even earn her a second glance.

Harmless civilian, she thought as she offered a smile to one of the detectives.

He gave her a wave.

And less than a minute later, she was in the SUV, armed with only the bear spray, the address and the surety that she was doing the right thing to get Lucien back.

Chapter 19

Lucien wasn't sure if the water was rising more quickly, or if he was just hyperaware of its presence now. It was midway up his thighs. Soon, it would cover his legs completely, and that fact was sending muted panic up every fiber of his being. He was a good swimmer. Excellent, even. Except that didn't matter at all if he was pinned down with zip ties.

How long? his mind kept asking.

The passage of time was hard to determine. It felt like hours had gone by, but he knew that was impossible. Hanes would be sticking to his schedule, which meant the other man would have to get back to Sally Rickson within a certain time frame. No way was he simply going to let Lucien die without sharing the reason why.

And there has to be a reason, even if it's a crazy, utterly misguided one.

For *however* long he'd been secured to the pipe, Lucien had been floating between searching for an explanation and trying to find a way to free himself. The only conclusion he'd come to was that in order to make the latter happen, he'd have to figure out the answer to the former.

What does Georges Hanes want?

Lucien truly didn't know. If the man wanted him dead, he could've simply killed him. A quick gunshot. A harder smack over the head. There'd been ample opportunity. Hell. *Now* was an opportunity. He and Raven hadn't been subtle in their movements. They hadn't been under guard. Lucien himself was the guard, and he'd clearly let himself be vulnerable.

Too vulnerable.

He shoved down the thought. He couldn't waste time beating himself up over what he could've done differently. There'd been no reason to suspect Hanes would grab him. In fact, if it weren't for the current, overly complicated scenario—which seemed to be deliberately catered to Lucien—then he would've simply carried on as he had been. Searching out the clues. Letting Raven in on the process.

Sure you don't regret that? At least a little?

"Shut up," he growled under his breath.

He switched his focus away from thinking and forced it on to doing instead. He vigorously rubbed the zip-ties on his wrists back and forth over the pipe, ignoring the way it made his arms ache. It was an effort he'd been making on repeat, and his muscles were sore. But the awkward angle and multiple ties gave him little hope. Not one had broken. They still felt no looser. If anything, it was his skin that was taking the brunt of it. His movements were a testament to the fact that his wrists were growing raw.

He'd experimented a little with his plan to stand up, if it came to that. So far, all he'd managed to do was discover a remarkable lack of flexibility in his body. In spite of his habitual running and natural physical strength, he was far from a contortionist. Every time he'd bent his knees, then tried to push his way up the pipe, his shoulders had twisted, then simply stopped co-operating. He tried again now anyway. Inching, inching, inching up.

"C'mon," he muttered as the pain seared across his back. "Cut me the tiniest bit of slack."

His words didn't earn him anything. The biting protest of his muscles and bones only intensified, and his eyes started to water.

Okay, he said to himself. *Maybe now* is *the time to think. Concentrate on something else and keep moving.*

The elaborate setup was all Hanes. No one could say the serial killer didn't enjoy complicated. He'd obviously staged the strange room—which Lucien still hadn't found a definition for—ahead of time. So Hanes had definitely been planning to use it.

But maybe it wasn't intended for you.

The thought made Lucien pause in his efforts, and he nearly collapsed as the burning pain lessened. He drew a breath and made himself try harder.

Maybe it really *hadn't* been for him. Maybe Lucien had just been in the way when Hanes came along for his true target. It was a possibility, at the very least.

He inched up a tiny bit more. The eye-watering had become a gush that spilled over to his face and tickled unpleasantly at the stubble on his cheeks and chin. But he was up farther than he'd gotten yet, so he kept pushing.

If he'd simply been in Hanes's way, then Lucien

needed to consider who *had* been the target. Hanes's pattern dictated that it was Jim and Juanita's son. If that was the case, then the other man obviously knew more about Sally Rickson's brother—or half brother, as the case might be—than Sally Rickson herself did. More than Jim did, too, because he couldn't picture the caretaker lying when both his wife's and daughter's lives were at stake. So how had Hanes acquired the information? Where *was* the brother in question?

"You need a hint?"

The question floated down from above, startling him both because he hadn't heard Hanes's approach, and because it seemed to synch so well with his own thoughts. He lost his momentum and slipped back down, sending up a splash of water.

"I hope you haven't drowned already." Hanes punctuated the statement with a dark laugh.

Lucien's jaw ticked. "Still alive, still planning on seeing you back behind bars."

"Oh." Hanes paused dramatically. "So you've got all the answers, then? You know where you are. And why. You know who I saved this spot for. And also why. So I can just go?"

The tick became a pulse. Lucien hated the overblown display of cockiness mixed with amusement, and it took a serious amount of effort not to react.

"I told you before," he said calmly, "I'm not interested in playing along. So unless you're here to unlock me and turn yourself in, you can just crawl back into whatever dark hole you came out of."

"I'll take that to mean you're still clueless and *do* want the hint. And you know I'm a fan of hints, Detective."

The air went silent for a moment before a nearly inaudible flutter carried through it. A second later, a flash of something white caught Lucien's eye as it floated down in front of him. It was a single sheet of paper. It landed on the water, featherlight and just out of reach. And overhead, the scrape of Hanes's exit provided no further explanation.

This was a mistake.

Raven swore it was the three hundredth time she'd had the thought in the last minute or so. She'd felt confident until she'd actually turned into the industrial district. Now the adrenaline—brought on by the exhilaration of having outsmarted the police—was clearly wearing off.

You didn't outsmart the police, said her subconscious. *You outsmarted common sense.*

Her pulse fluttered a little faster as she turned a corner and caught a whiff of charred air. It was a foreboding scent. The fact that it hung on so strongly, weeks after the fire, was a testament to its destructive power. It made Raven's hands itch to swing the wheel and drive at full speed back in the opposite direction.

Her subconscious piped up again, louder than before.

You're not just making a mistake, it said. *This isn't the spontaneous, online purchase of an overpriced pair of shoes. This is knowingly walking into a serial killer's territory. Knowingly putting yourself in the sight lines of the man who murdered your whole family.*

Pain stabbed at her chest, and she fought it.

"Don't you think I know all that?" she responded aloud. "Because I do. And I know more, too. Hanes took Lucien. And all I have is the dumb bear spray to protect myself. But I'm going in anyway, so you might as well just cool it."

As she finished, her voice rose to a near yell, and a semihysterical laugh at the absurdity of the self-directed argument nearly burst free. But any hint of mirth abruptly disappeared as she rounded a street corner and spotted the gated industrial park. The burned-out building stuck out from the rest, even in the dim light. Its sides were black and broken, and reams of yellow caution tape underscored the danger and blocked the way in.

Are you still sure about this?

"Yes," she murmured, pulling the SUV to a stop as close as she could get. "I'm sure."

She had the first aid kit in the back, and she was trained in how to use it. She'd been the one to figure out how to help Jim. And no one knew better than Raven did that in this situation, the mere presence of a friendly voice was the more important than all the rescue equipment in the world.

With that in mind, she cut the engine and gazed at the shell of a building. She tried to picture what it might've looked like before. A big sign overhead, maybe, with the Magic Fire logo? A color scheme that suited the place? Red and orange and a bit of black and gray to add to the mystery? Raven stared for a second longer, then shook her head and told herself to quit stalling.

The moment she opened the door, the smoky scent went from a light trace to a thick slap. It was cloying. Too much, really. And it got worse the closer she got. But she made herself ignore the smell and move forward anyway.

There was no door to step through, but a large open space at the front was entrance enough. Raven picked her way over the rubble, then stepped through into what had once been a large two-level warehouse. She stood still for a moment, her eyes roving over the place. There were bits of pieces of utterly unidentifiable equipment and piles of ash littered throughout. In spite of the missing chunks of roof and broken-down walls, it still seemed big. Overwhelming. And very unstable. Raven had the feeling that one wrong move was going to equal a broken leg. She realized that she'd somehow expected to walk into an empty space with a clear path to Sally Rickson.

This is Hanes, she chastised. *You should've known better.* She swept her eyes back and forth again. *So what now?*

Did she yell out Sally's name? Would it draw unwanted attention? She hadn't seen any other cars in the area, but that didn't necessarily mean she was alone. *Was* she alone?

She worried at her lower lip with her teeth and silently urged herself to make a decision. But another moment of hesitation saved her from having to do it. A sound—a whimper—carried through the building, echoing a little. Then it stopped abruptly.

"Sally?" she called.

The whimper came again, and Raven drew in a breath then held it while she tried to pinpoint the sound's location. She tipped her head to the side and listened hard.

It's coming from above.

Her eyes went up, and the whimper turned to a plea.

"Is someone there?" asked a voice—raspy but still undeniably female. "Please…"

"I'm coming," Raven replied, hoping she could keep the promise.

Carefully, she moved a little farther into the space. Even more carefully, she climbed over a pile of charred metal. She nearly lost her footing twice in the process, and once she got to the bottom of it, she did stumble enough that she bit down on her tongue and let out a yelp. But finally she reached the other end of the warehouse. And there she was forced to stop. A set of stairs led to the next floor. Or they once had. Now the steps ended halfway up, and a large chunk of the floor above was missing. As Raven stared up, wondering how she could possibly make it to Sally without breaking her own neck, an ominous *cr-r-rack* sounded overhead. And the noise was immediately followed by a piece of tumbling debris. Raven's eyes followed it as it bounced down the first few stairs, slipped through the gaping hole, then hit the ground below and carried on until it smacked into the nearest wall.

Not a good sign.

"Sally?" she called. "I'm just going to need to—"

Her words cut off as her gaze dragged up the wall, and her throat went dry. A large piece of black paper—the kind children used for crafts—had been taped there, and across it, in streaky white lettering was Hanes's message.

CHILDHOOD IS SWEET, it read. *ALL FUN AND GAMES. AN EYE FOR AN EYE.*

The words gave Raven a chill, but she shook it off as she remembered that it wasn't the clue that mattered—it was the substance used to write it. Momentarily forgetting her concerns over the instability of the floor and ceiling, she moved closer. Ten steps in, and she caught a whiff of something. And the smell made her understand the odd appearance of the letters.

Chlorine bleach.

The words had been painted on with the stuff, and it reminded Raven of something. And not in a household-cleaner kind of way. She stared a little longer, trying to figure out what it was. While she couldn't quite put a finger on it, she was filled with a sudden need to go to Lucien's apartment. She had no idea where the urge came from, but it very nearly spurred her to turn and run for the SUV. The only thing that stopped her was Sally. Raven couldn't leave her. She *wouldn't*. Because she knew exactly how the other woman must feel, and being alone was the last thing she needed.

Quickly, she pulled out Lucien's cell phone and snapped a picture of the message, then refocused her attention on finding a way up to wherever Sally had been trapped. But as she scanned the area in search of a viable option, sirens filled the air, and Raven realized that *she* wasn't the person most equipped to handle the situation.

As if you couldn't figure that out before you came?

She ignored her conscience's sarcasm and called out, "Do you hear that, Sally? Help is on the way."

The response was faint, but still audibly relieved. "Thank you."

"Don't thank me yet," Raven muttered under her breath.

The sirens grew louder, and she eyed the door. She had to make a decision, and she had to make it fast. If Sergeant Gray got there, he'd undoubtedly try to stop her from leaving. And she wouldn't blame him for trying. But she wouldn't let him do it, either. She waited until the sirens reached a crescendo, sent up a silent apology to Sally for not sticking around, then slipped back out to the SUV and headed toward Lucien's apartment, determined to follow her gut.

The water was up to Lucien's hips. A little bit past them, if he was being honest. His body was heavy with

a combination of sopping clothes and exhaustion, and
he hadn't yet managed to lift himself to a standing position. He hadn't made much progress in determining
Hanes's purpose, either. The sheet of paper that the
other man had dropped down had floated to one corner
of the concrete space, propelled by the influx of liquid,
and there it stayed.

Some clue that turned out to be.

Lucien knew the thought was bitter, and he knew he
couldn't afford to give in to the dragging hopelessness
that threatened to go along with it. He'd called out to
Hanes a few times, hoping that the other man would
be disappointed that his hint had failed. So far, he'd
received no response. It made him assume Hanes had
actually left the premises, and he wasn't sure if that
was a good thing, or a bad thing. Lucien's concept of
time was still skewed, but if he had to think about it,
he might guess that it was about time for the killer to
be checking on Sally Rickson's status.

They'll have her, he assured himself.

Maybe it wasn't a completely realistic thought, but
anything that buoyed his confidence was a positive. He
didn't have a whole hell of a lot more going for him at
the moment.

Stifling a curse, Lucien leaned his head against the
pipe and closed his eyes for a second. He took a deep
breath and dug into his own mind in search of something to grasp at.

You need to get that paper.

"No kidding," he muttered.

It was true that after his first couple of attempts to
swish the so-called hint in his direction, he'd given up
and gone back to simply trying to free himself. But
those efforts seemed to be growing more futile by the

minute. So maybe it was time to try something new. He opened his eyes and turned his attention to the corner where the single sheet sat. It was bobbing up and down a little with the continued flow of water.

Five feet out of reach.

That was Lucien's estimate. If he'd had a single arm free, he probably could've stretched out and grabbed it.

"But you *don't* have a free arm, do you?" he muttered. "All you have is a free leg, and it's not exactly helpful in this situation."

But then his gaze dropped to his foot, and he wondered if it *could* be helpful. Could he reposition himself and stretch it out far enough? It was at least worth a shot, wasn't it?

With a grunt, he pressed his heel to the ground and pushed to the right. The water slurped a protest. His pants stuck to the pebbled surface underneath him. But he'd *moved.* At least three inches. It was enough to spur him on. He repeated the same steps again.

Grunt-dig-twist.

He could already feel the sweat forming over his face.

Grunt-dig-twist.

His beat-up muscles were deepening their resentment.

Grunt.

Dig.

Twist.

His rear end felt like it was scraping against sandpaper, and he was 99 percent sure that a hole was wearing through the fabric of his pants.

Grunt, diiiiiig. Twist.

He collapsed against the pipe and eyed his target again. He was angled directly toward it now, but as he stretched out his leg—even pointing his toe—he realized his efforts had been in vain. The paper was still about a foot farther away than he could reach.

I'd have to be lying down to get it. As soon as the thought popped into his head, it stuck.

If he *could* lie down, he truly might be able to reach. And as many times as he'd tried to push himself up and out of reach of the rising water, he hadn't once attempted to sink into it.

Yeah, he thought sardonically. *That might be because drowning isn't on the agenda.*

Which might very well happen if he got down there and couldn't get back up. As his stare hung on Hanes's "hint," though, he realized doing the opposite of what he *wanted* to do might be the best option. Thinking he was probably going to regret it, he dug his heel into the ground again. Only this time, instead of twisting, he pulled forward. Almost immediately, his bound hands hit the ground. He was so surprised by the quick success that he cracked his head on the pipe, which wobbled awkwardly sideways.

"Easy, Match," he said as he steadied himself. "Let's try to avoid any *actual* drowning, okay?"

He eased down a bit more, his eyes on the paper. It was only an inch or two away now. Lucien took a moment. He pinpointed the location. Lined up his toe and dipped it down under the water. He leaned his head back and prepared to scoop up the clue. Then stopped. Because it was then that realization hit him. The ceiling that he'd vaguely recognized before—crisscrossed and gray and way higher than it ought to be—abruptly found a place in his mind. He wasn't sitting in the middle of some strange room. He wasn't in a *room* at all. He was at the bottom of a swimming pool.

Chapter 20

Sergeant Gray was furious. Raven knew, because his name had appeared on Lucien's cell phone five times over the course of her drive from the burned-out warehouse to the apartment building. Three calls, two texts to be exact. The former went unanswered, the latter went unread.

He's not my *boss.*

The thought was as true as it was petulant. The only hold the older man had over her was the fact that he was in charge of Lucien's career. And even then, she was pretty sure he couldn't fire a detective based on the behavior of an autonomous individual. She hoped, anyway.

As Raven used the key card Lucien kept in his sunshade to open the gated, underground lot, then guided the SUV into its designated spot, the phone rang one more time. She grabbed it from the console and prepared to hit the Ignore key. But it wasn't the sergeant's name scrawling instantly over the screen; it was the hospital.

Raven's heart did a nervous skip, and she swiped to answer it, her voice tentative as she issued a greeting. "Hello?"

The woman on the other end sounded puzzled. "Is this Detective Match?"

"No, this is—" She cut herself off.

What *was* she? Not his witness. Not the woman he was protecting. She was definitely more than those things. But girlfriend didn't seem to fit. Not without a discussion. If Lucien even wanted to take things there. *Did* he want to? A wave of doubt swept through her. What had their time in bed meant to him?

And why am I only really thinking about it now?

"Hello?" The voice on the other end jerked her attention away from her ill-timed tumble of thoughts.

"I'm here," she said quickly.

"But you're not Detective Match?"

"No. This is his number, though. I'm his…partner?" She knew it sounded more like a question than a statement, but it felt almost right, so she just left it.

And the woman on the home phone seemed to accept it, too. "Oh. Good. I was pretty sure that Mrs. Rickson had called Detective Match *he* a couple of times, so it just threw me a little when you answered."

Raven's heart thumped again. "Mrs. Rickson? She's awake?"

"Awake and lively." A light laugh carried through. "Unfortunately, she's still in the intensive-care wing, and the doctors discourage phones from being allowed in."

Phones.

A little belatedly, Raven remembered that unexpected calls hadn't worked out in their favor recently.

"I'm sorry," she said curtly. "Did you say who this was?"

There was a pause on the other end. "Pardon me?"

"How did Mrs. Rickson know to call Detective Match? And how did you get this number?"

"I think there's been a misunderstanding."

"Has there?" Raven kept her tone cool.

"I think so," replied the other woman. "My name is Rita Marshall. I'm a nurse at Vancouver Hospital. Mrs. Rickson—Juanita—is a patient here, and I'm trying to get a hold of Detective Match."

In her head, Raven wavered, but out loud, she held her ground. "So if I hang up the phone, then call back and ask for Rita Marshall, they'll put me through?"

"They're more likely to put you through if you ask for the intensive care unit, but yes."

Raven hesitated. Her paranoia didn't quite abate. And she didn't think it should. Quickly—before the so-called nurse could say anything that was even more convincing—she tapped the phone off and dropped it in her lap. She stared down at it for a second, half expecting it to ring again right away. When it didn't, she picked it up again and started to hit the callback button before realizing that it might just lead back to the same faked number. She needed a different line.

"If I'm *ever* in the mood to change jobs again, it won't be for police work," she muttered.

Sure that Lucien was the kind of man who wouldn't rely solely on a cell phone, she swung the door open, then made her way up to his apartment. Thankfully, the garage had an elevator that led directly to his floor.

Even more thankfully, the short journey wasn't interrupted by other residents or guests.

When Raven turned the key and took the first step into Lucien's private space, though, she wished—a little strangely—that there *had* been an interruption of some kind. In the months that she'd lived with him in the safe house, they'd talked about his living arrangements, just like they'd talked about everything else. But aside from sitting outside like a stalker, she'd never been inside. It felt a little wrong to be there.

But as she flicked on the light and took a small spin around, she could see that it didn't contain anything particularly personal. The condo was supposed to be a temporary fix until he settled on a neighborhood where he wanted to buy a place. He'd been there about six months when she first met him, and he'd told her he'd left many of his things in storage. Except now it'd been three and a half years, and there was still almost no evidence of the man Raven knew so well. Spartan decor. Furniture that screamed *showroom*. A treadmill and a TV.

Even when she moved from the open living area to the single bedroom, she didn't find anything. Not a framed photo or a book or a notepad with something scrawled on it.

How am I going to find something that supports Hanes's clue in here? Raven wondered a little hopelessly.

She let her eyes rove over the room once more, thinking that she probably would've had a better chance of finding a bigger glimpse into Lucien's life by going back to the safe house. Which might have sent a warm shot to her heart if not for the fact that it was currently making the situation that much harder. She nearly sank down onto the bed in despair before she remembered that she had another objective to follow up on—the call to the hospital.

Hoping that would give her something to go on, or that it would at least boost her hope, Raven exited the bedroom in search of the phone. She found an older-model portable tucked in a corner in the kitchen, conveniently sitting on top of an old phone book. A quick flick through the emergency pages got her the general number for the hospital. She dialed, listened through the automated prompts, hit 9 to talk an operator then asked for the ICU.

Five seconds later and two rings later, a crisp voice came on the line. "This is intensive-care desk."

Raven did her best to sound authoritative. "Hi there. My name is Raven Elliot, and I'm working with the Vancouver PD on the Rickson case. I received a call from a nurse named Rita Marshall. Is she available?"

Does she even exist? she wanted to add.

But the woman on the phone was quick to assuage her unasked question.

"Rita?" she replied. "Yeah, you bet. Hang on one second and I'll track her down."

Raven exhaled as cheesy hold music filled her ear. Knowing that the nurse wasn't one of Hanes's tricks lifted about a million pounds of tension from her shoulders. Feeling like she could relax for just a moment, she pulled out one of the tall stools from the breakfast bar and moved to lift herself into it. But as she shifted her body, she also shifted her view. And something unexpected drew her eye. Her breath caught.

Tacked to the side of the fridge with a plain black magnet was a photograph. A little grainy. An odd shape and size for a picture—square, and probably two inches by two inches. But that wasn't what made Raven do the double take. It was the subject matter. Because it was a photo of *her*. Her eyes were on the camera, her mouth open in a laugh, one hand lifted in a protest. And she remembered exactly when it was taken.

It was about three weeks in to their stay. Raven had had a particularly rough time that day because it would have been her brother's birthday. Lucien had let her cry. Multiple times. He hadn't complained when she got up in the middle of a card game and simply walked away. And when she'd come back, maybe an hour later, and said how sorry she was, he'd pulled her in and held her close and told her she had nothing to apologize for. It was the first time he'd wrapped his arms around her since carrying her out of the hole where Hanes had left her. And Raven had sensed it was a turning point of some kind. For her, anyway. She'd wanted to stay there forever. Safe with Lucien. And she'd known that no matter what happened next—with the case, with her life, with the killer himself—she would never feel something platonic for Lucien again. If she'd ever felt it at all.

Then he'd made a joke. Something silly that she couldn't remember the specifics of at the moment. But it'd made her laugh. And Lucien had grabbed his phone and snapped the shot and told her that even in the darkest moments, there could still be light.

And here it is.

Unconsciously, she stepped to the fridge and ran a finger over the photo. He'd held on to it. Gone out of his way to print it. And kept it in view for three entire years.

A thick lump formed in Raven's throat. She *had* to find him. She *had* to get him back.

Fighting tears, she closed her eyes. She was thankful that a second later, a slightly breathless greeting interrupted the increasingly desperate turn of her thoughts.

"This is Rita Marshall speaking."

Raven forced herself to turn away from the photo and brought her attention back to the phone. "Hi, Rita. This is Detective Lucien's partner. Raven Elliot. I just want to start by saying sorry for hanging up before."

"No, it's fine. I'm sure you have to be—" the nurse stopped. "Wait. Did you say Raven?"

Raven's pulse bumped up. "Yes. Why?"

"Ohhhh." The other woman dragged the word out. "Mrs. Rickson was talking about you. She called Detective Match *yours*. I thought that meant...whoops! This makes much more sense."

Raven's face burned. She knew she'd mentioned Lucien to Juanita over the years, but she'd thought she'd kept it casual.

She cleared her throat and steered the conversation back to the topic at hand. "About Mrs. Rickson, Rita... Is there a way we can bend the no-phone rule so that I *can* talk to her?"

"They're keeping her under pretty tight watch. That's why I agreed to call for her, actually. She was a little distraught after speaking with her husband, and she said she had something to tell Detective Match. But *only* Detective Match. So I was hoping to get him to come *in*." The other woman's voice dropped to a near whisper. "But Detective Elliot..."

Raven winced, but didn't correct the nurse. "Yes?"

"Are we in danger at the hospital? Right after you hung up, one of the other nurses overheard the policewoman at Juanita's door say this has something to do with the Kitsilano Killer."

Raven channeled her own inner cop, pulling from everything she'd ever heard on TV, then using the even tone she'd heard Lucien apply during official business. "I'm sure you know we can't comment on that."

"Right. No. Of course not." The nurse let out an audible sigh. "Do you have a way of getting in touch with Detective Match to let him know what's going on?"

Raven's chest compressed. "Not at the moment. But I could come down myself."

"Could you? That would be amazing. I'll let the other officers know that—"

"No!"

"What?"

Raven bit her lip. "It's a…uh…hierarchy thing. I don't want anyone to feel like I'm stepping on their toes."

Rita laughed. "Lord knows I understand that. Why don't I text you my personal number, and you can let me know when you're here, and I'll bring you up myself?"

"Sounds like a plan."

Raven tapped off Lucien's home phone, set it on the charger and let her eyes drift to the photo on the fridge once more. Her gaze lingered for a few seconds longer, and then she pushed up off the stool and snagged the keys from the counter. She was sure she wasn't going to find the key to solving Lucien's whereabouts by searching his apartment. It didn't have enough of *him* in it to make a difference. But Juanita might have something to contribute. It gave Raven hope as she stepped out of the condo and made her way back to the elevator. And she'd be just plain glad to see the other woman, too. It felt like a lifetime since she'd found her sitting in her husband's office.

And speaking of her husband…

Raven frowned a little. Why had Juanita gotten upset after talking to Jim? She started to make a mental note to ask the question if the other woman didn't volunteer an explanation from the get-go, then paused, midthought, as the elevator slid to a stop on the first floor. Raven tensed. But when the doors slid open, the tension turned to something else. Recognition. Because as a damp-haired woman stepped in, a folded towel in her hands, a familiar scent hit her nose.

Chlorine.

She knew it must've come from the hot tub in the condo's gym. But what it reminded her of was Georges Hanes's most recent message.

After several failed attempts and a frustrating block of time where the sheet of paper had sunk down below the surface of the water and threatened not to float up again, Lucien finally had it in his lap. And now he knew exactly what it was—the same family tree he'd spotted at Sally Rickson's house. He squinted down at the slightly blurred words, trying to discern the significance. He was sure it had something to do with Sally's brother. It was the only thing that made sense. As he found Jim's and Juanita's names, though, he saw nothing to indicate the existence of some secret love child. The couple's names were there. Sally's name connected the two of them. That was it.

Frustrated, Lucien ran his eyes from the top of the page to the bottom. The tree started three generations back. Great-great grandparents. Birth years and places. Surprisingly few aunts and uncles and cousins. Sally's family seemed to stick to one or two children per couple. His gaze and mind roamed over it together.

Greg married Lucinda. One son, daughter. The daughter, named Wanda, had married James. James

*married Lisa, and they two had Jim, an only child. Jim
went on to marry Juanita, and Juanita and Jim had—*

Lucien abruptly stopped cataloguing. There was
something off. Not in the names. Those lined up just
as they should. There was something *physically* off
about it.

He bent his knee to bring the paper closer, and he
scanned it again, this time paying attention to how the
names and boxes fit next to each other. They were tidy.
Exactly right for the page. Except for the very last spot.
Beside Juanita's name, on the far right side of the page,
there was a space.

"And there shouldn't be one," Lucien murmured.

If he could've, he would've run his thumb over it. His
attention flicked to the other side of the paper.

No space.

It was like someone had deleted an entire name from
under Juanita's spot. His cop instinct reared its head.
Earlier, he'd posited the idea that Jim might have a son
somewhere that he didn't know about. It wasn't out of
the realm of possibility. But what Lucien *hadn't* considered was that Jim might not be the one with an out-
of-wedlock child. He glanced down again. If his new
suspicions were correct, then the brother in question
wasn't an unknown; he was a secret. Which added a
new pile of questions. They reeled through Lucien's
mind.

Did Jim know about the child? Was it his? The latter
seemed unlikely, but it wasn't impossible. If it wasn't
his, then whose was it? Sally had obviously found out.
Had she told her father, if he hadn't known before?
Most important, though…what had happened to the
boy? Who was he? Where was he now?

Lucien frowned as an idea tried to worm its way

into his mind. There was a candidate right in front of his face. A man with a questionable past and uncertain parenthood. A man who'd centered his existence on destroying perfect families.

A chill slipped between Lucien's shoulder blades, and it had nothing to do with the fact that the water was nearing his waist. He let his knees drop, and he lifted his gaze overhead. There was nothing for him to do but wait for Hanes—who probably wasn't Hanes at all—to return so he could let the man know that he'd finally figured it out.

Chapter 21

Raven followed the well-curved fiftyish woman up the stairs, glad the nurse was moving at a quick pace. She was eager to get into Juanita's room. She wanted to hear what the caretaker's wife had to say, even if it wasn't good news. But more than both of those things, Raven wanted to get back to the safe house. Because on the drive over to the hospital, she'd remembered something. Lucien hadn't brought much with him for those months they'd lived together, but one thing he *had* packed was a memory book. And it seemed strangely important to retrieve it, even if Raven couldn't put her finger on why.

She remembered the story he'd told her about why he'd brought the book along. He'd explained to her that it wasn't nostalgia that made him cart it around. It was superstition.

Through a series of events that involved Lucien grabbing the wrong bag on the way out the door, the memory book had been with him on his first shift. To keep it hidden from his training officer, he'd tucked it under his shirt. That day, they'd unexpectedly busted a major drug dealer.

Three months later, when Lucien was moving out of his parents' place, he'd been called in to attend an armed robbery. With little time to spare, he'd simply gone into work with a moving box in the back of his car. The memory book was sitting on top, and it had been Lucien who brought down the shooter.

And the book had been there on a third occasion, too. On the evening before his father's funeral, Lucien had tossed it into the car with the intention of bringing it with him the next day. And that night, he'd been thrown into the middle of a domestic-abuse situation that had spilled over into the street. His quick reaction had saved a child's life. And he spied a pattern. He'd started carrying the memory book in his glove box for luck. And nostalgia or superstition, it didn't matter. If there was anywhere that held a hint as to where Lucien's and Hanes's lives intersected, that would be it.

Rita Marshall stopped abruptly just then, and Raven nearly stumbled into her. The other woman didn't seem to notice the near collision. She just gestured to the end of the hall.

"This is it," she whispered. "Juanita's room is around the corner. There're two other cops in front of the door."

Raven nodded, ignoring the words *other cops*. She was just glad that Rita wasn't questioning the need for secrecy. And she was even gladder that the nurse hadn't asked for ID.

She inhaled and did her best to sound confident. "This is great, Rita. Is there any means of getting them to step away for a few seconds?"

The other woman lifted an eyebrow. "You want me to create a distraction? Like in the movies?"

Raven flushed, guessing that she probably did sound like caricature of actual police work. But Nurse Marshall just smiled and snapped her fingers.

"Got it!" she crowed, then turned and hurried the rest of the way up the hall.

Raven winced, and she braced herself for something big. A crash. A scream. A sudden fire alarm. Instead, there was just silence. And a moment later, Rita reappeared.

"Come on," said the other woman. "You've got at least a few minutes."

Raven stared at her, and she couldn't help but ask, "What did you do?"

"Told them there were free doughnuts in the lobby, of course." Rita laughed. "I'm kidding. I told them I saw a petite dark-haired woman sneaking around by the elevator. But seriously…do those jokes ever stop being funny?"

Raven bit back an urge to suggest the nurse ask an actual cop, and made herself smile. "No. At least not when they're a lead-in to getting me what I need."

Rita grinned. "Okay. You do your thing. I'll sit outside the room, and if the cops come back, I promise to let out a bird noise or something."

"Thank you."

She followed the other woman to the room, hurriedly stepped in and then just as quickly stopped. Juanita was lying in the raised bed, tubes attached to her hand, her nose and her head. Bandages obscured her face. She looked weak and small. Not lively as Rita had said. But Jim was beside her in a chair, his fingers curled over her IV-free hand, his head resting on one of her blanket-covered thighs. His eyes were closed, his mouth open, a soft snore escaping his parted lips. It was heartbreaking and sweet at the same time. Raven's throat was immediately raw. And the going-to-cry feeling only intensified when Juanita spotted her and sent a big smile in her direction.

"Raven," she greeted in a pleased whisper. "Come in."

Raven's gaze went to Jim, and she answered in an equally low voice. "I don't have to."

The older woman shook her head. "Please. We owe you our lives. We owe you *Sally's* life, from what we were just told. Don't mind Jim. They wouldn't let him have a bed in the room, so he forcibly discharged himself, and here he is, out like a light." She smiled again. "But I wasn't expecting to see *you*."

Raven swallowed. "Lucien—Detective Match—is indisposed. I came instead."

"Oh. That's too bad. Well. Not the 'you coming instead' part." The older woman eyed Raven with concern, taking in her expression, and her smile faded. "Is he okay?"

"He's…" She couldn't quite make herself say it aloud, so she opted for something else. "I *want* him to be okay. That's why I'm here. One of the nurses said you had some information for Lucien?"

Juanita cast a quick glance down at Jim, then sighed, her face full of devastation. "It's probably better that he's asleep. He doesn't know. Or I should say he *didn't* know. He does now. We've never had many secrets from each other. But this…"

Raven stepped closer. "What is it?"

"I was sixteen, and I thought I was in love. His name was Lincoln. He rode a motorbike, and—sorry. I guess none of that matters at the moment. When I found out

I was pregnant, he took that motorbike and he left." The older woman met Raven's eyes. "Jim said the police asked him about Sally having a brother. She does have one. Nine years older. He was adopted before I did more than see his face. It was the best thing for him. Or I thought it was."

Raven felt the air go out of her lungs. "Oh, Juanita."

"Sally found out. Something about a DNA database." Juanita exhaled a regret-filled sigh, then nodded toward the night stand. "My purse is in the drawer. The police said they found it at the scene, too. They thought it was strange, but I've been lying here thinking about it, and I'm sure it was on purpose. Open it up and pull out my wallet?"

Careful not to disturb a still-snoring Jim, Raven did as was requested.

"Open the wallet, too," Juanita said. "Then reach into the crease behind the cards."

Raven complied, and her fingers immediately brushed something she recognized by feel. A photograph. With her heart beating a little faster, she dragged it free. It was dog-eared and faded, but the subject was still clear. It was a shot of a little boy in swim trunks, standing in front of a pool.

A pool. The chlorine smell.

Blood rushed through Raven, making her so lightheaded that she nearly missed Juanita's next statement.

"I asked the adoption agency if they could get me a photo," she was saying, "and that's the one they sent."

Raven forced out a thick-feeling breath. Because she knew now why the memory book had sprung to mind. She'd only caught a glimpse into it once. Just inside the front cover, actually, where—tacked down to the first page—was a blue ribbon from a swim meet.

* * *

The water seemed to be rising quicker than it had before, and it was sloshing up past Lucien's elbows. A deep knot of worry had taken root in his stomach, and it burned as much as his shoulders did. Since giving up on the idea of forcing himself to his feet, he'd latched on to a new idea—that he could turn to buoyancy. As tightly as he was bound, there was at least a little give. If he could stretch his arms to give himself enough space, he'd float up. The only problem with the plan was that he wouldn't know whether or not it was going to work until it was essential that it *did* work. So—as much as Lucien hated to admit it—he was relieved when the scrape overhead signaled that Hanes was back. The other man still sent his gut churning and his teeth on edge, though, when he called out a too-casual, slightly condescending greeting.

"How're we doing down there, Detective? Any luck?"

Lucien flexed his fingers, but it was the only bit of anger he let escape. "Oh, I think so, Hanes. Why don't you come closer so we can talk about it?"

Irritatingly, Hanes's reply was a chuckle. "Why? Have you devised some clever plan to kill me using only a shoelace?"

"If I were that clever, *I* wouldn't be the one sitting at the bottom of a swimming pool."

"Aha. You figured that part out."

"Disappointed?"

"I think you know me better than that, Lucien."

Bile rose up in the back of Lucien's throat. He didn't like the intimate tone, nor the use of his name. He wished he didn't know a damn thing about Hanes, let alone to have the man presume—correctly—that he understood how much the other man liked his game.

Out loud, he kept his tone measured. "Shoelace notwithstanding...why don't you come down and find out what else I've figured out?"

"You wish it were that easy," Hanes replied. "But I'm going to need more of a hint that you're on the right track before I discuss things face-to-face."

"What kind of clue would you like?" Lucien asked. "Do you want me to tell you I know about Sally Rickson's DNA test? That she found some results she didn't like, and that she wanted to erase them? That she realized she had a brother...but wished she didn't know?"

Drawn-out silence reined, and for several seconds, worry threatened. Had he gotten it wrong? Was he off the mark by a mile? He'd been sure he was right. Finally, after a few more protracted moments, Hanes's voice carried down again.

"Yep," said the other man. "All that'll do just fine."

Then the sound of shoes tapping on something metallic lifted from behind Lucien, and he knew the other man was descending. He just wasn't sure what that would lead to.

Raven was back to cursing her own recklessness. It had subsided somewhat at the hospital. Maybe because talking to Juanita had seemed so normal, even though the subject matter was anything but. There wasn't anything too odd about going to see an injured friend in the hospital. And there wasn't even anything that weird about that same friend confessing a secret while experiencing such a close call with death. But it was utter insanity to walk directly into the path of a serial killer. And unlike when Raven had gone after

Sally, this time, she was sure she was going to encounter Georges Hanes.

A little wave of dizziness hit as the reality came crashing properly in for the first time.

Oh, God.

She had to tighten her hands on the wheel to keep from yanking it to the side and pulling herself off the road.

Am I really doing this?

"Yes, I am," she said aloud to Lucien's empty SUV.

She had no choice. As she'd left the hospital, she'd caved in and called Sergeant Gray. His phone had gone straight to voice mail twice, and a glance at the clock in the car had told Raven that Lucien's time was running short. So she'd texted the information to Sergeant Gray instead. And she'd called Dispatch, as well. But she'd tuned out their immediate response.

Wait, they'd told her. *Sit tight. Let us do our job.*

All very reasonable. But the problem it*self* wasn't in the realm of reason. Raven's heart had no interest in waiting. If she did, and Lucien died, she didn't know how she'd push past it. All of the tools and all of the training and all of the experience she had as a grief counselor did nothing to assuage the surety that if Hanes took this one final piece of her life away from her, she might never get over it.

Raven stepped on the gas.

She had no firm proof that Lucien was where she believed him to be. But she remembered what he'd told her about his instincts. How when he'd seen the guy putting up the posters about the mining museum, he'd just *known*. And he'd felt compelled to follow through. That was exactly where she was now. In her head. In her heart. And deep down in her gut. She was completely certain, and she didn't dare waste time on *sitting tight*. And she could swear that as the miles and minutes ticked by, she could feel herself getting closer to Lucien.

Her foot lowered a little more, and a glance down told her that she was already cruising well past the speed limit. She didn't care. The drive had taken her off the highway, away from the city traffic and into a surprising pocket of wilderness. The winding road was blissfully empty. The time and the weather weren't exactly conducive to the hiking crowd that normally frequented the area. So she didn't slow at all. Not until a billboard came into view just ahead. Then, she eased her foot up just enough to peruse the advertisement.

In faded lettering, the sign announced the grand opening of a state-of-the-art aquatic center. Greenview Waterpark. It promised the best experience right in the heart of a natural setting. A smiling boy in retro swim trunks stood beside a picture of the facility in question, and tall trees dotted the background. Below that, a date—thirty years in the past and punctuated with three exclamation points—stood out. And across the whole thing was a red banner with the words NOW CLOSED in bold black. But even that was somewhat washed out.

Raven had been a teenager when the popular destination had shut down, and she remembered the news coverage quite well. The privately owned facility had suffered a blow when an elderly man drowned in one of its pools. A lawsuit had followed. The owners had never recovered, and the place had simply been abandoned. Raven hadn't thought of it in years. But that didn't stop her from being convinced that Hanes would have chosen it.

A few hundred feet ahead, another sign came into

view. It beckoned with a green arrow and announced that the waterpark could be found by taking the next left.

Almost there now.

Anticipation mixing with fear, Raven flicked on her turn signal and guided the car onto the narrower road. It was still paved, but also cracked and uneven, forcing her to reduce her speed again. But when she rounded the corner, she was glad she wasn't going terribly fast. If she had, she might've missed the strange, dawning moments of realization. As it was, she felt like she was watching a slow-motion movie reel.

First came a broken-down sign that has an ominous drunk-driving message about taking lives. It was out of place, and even though it was overgrown and looked like it'd been there a while, it'd obviously never been intended for the space it now occupied. But it wasn't that which caught and held Raven's attention. It was the words in the ad.

Taking lives. Would you give yours?

They were eerily similar to the message that Hanes had left at the scene of the caretaker's abduction, and Raven couldn't help but see the crimson lettering flash through her mind.

A LIFE IS OWED TO ME. SO I'LL TAKE ONE EVERY DAY UNTIL YOU GIVE ME YOURS. And as she moved past the sign, it happened again. A small but very vibrant patch of yellow flowers demanded to be seen. And the hint in chalk—the one left where Jim was found—jumped up.

PRETTY YELLOW FLOWERS, ALL IN A ROW. I'D GO BACK, IF THEY'D LET ME.

A moving-underwater feeling hit Raven. It couldn't be a coincidence. Not where Hanes was concerned.

Fear made her shiver, and her foot wanted to lift off

the gas pedal completely. But she forced herself to push on. And for a few seconds, there was nothing further. She started to relax. To question her paranoia. But as she reached the large gravel parking lot and came to a stop, she noted—back in underwater mode—that the nearest building was decorated with a mural. It had been painted with a row of cartoon kids, each one a little bigger than the last. And there was no denying that it matched up with Hanes's third clue.

SHORTEST TO TALLEST, SIDE BY SIDE. TAKING ONE IS THE ONLY CHOICE. Raven put the SUV into Park, cut the engine and sat there staring at it. Hanes had been leading up to this place. Maybe even to this moment. But knowing it provided no relief. And on top of that, there was the final clue to consider. The one that the evil man had written in bleach before taking Lucien.

CHILDHOOD IS SWEET. ALL FUN AND GAMES. AN EYE FOR AN EYE. An eye for an eye couldn't lead to anything good.

Raven exhaled, counted to ten and swung open her door. She stepped over the gravel, averting her eyes from the row of cartoon children, and bypassed the smaller building completely. She ducked under the turnstile that led into the main area, then moved past the remnants of waterslides and splash pads. She had her sights set directly on the large structure at the very back of the park. She knew what was inside. Two indoor, year-round pools. Both of which had been home to a swim club when Lucien was a teenager.

Outside the building, she paused to decide how best to enter. The glass doors at the front seemed too obvious. Yet she didn't relish the idea of trying to find another way in. Scanning for a side entrance, she moved along the outside of the pool. But halfway up the cement path, she froze. Because from one of the large, very cracked windows, a familiar, terror-inducing voice carried out.

Georges Hanes.

It sent Raven spiraling back three years. All the healing she'd done on her own, all the healing she'd helped others achieve…it was gone in that instant. She was helpless all over again. Bound by the killer's words, clinging to them because they were the only human contact she had. But hating them, too, because she was so sure they'd be the last thing she ever heard.

And now she was stuck again. Equally bound. Equally hateful. All she could do was stand there and listen as he spoke.

Chapter 22

Hanes had been rambling for minutes. How many, Lucien didn't know, but the water had climbed over his belt, and was halfway up his chest. The other man seemed to want to rehash every moment of his trial. The details of his kills. The elaborate plans. Far, far more details than he'd given near the end of his trial. He sounded almost giddy—almost drunk, almost non-sensical—with the revelations.

Truthfully, Lucien would've gladly done without it all. The man was already convicted. His victims were all found, all laid to rest. There was no need for further detail. But Hanes had something Lucien didn't. *A gun.* And the solitary interruption that Lucien had made had earned him a barrel in the face.

This was how it had ended for Hanes's other victims. The time limit expired, and the murderous man ended their lives with a single shot to the head. So

Lucien didn't try again to hurry things along. He let Hanes slosh around, wave the weapon and go on. At last, though, the other man seemed to be winding down. Coming to some conclusion. He whipped toward Lucien, his eyes glittering, a pleased smile on his face.

"So now…" he said. "Now we get to Sally Rickson's brother. And you see why, don't you? You—and I mean that in a general, police sense, not in a Lucien Match sense—always assumed that it was a contest of wits. And at first, I thought so, too. You—" He paused to chuckle. "*You*, you, this time, I mean—you outsmarted me. I was pretty damned pleased about it, when you found the girl. There was an 'at last' moment. But somehow the great, cosmic karma bungled things. That rookie found me and I was stuck in that cell for three years. And then…" He stopped again, and gestured to Lucien. "Well. You fill in the blanks."

Lucien proceeded cautiously, wary of the other man's gusto. "And then…the DNA test."

"Exactly!" Hanes crowed. "Damn, was I not expecting *those* results. Though really, maybe I should've. Because cosmic karma *did* have something to answer for."

"But what now?" Lucien asked.

The other man blinked. "What do you mean?"

"How do you win this one, Hanes?"

"By killing you."

Lucien didn't know what response he'd been expecting, but for some reason, it wasn't that. He blinked up at Hanes, his mind more puzzled than chilled. "That doesn't make any sense."

The serial killer's expression grew equally confused. "What do you mean? You put the pieces of the puzzle together yourself, Detective, so you should know just how *much* sense it makes."

Lucien shook his head. "It doesn't fit your pattern. And I know that matters to you. A lot. You just spent all that time explaining it to me."

Hanes lifted his gun-free hand and ticked off the words like they were a grocery list rather than people's lives. "Father. Mother. Sister. Brother."

"Exactly."

"Exactly?"

Under any other circumstances, the exchange might've been comical. But Lucien was far from amused. And he was seeing a way out. A tiny bit of potential light.

"So…" he said slowly. "By that calculation…you should be aiming that weapon at your own head."

Hanes's brow creased. "My *own* head?"

"Not only did I win your game by putting all the pieces together—to quote you—but you should've been the target in the first place."

"Me? I—oh, I see where you're going with this." The other man's expression cleared for a second, then darkened. "I'm actually disappointed. I really did think you were cleverer than that."

With no further explanation, the barrel of the gun came up. As visions of Raven's face filled his mind, Lucien refused to look away from imminent death. If he was going to go, he was going to do it with eyes open and the woman he loved at the forefront of his thoughts.

Long, dark hair.

Beautiful blue eyes.

Her skin.

Her voice.

But then—like he'd conjured it—her voice came to life for real, in a single-word scream.

"No!"

Hanes jerked his attention up, the weapon wavering. But Lucien couldn't find even a sliver of relief in the fact the gun was no longer pointed his way. Up above, staring down at them, was Raven. Seeing her made his heart tighten. The dark, beautiful hair he'd just envisioned was a mess. Even in the poor lighting, he could see the mix of fear and determination on her face. He was desperately glad to see her. But also desperately wished she weren't there. He suspected she knew it, too, because she directed her gaze toward Hanes rather than toward him.

"I know," she told the other man, her voice surer than her expression.

The other man's arm lowered, just a little more. "Do you?"

Raven nodded. "Yes. Can I come down?"

Hanes sighed. "No. But if you do a little spin, lift your shirt and convince me that you're not armed, I'll let you sit on the edge and tell me what it is you think you know."

Lucien bit down to keep from snarling that Raven didn't have to do a thing the other man said. He knew that whatever she had to say, it was buying them time—something they direly needed. He still didn't like it, though, when she complied. White-hot anger built up under the surface as he watched her turn in a circle, shirt lifted up to expose her sports bra. Hanes, however, seemed satisfied.

"Good girl," he said with a nod toward the edge. "Have a seat."

Raven took a visible breath, then sank down, her feet dangling over the mostly empty pool.

"Lucien thinks it's you," she said.

Hanes nodded again. "Yes. It would appear that he does."

Lucien frowned, but kept his mouth shut.

Time, he reminded himself.

But a second later, thoughts of coming up with any kind of plan completely flew away.

"It's him, though, isn't it?" Raven said.

Two sets of eyes turned his way. The water under him seemed to be making the whole room sway, and he could barely manage to get out the obvious question.

"What are you saying?" he asked.

"You're Juanita Rickson's son." Raven said it softly—kindly.

But the air still went out of Lucien's lungs so fast that he had to draw in a gasping breath that burned in his chest. Juanita Rickson's son? It was impossible.

"My mother died when I was born," he said.

"No," said Hanes. "Your mother gave you up to a lovely couple named Robert and Daphne Match. And six months later, Daphne died."

"I would've known."

"Would you? Think about it. Your father abruptly moved from Saskatchewan to BC. He cut himself off from every bit of family her ever had."

Lucien still shook his head, but he couldn't deny that what Hanes said was true. Lucien's father *had* isolated himself. He didn't keep a single photograph around. He never sent or received a Christmas card.

Hanes smiled. "Don't worry, Detective. People *did* die the night you were born. But your biological mother wasn't one of them."

"Back it up," Lucien growled. "Tell it from the be-ginning."

Hanes shrugged. "Have it your way. I'll even start

the story with a dark and stormy night. I was seven, and I remember it perfectly, because it was one of those rainy days where even if you wanted to, you couldn't go outside. I was driving my mom crazy, and my older sister was having some kind of emotional crisis like only twelve-year-old girls can. My dad was home from work with the flu." He paused. "You might not remember the day, Detective. But the date will stand out. September nineteenth. Sound familiar?"

Lucien's throat was dry as he replied, "I think you know already that it's my birthday."

"That's right. I *do*." The other man smiled. "And the place might mean something to you, too. Waterville, Saskatchewan. Your dad ever mention that little town to you?"

This time, Lucien said nothing. He was more than aware of the existence of the postage-stamp-sized community. His father—for all his failings—had spoken fondly of it, because his only son had been born there.

On a very dark, very stormy night, said a little voice in Lucien's head. He tried to slough off the thought; another one crept in right behind it. *And coincidentally close to the place Juanita Rickson grew up.*

It still seemed too incredible to be true. Yet wasn't that just what made it *more* believable?

As the other man went on, Lucien listened and his mind was open just enough to not dismiss the story as absurdity.

"It wasn't me, who started the fire," Hanes told him. "So we might as well just get that out of the way. If it had been, I'd take responsibility. I don't want it to come back to me, or to make that part more than it is." He paused to scratch at his chin with the gun, then gave his head a small shake. "But the fire was just the first thing, anyway. It lit up the house, blocked the exits, and we were stuck on the second floor. The sirens came, and the smoke was so bad…but my dad said the engines were on their way. That it would be okay. Except he didn't know that the road was mostly washed out. He didn't know that the ambulance had come in before and was trying to get back. And he didn't know about *you*." He stopped again, this time to shoot a dark look toward Lucien, and then he started pacing, his words coming faster. "Two emergency vehicles headed straight for each other at full speed. On one very narrow road. Someone had to swerve. And the fire-truck driver made the choice. Neither he nor the truck could be saved. They told me later about the baby. How he'd lived. How that, at least was a miracle. They didn't seem to care that the baby had murdered my family, just with his very existence." He laughed a bitter, unamused laugh. "When I was a kid, I heard the term *second-degree murder*, and I was sure that was what it meant."

As Hanes ceased in his sloshing walk, Lucien realized that his own incredulity had already faded into a grudging acceptance. The other man had no reason to lie. No reason to fabricate such an unbelievable chain of events. Even if he had, his story could easily be verified or refuted by the DNA results in question, and Lucien's rarely wrong gut assured him that it would be the former. And really, it explained a few other things, too. His father's constant anger. His rabid bitterness toward Lucien himself.

"Want to know how I figured it out?" Hanes asked, then didn't wait for a reply before explaining, "I was curious about you. I wanted to know what made you smart enough to solve my riddle when no one else could. So I thought…why not *become* Lucien Match?

The DNA website isn't flagged in prison. So I got myself in using your name. And lo and behold, there you were. And there was your perfect family. Jim. Juanita. Sally. An exact replica of the one that should've been mine." Hanes's voice dropped low with a dangerous-sounding awe. "Imagine. Just *imagine*. Learning that the person who was chasing you down was the very one who'd made you into the monster you are." He stopped yet again, and lifted his eyes to Raven. "I'm sorry. You weren't supposed to be here for this. And I really meant for you to live."

The meaning of Hanes's words slammed into Lucien like gale-force wind, and he pulled uselessly at the zip-ties as the other man took aim.

Raven heard the change in Hanes's tone. She saw the sudden flash. And a heartbeat before the shot rang out, she jumped. Forward and down. At the same time, she dipped a hand into the center of her sports bra and drew out the small cylinder she'd hidden there. Her landing sent a cascade of water up, soaking her. She ignored it in favor of finding Hanes. He stood directly in front of her, visibly stunned. Raven took advantage of the brief surprise Her hand shot out, her finger pressed down and the hiss of bear spray filled the air. More important, it filled Hanes's face.

With a thick stream of curses leaving his mouth, Hanes stumbled back. His hands came up to his face, the gun dropped to the water, and Raven jumped again. Forward and down again. And her fingers found immediate purchase. Metal—warmer than the water that surrounded it—filled her palm, and for a second, triumph reined. But it was ripped away as Hanes lunged toward her.

Reflexively, Raven dived to the side. The evasive maneuver made her lose her footing. She toppled sideways. Her elbow plunged into the water, then slammed against the hard, pebbled bottom of the pool. And both the gun and the bear spray slid from her grasp.

No. No, no, no!

She flailed her hand around under the water, searching for either of her weapons. She came up blank.

And Hanes was already charging at her again. Raven pushed to her feet and stumbled out of reach again.

Hanes didn't let up. He was out of control. Still blinded. But he was like a wounded animal, desperately seeking his prey. Screaming furiously and nonsensically, he leaped her way. Only this time, he went the slightest bit wide, giving Raven the briefest moment of reprieve. She spun in a frantic circle, trying to find the gun or the bear spray through the swirling water.

Where?

For a moment, she couldn't see anything but ripples.

Vaguely, she was aware that Lucien was hollering a protest. Telling her to get out while she could. But she wouldn't leave without him. He was crazy to suggest it. And his voice faded out when she spotted an anomaly—an even darker break in the murkiness—about six feet away. She stepped toward it. Immediately, her foot caught on something, sending her down. For a second, she was crawling through the water. Slogging against it. Then she realized there was an easier way. She drew a breath, pushed her face into the wetness, kicked out her leg and *swam*. And a heartbeat later, there it was.

The gun.

She stretched out her arm, yanked it up and spun. Her rear end hit the bottom at the same moment the barrel lifted from the water. It was a second too late.

With red-faced, eyes-shut fury, Hanes bore down on her. His shoulder clipped hers, and sent the gun flying yet again.

If she'd had time to do it, Raven would've cried. But there wasn't a moment to spare. In spite of the fact that Hanes couldn't see her, he'd obviously zoomed in on her location. He flung his body at her, and knocked into her a second time. And before Raven could react, his hands were on her. One drove into her stomach, winding her. The other came up and closed on her throat. But it didn't squeeze. Instead, it pushed her down and held her there. And Raven realized his goal wasn't to choke the life out of her—he intended to drown her.

No, she thought, a surge of determination rushing in. *I'm not going to let him win.*

She closed her eyes. She focused. And she saw a way out.

Eyes or baby-maker, Lucien had always said.

The oldest trick in the women's self-defense handbook.

Lucien felt more powerless than he'd ever felt in his life. The woman he loved—the woman to whom he still hadn't expressed that love—was on the brink of death, and there was nothing he could do. It didn't seem real.

"Stop!" he hollered uselessly, slamming his wrists against the pipe and pleading with the universe to cut him some slack.

He'd saved her three years ago.

And for what?

To just die at the hands of the same man who he'd rescued her from in the first place? It was viciously cyclical.

"Hanes!" His voice was harsh and hollow at the same time. "Please. For the love of all that's—"

His words cut off as the painful tableau in front of him exploded into action. Water surged up, and a blur surged with it, slamming straight between Hanes's legs. The evil man cried out and doubled over. Raven's foot—which Lucien belatedly realized was what made up the blur—came flying up again, hitting its mark a second time. And with the repeated blow, Hanes went over backward. His head smashed straight back against the concrete, and very abruptly, the killer went silent.

Stillness hung in the air for a long moment. Then Hanes slid sideways, crimson pooling from his skull, and Lucien was 99.9 percent sure that the other man had left the world for good. Relief hit, but only for as long as it took him to realize that Raven hadn't yet resurfaced. Lucien whipped his attention away from Hanes's body back to the place where she'd been just a moment earlier. What he saw stopped his heart. She was there. Faceup. But motionless except for the water lapping against her.

"Raven!"

Lucien smacked his wrists so hard against the pipe that he was sure he was going to come away with broken bones. He didn't care.

"Raven. Oh, God. Please."

He gave up on the zip-ties and stretched out a foot. *If I can just reach her. Pull her closer.*

He was too far away. Despair and hopelessness washed over him. He closed his eyes, frantically searching his mind for an answer. And then her voice—weak and small—carried to his ears.

"Pick me," she said.

His eyes flew open, and he saw that she was righting herself. But she didn't move toward him.

"Pick me," she said a second time, a little stronger.

"Raven…" his voice was hoarse. "Pick you? What do you mean?"

"I don't care if it's selfish."

"What are you talking about? Come here."

"The choice," she told him, a hint of stubbornness creeping into her tone.

Her tone almost made him laugh. "What choice, Raven?"

"Between me and the job."

"There was never a *choice* between you and the job."

"But you said it. And that's why you left." The pain in her words palpable. "You chose work."

Lucien's heart throbbed. "That's why I…no. I left because I didn't think I could make a life for you. I thought my job would stop me from being the man you deserved."

Her face creased. "How could you think that? You saved my life. You're not just *my* hero. You're *literally* a hero. I never wanted to get in the way of that."

This time, he did laugh; he couldn't help it. "Raven. Trust me on something. You're your own hero. But please—I'm begging you—come here."

She didn't move, and he realized he still hadn't said the all-important words.

"I love you. I've always loved you."

At last she surged forward, then collapsed against him. "I love you, too, Lucien."

"And just so we're clear it was never a choice. It was you over the job, the whole time." He bent to press his lips to her forehead. "Now… One small favor?"

"Anything."

"Break these stupid zip-ties so I can kiss you properly."

And thankfully, this time, she didn't stop to argue.

Epilogue

Lucien stepped into the kitchen of the former safe house—their house now—and frowned when he didn't spot Raven right away.

"Sweetheart?" he called.

"Down here," she replied. "I knocked your phone off the counter, and now I can't find it."

Chuckling, Lucien slid around the counter and found her kneeling down on the ground. His mouth twitched a little. He'd been working on a speech for the last two hours, and all of it required *him* to be the one on bended knee. He started to ask her to stand up, then stopped as a familiar ringtone came to life.

"Well," he said, "my best guess is that it's coming from under the fridge."

Raven groaned. "It is, isn't it?"

She started to flatten herself down, but Lucien stopped her. "Hang on. Wait a second."

She paused and looked up at him. "What? Why?"

"Because ten bucks says that's my boss and his bad timing."

"His bad timing? What's he interrupting now?"

In response, Lucien lifted an eyebrow, dropped down beside her, and—thinking it suited them to be on equal ground anyway—he pulled the velvet box from his pocket.

* * * * *

WE HOPE YOU ENJOYED
THIS BOOK FROM

HARLEQUIN
ROMANTIC
SUSPENSE

Danger. Passion. Drama.

These heart-racing page-turners will keep you guessing
to the very end. Experience the thrill of unexpected
plot twists and irresistible chemistry.

4 NEW BOOKS AVAILABLE EVERY MONTH!

HRSHALO2020

COMING NEXT MONTH FROM

HARLEQUIN

ROMANTIC SUSPENSE

Available September 1, 2020

#2103 COLTON 911: DETECTIVE ON CALL
Colton 911: Grand Rapids • by Regan Black
Attorney Pippa Colton is determined to overturn a wrongful conviction but must find a way to get the truth out of the star witness: Emmanuel Iglesias. The sexy detective is sure the case was by the book. When Pippa starts receiving threats, her theory begins to look much more convincing, if they can unearth evidence before the true killer stops them in their tracks.

#2104 COLTON'S SECRET HISTORY
The Coltons of Kansas • by Jennifer D. Bokal
When Bridgette Colton's job with the Kansas State Department of Health sends her to her hometown to investigate a cluster of cancer cases, she uncovers long-hidden family secrets that lead her back to her first love, Luke Walker.

#2105 CAVANAUGH IN PLAIN SIGHT
Cavanaugh Justice • by Marie Ferrarella
A feisty reporter has always believed in following her moral compass, but this time that same compass just might make her a target—unless Morgan Cavanaugh can protect her. Her work gets her in trouble and anyone could want to silence her—permanently.

#2106 HER P.I. PROTECTOR
Cold Case Detectives • by Jennifer Morey
Detective Julien LaCroix meets Skylar Chelsey, the daughter of a wealthy rancher, just when she needs him the most: after she stumbles upon a murder scene. Now they fight instant attraction and a relentless killer, who will stop at nothing to silence the only living witness.

YOU CAN FIND MORE INFORMATION ON UPCOMING HARLEQUIN TITLES,
FREE EXCERPTS AND MORE AT HARLEQUIN.COM.

HRSCNM0820

SPECIAL EXCERPT FROM

⬥ HARLEQUIN

ROMANTIC SUSPENSE

*Detective Julien LaCroix meets Skylar Chelsey, the
daughter of a wealthy rancher, just when she needs him
the most: after she stumbles upon a murder scene. Now
they fight instant attraction and a relentless killer, who
will stop at nothing to silence the only living witness.*

Read on for a sneak preview of
Her P.I. Protector,
the next book in Jennifer Morey's
Cold Case Detectives miniseries.

Great. She'd get to endure another visit with the dubious
sheriff. Except now he'd be hard-pressed to doubt her
claims. Clearly she must have seen something to make
the hole digger feel he needed to close loose ends.

Julien ended the call. "While we wait for the sheriff,
why don't you go get dressed and pack some things? You
should stay with me until we find out who tried to kill
you."

He had a good point, but the notion of staying with
him gave her a burst of heat. Conscious of wearing only
a robe, she tightened the belt.

"I can stay with my parents," she said. "They can
make sure I'm safe." Her father would probably install a
robust security system complete with guards.

"You might put others in danger if you do that."

Her parents, Corbin and countless staff members might be in the line of fire if the gunman returned for another attempt.

"Then I'll beef up security here. I can't stay away from the ranch for long."

"All right, then let me help you."

"Okay." She could agree to that.

"Don't worry, I don't mix my work with pleasure," he said with a grin, giving her body a sweeping look.

"Good, then I don't have to worry about trading one danger for another." She smiled back and left him standing there, uncertainty flattening his mouth.

Don't miss
Her P.I. Protector by Jennifer Morey,
available September 2020 wherever
Harlequin Romantic Suspense
books and ebooks are sold.

Harlequin.com

Copyright © 2020 by Jennifer Morey

Get 4 FREE REWARDS!

We'll send you 2 FREE Books plus 2 FREE Mystery Gifts.

Harlequin Romantic Suspense books are heart-racing page-turners with unexpected plot twists and irresistible chemistry that will keep you guessing to the very end.

FREE Value Over $20

YES! Please send me 2 FREE Harlequin Romantic Suspense novels and my 2 FREE gifts (gifts are worth about $10 retail). After receiving them, if I don't wish to receive any more books, I can return the shipping statement marked "cancel." If I don't cancel, I will receive 4 brand-new novels every month and be billed just $4.99 per book in the U.S. or $5.74 per book in Canada. That's a savings of at least 13% off the cover price! It's quite a bargain! Shipping and handling is just 50¢ per book in the U.S. and $1.25 per book in Canada.* I understand that accepting the 2 free books and gifts places me under no obligation to buy anything. I can always return a shipment and cancel at any time. The free books and gifts are mine to keep no matter what I decide.

240/340 HDN GNMZ

Name (please print)

Address   Apt. #

City   State/Province   Zip/Postal Code

Email: Please check this box ☐ if you would like to receive newsletters and promotional emails from Harlequin Enterprises ULC and its affiliates. You can unsubscribe anytime.

Mail to the **Reader Service:**
IN U.S.A.: P.O. Box 1341, Buffalo, NY 14240-8531
IN CANADA: P.O. Box 603, Fort Erie, Ontario L2A 5X3

Want to try 2 free books from another series? Call 1-800-873-8635 or visit www.ReaderService.com.

*Terms and prices subject to change without notice. Prices do not include sales taxes, which will be charged (if applicable) based on your state or country of residence. Canadian residents will be charged applicable taxes. Offer not valid in Quebec. This offer is limited to one order per household. Books received may not be as shown. Not valid for current subscribers to Harlequin Romantic Suspense books. All orders subject to approval. Credit or debit balances in a customer's account(s) may be offset by any other outstanding balance owed by or to the customer. Please allow 4 to 6 weeks for delivery. Offer available while quantities last.

Your Privacy—Your information is being collected by Harlequin Enterprises ULC, operating as Reader Service. For a complete summary of the information we collect, how we use this information and to whom it is disclosed, please visit our privacy notice located at corporate.harlequin.com/privacy-notice. From time to time we may also exchange your personal information with reputable third parties. If you wish to opt out of this sharing of your personal information, please visit readerservice.com/consumerchoice or call 1-800-873-8635. **Notice to California Residents**—Under California law, you have specific rights to control and access your data. For more information on these rights and how to exercise them, visit corporate.harlequin.com/california-privacy.

HRS20R2